the CREEK DON'T RISE

*Yatesboro Yarns
Down Company Row*

MARY KATHRYN KOMA

WORD ASSOCIATION PUBLISHERS
www.wordassociation.com
1.800.827.7903

ISBN: 978-1-63385-417-8

Designed and published by
Word Association Publishers
205 Fifth Avenue
Tarentum, Pennsylvania 15084

www.wordassociation.com
1.800.827.7903

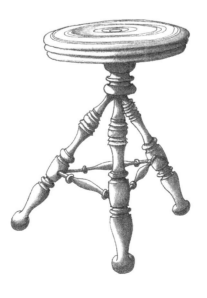

Dedication

I dedicate this book to my mother, Doris Jean (Dotsy Enterline) Maffei. You taught me the love of family and what we call home. We lost you on January 13, 2019. You helped me find my way back to where I felt your heart, and especially your warmth which is ever present in our home. I began to write. Your memories and love guided me through the next two years of writing. On the anniversary of your death, January 13, 2021, I completed my story. I hope you are proud.

Acknowledgements

A unt Peggy (Enterline) Klodell, Thank you for sharing with me your memories of Yatesboro and your experiences growing up. You are my Patsy. With your memories, I was able to create this fictional story, yet include the true life of a young girl growing up in Yatesboro. At 90 years old, you are an amazing woman. I love the life you lived. Thank you for helping me create this heartwarming story of prankishness, mischief, happiness, camaraderie, compassion, despair, sorrow and love.

To **Karen Coulter**. My mentor and friend, who was the first to begin with me on this journey. Thank you for your endless hours of work editing, and for your constant support. I learned so much from you about writing. You were always patient and encouraging. I could not have accomplished this without you. You have a gift. Thank you.

To my sister, **Cheri Wolff, and her children, Ian and Emma** for designing the cover. Cheri, a brilliant artist. Ian, a technological wizard. Emma, an artist with the same eye for excellence as your brother and mother. I hope you all share your gifts with the world someday. You simply must. Thank you!

To my mother, **Dotsy (Doris Jean Enterline) Maffei** and my **Aunt Kakern (Ida Enterline) Millikin for** talking so much about Yatesboro and the past. Two wonderfully loving women who cared enough to share their lives with us. I was so lucky to have you both, and miss you to the moon and back.

To my father, **Joseph James (J.J.) Maffei**, for handing down to me his passion for putting words on paper. I hope you are writing in Heaven. Thank you, Dad.

To my son, **David Koma**, for your technical support and constant encouragement. Through your patience and diligence, you made this possible for your "non-tech" Mom. Thank you!

To my family: My sons **Michael Koma** and **David Koma**, daughter-in-laws **Susan** and **Melissa** and my grandchildren: **Megan, Mason, Dylan, Lauren, Peyton, Ellie, Dawson.** For cheering me on and never losing the faith. Thank you.

To my proofreaders: **Marilyn Clark, Megan Koma, David Koma, Michael Hlebik, Jen Schlosser, Cathy Patterson, Cheri Wolff, Mike Koma**. You were an important and integral part of this journey. Thank you.

Thank you to the following for help with history and photographs:

The Armstrong County Historical Society, Ron Juliette, Rich Covola, Judy (Kashur) Lazzeri, Dennis and Janet (Palilla) Hellgren, Ed and Mary (Cicchiani) Alwine, Jim and Cathy (Bohan) Patterson, Tom and Carolyn (Davidson) Maffei, Carmella (Platania) Ashbaugh, Marilyn Clark, Tim and Marian Stockdale, Miriam (Arbuckle) McCullough, Jolene (Maffei) Formaini, Cheri Wolff, Kyle Heide at Staples Indiana, The Kittanning Leader Times, Mike Passerini, Linda (Nagy) Brown, Bev Stewart, Donna Galentine.

Thank you to **Erma Dovenspike**, who had faith in me and inspires me every day.

Special thanks to my husband, **Mike**, for his love and support through hours, days, months he spent alone as I wrote.

You never lost faith and you always encouraged me to keep going. I am lucky to have you. I love you.

To **April Urso** and **Francine Costello** at Word Association Publishing Company for helping me navigating the process with patience and encouragement.

Thank you to the families who allowed me to share their tragedies.

To **ALL MY FRIENDS AND FAMILY** who had faith that I could. I did. Thank you.

THE CREEK DON'T RISE

one
In The Beginning

The Blackhands that live in and around Yatesboro are evil men. They gamble, they steal, they fight, and they kill.

I am Patsy. I am just a kid. I was born in 1930. Yatesboro is my home.

People here are mostly good, but not all. My daddy often talks to me about the Blackhands. "Patsy, these are evil menacing men. You stay away from them! You know that red brick building down by the dam? They make moonshine there. Whatever else they do, no one knows; but people have disappeared from town. We all know the Blackhands got them! Don't you ever go near that red brick building, Patsy!"

It horrifies me, yet I am intrigued and curious. "I want to see that building, Daddy. Will you take me?"

"I said stay away from it, Patsy! I mean that! We don't go there!"

I know when it is time to shut-up. Now is the time.

Until the turn of the 19th century, Yatesboro was just farmland. My daddy told me all about it. The discovery of coal seams in the hills of Yatesboro brought the opening of coal mines. He said it was an exciting era of change for our valley. In 1899, Daddy said a man named Lucious Robinson purchased 1,000 acres here and he opened coal mines, erected mine buildings, and built our company town for his employees. In 1900 he named it Yatesboro after Arnie G. Yates, President of the Buffalo, Rochester and Pittsburgh Railroad.

The railroad goes through Yatesboro, and connects all of the five mines. Daddy said that immigrants from Europe flooded to Yatesboro. They were called unnaturalized foreigners. They came into New York. Then they came by train to Yatesboro. They stayed at the Valley Hotel until the 250 single and double company homes were built.

Yatesboro grew very fast once people started making money in the mines. They sent for their families to come from other countries. Daddy said at first only four hundred men worked in the mines. Now, over a thousand do, and they produce 825,000 tons of coal a year.

Across the black road of Yatesboro is the Flats and Yatesboro Hill. There are many company houses built there. They all look the same. I like to go to the Flats when the train is coming through. I love the train. If I stand in front of the Kashur house, it will stop right in front of me. Right on time! The whistle is loud as the train screeches to a stop.

Suddenly, a door opens on the first boxcar of the train. A burly man is standing there with chickens in crates behind him. Mrs. Kashur hollers to him, "One please." The man grabs a chicken, takes a hatchet, lays the chicken on a wooden block, and chops off the head. The chicken is still squirming as he hands it to Mrs. Kashur, holding it by the feet. She hands him her quarter. That was sickening! Maybe I'll quit rushing to see the train, at least on the days they are chopping chicken's heads off! I hurry home.

Daddy just came home from his shift in the mines. He is at the garden hose washing off. "Hi, Daddy!" I run out to greet him. I can only see the whites of his eyes.

"Hey, Patsy!" He is always happy. "Grab me my towel, will you?"

His towel is always hanging on the nail on the back porch.

Wearing threadbare, blue cotton trousers and over-stretched suspenders, in my eyes, my daddy is a towering, slim-cut, sturdy tree. Daddy talks softly and rarely hollers, and he teaches me things. If he isn't in the coal mine working, he is in the garden. I beg him to tell me more about the Blackhands. Instead, calmly, he says, "You don't need to know more, little girl. All you need to do is stay away from them and that red brick building!"

I don't like that answer. I do not disobey Daddy though. At least most times.

It is 1938. Franklin D. Roosevelt is President, a democrat. Daddy is unhappy about that, since he is a true republican.

Last year, there was a quarantine for scarlet fever. Scarlet fever is a bacterial illness that develops in some people who have strep throat. My sister, Dee, got it. She had a bright red rash all over her body. Her fever was so high that Mama had to put ice around her. We all had to stay in the house for weeks. No one else in our house got it, though. Thank goodness, the quarantine is over now

I am 8 years old, and I am a tomboy, a tomboy in a dress. I love to wear pants but Mama most times won't let me. My dark brown hair is curly and falls in spirals. Mama calls them ringlets. I call them ugly. Because I have green eyes, my friends say I have an Irish temper. I suppose it is because I stand up for myself pretty darn good. Mama and Daddy are Scottish and love their heritage. My daddy's brother, Uncle Frederick, owns a Blacksmith Shop here. Daddy hangs out there sometimes along with my Uncle Tip.

I live on the side of the hill where the Catholic Church and the Cowanshannock High School are. On this side of the hill, mostly Catholics live. Our family is one of the few protestants on our street. The coal company owns all the houses here, and they all look alike. Old gray beaten wood with the same front porch, the wooden screen door that bangs and bounces at least twice when it closes. An old coal furnace burns in our primitive basement. There is a big register between the living room and dining room where we all want to stand in the winter, the hot air blowing up our dresses. Mrs. Woods owned our house first. She sold it to Mama and Daddy. She left a refrigerator they paid her ten dollars for. It has a foot pedal to open the door. We even have ice in there!

Mama and Daddy had lots of kids and I am the youngest. I've got two older brothers, Sid and Doug, and the rest are girls. Ina is the oldest girl. She thinks she is the boss of us all, and she is clever. Dee is the goodie-two-shoe and does everything to please Mama and Daddy. My sister, Bella, is one year older than me. She and I can get into a lot of trouble. Mama's second baby, Thomas, died. He died of the flu at nine months old. I don't think Mama ever got over that. Since she lost Thomas, she panics at the slightest sign we are sick. Last night I was coughing, so she made a mustard seed poultice for my chest. She puts it in flannel and it stinks. I quit coughing though. I had a boil on my back last year. She put ground up egg shells on it. That worked too. Mama knows how to fix everything.

Today is a pretty day. I love when I wake up to the birds singing and the sound of Mr. Roebuck's lawnmower. At breakfast I eat my oatmeal as fast as I can. "Going for a walk, Mama!" I yell as I run out the old screen door.

Across my street and turning left, I walk past the Catholic Church. I admire the beauty of it. The tall bell tower looms over the white wood of the massive building. Every morning the bell rings at 8:00 am. The chimes fill the air a mile away. Walking into the church is an awesome sight. The altar is very high. It is white carved wood that goes up into peaks. There is a cross in the middle with Jesus, the blood runs down his hands and feet. There are statues beside him. Little red glass candles are always burning. The first priest here was Father Federici, but he died a few years ago. Now the priest is Father Berto.

Bella and I go to the church parking lot every time there is a wedding, with all our friends. We sit out front in the grass, waiting for the bride and groom to come out. We throw rice at them. Then we make sure we are at the bride and groom's house when they return from their honeymoon. We throw rice again until they give us candy.

Husker is working at the church today, helping Father Berto rake the lawn. Husker is my age, and a quiet kid. He works hard, as he helps make money to feed his family. Husker is always a little dirty. His blonde hair is long only on the top and falls over his forehead. It looks today like it needs washed. The grease is keeping it from flying in the wind.

"Hey, Husker!" I holler, smiling and skipping as I go. He looks at me, then looks down. He is so darn shy, and all he does is work. I mostly hang around boys, not girls, except for Ethel. She is my best friend. Boys like what I like: baseball, dissecting frogs, and getting dirty. Girls are too prissy, except for Ethel.

I like to embarrass Husker, especially in front of the priest. He lives at the end of my street. He often is in his yard managing all his younger brothers and sisters, pushing them on the tire swing hung from the big maple tree, or playing hide and seek with them. He is a good brother.

I stop and lean over, my hands on my knees, "Husker???" I think maybe if I say it as a question he will reply. He does not acknowledge me, as usual. Father Berto winks at me. I smile and wave goodbye, as I move on down the hill and turn left.

I am on Main Street. I'm passing my church, the Yatesboro Presbyterian Church. Rev. Murphy is at the side of the church pounding a nail as he glances over at me. "Hey, Patsy!" I was hoping he wouldn't see me.

"Hey, Rev. Murphy. What cha doin'?"

He stops pounding, "Fixing this frame here. Will we see you Sunday?"

I want to say I'd rather not but I don't dare. Mama would kill me. "Sure thing!" I keep on moving down the street. I am not in the "visiting my preacher" mood today. Got things to do.

There are lots of kids in every house. The company boss, Jim Craig, owns the biggest one on Main Street. He even owns a Model A Ford! He is big and burly with a loud voice. I am passing his house when I hear Mr. Craig holler, "Hey Patsy, I've got the game on!" He knows of my love for baseball. "Come on up! The Pirates are playing the Reds!" Our little town had only gas lights until 1929, when we got electricity. But few have radios. The company boss is one of the first to have a radio. There on his porch he has set his radio, so everyone around can listen to the baseball game. I scurry up the stairs. I sit on the top step. I don't remember even combing my hair this morning but I don't care. Can't manage these crazy curls anyway!

It is already in the third inning. The game is a close one. I listen intently to each play as the crowd roars. Second baseman Pep Young is up to bat. Strike one! Strike two! Strike three, you're out! Inning after inning I listen intently, wistfully wishing I was there...excited for the next pitch.

Boomer Yates is walking by now on his way home from the Lias Livery Stable on Water Street in Rural Valley where he shovels horse poop. Boomer is skinny and dirty. His hair has been shaved down to nothing. He is always in his work boots, dirty pants, and the same filthy plaid flannel shirt. He sees me on the top step. "What's going on, Patsy?" Simultaneously, he has heard the game and the crowd cheering, so he runs up the stairs to sit beside me.

"Can't you sit somewhere else?" I want to know.

"Nope! Gonna sit right here!" He stares at my head, "Did a bat get tangled in your hair?"

He is an idiot. I punch him a good one in his shoulder. He just laughs. He thinks everything he says is funny.

The game is a good one, tied most of the way through. It is the last inning. The Pirates are in the outfield and they are winning by one with two outs. We all listen intently. Red Lucas is the pitcher for us. Red is thirty-six years old this year and Daddy says he'll probably retire. Wally Berger is at bat for the Reds. There is one more out to get and it is all over.

"Strike one!" the umpire yells, then "strike two!" I excitedly lean closer to the radio as my heart pounds. The pitch is thrown, and the ball hitting the bat is as clear as a paddle smacking a bare butt. The crowd hushes. The announcer exclaims, "Batter connects. Ball to short, Arky Vaughan scoops it up, throws to first baseman, Gus Suhr. HE'S OUT AT FIRST!"

The crowd roars. I give a scream clapping my hands. I hope someday I will go to a baseball game, but I know it is doubtful. We don't even have a car!

The game is over. Suddenly, I smell something like wet dog, but worse. I realize it is Boomer. "Boomer, you stink!"

He just laughs, "Here, smell my breath too!" He leans over and leaves out a huge exhale into my face. A little spit came with it too.

"Stop stupid! I HATE YOU!" I jump to my feet and push him over. I'm desperately trying to hold my breath. I think his breath shows on my face like dog poop stuck to a shoe.

Boomer falls onto the porch. I run down the stairs and begin running up the hill to home. "Run baby girl, run home to Daddy!" Boomer yells laughingly, as I faintly hear Mr. Craig scolding him.

I hate Boomer, and he is NOT going to get the best of me!

two
Mischief

Summertime is the best! I caught fireflies until late last night and slept in just a little. Today Mama is not at home. She is delivering another baby at the O'Connor house. Daddy is in the garden picking tomatoes and green peppers. There is a storm brewing. The dark clouds are forming from the west. I can hear thunder, and now and then, a flash of lightning. I look out the back door, "You need help, Daddy?"

He is starting to come towards the house, "No, pumpkin, I got it! Just as he gets onto the back porch, a downpour starts. He has the tomatoes and peppers in a kitchen towel that he holds by gathering the four corners. I hold the screen door for him and he throws them onto the table. He seems in a cheerful mood. "How about Mama delivering another baby? That will make those O'Connor's ten kids!"

I know Mama won't be home for a long time. "I never will understand why babies take so long to come out, Daddy."

He smiles at me. "Someday you will!"

Three hours later Mama returns home, but she tells us she has to go back to the O'Connor house. The baby hasn't come yet. "Just want to freshen up. Doc Griffith is there with her right now. I'll go back in a bit."

Mama's name is Isla. She is roly-poly and full of love. She has long hair which she never shows. It is always up in a neat bun at the back of her head. She starts to brush her hair out. I sit on her bed and watch, twirling my curls. She takes her hand to pull all the hair out of her hair brush that she has lost while brushing. She then rolls it onto a ball of hair she already has formed, which she keeps in her drawer. This makes the ball bigger. "This is my rat!" She holds it out to me, sitting atop her open palm. She has given a name to a stupid ball of hair.

I think it is rather disgusting, "A rat, Mama? A rat has four legs and a tail."

She smiles, "It is what I call it. Look here, it is my hair all rolled into a ball, my rat!" She then puts the ball of hair at the back of her head and wraps her long hair around it, making a large bun. "See?"

Not sure if I'm amused, "That's nice, Mama." She seems so proud of it. "If you like it, I like it!" I'm not going to tell her I think it is ridiculous!

Mama wears house dresses every day and her homemade feed-sack apron is always atop her dress. Mama is hard working. Not just at home, but always helping Doc Griffith deliver babies. When Mama is delivering babies, we have to mind Daddy.

Doc Griffith's office is the red brick building on Main Street, at the bottom of the hill. The coal company pays him fifty cents every month from each miner and he gets free rent. When we need medicine, he mixes it right in his back room for us. When we sled ride in winter down the hill, we can go into his office and sit on his velvet couch to get warm. Everyone loves Doc Griffith.

"Be a good girl for Daddy, Patsy. I'll be back in a little while." The screen door bounces as Mama heads back to the O'Connor house.

Bella and I have our chores to do later today. We are in charge of feeding our three beagles and the chickens. Bella and I always get the outside chores. My older sisters are in charge of the inside chores like washing, ironing and housework. This is a good split because I love being outside anyways. Bella talked me into giving her the job of feeding the dogs. I do the chickens. Bella is afraid of the chickens. Our rooster, Harvey, chases her. Harvey chased her yesterday and Bella ran around the yard squealing like a baby. I had to catch Harvey and throw him in the chicken coop, "You are ten times bigger than Harvey, Bella, and you act like a child!"

She gets mad, as usual, "Try letting him peck at your ankles, Patsy. Try that!" I can't win with Bella.

Daddy has plans for us today. He directs his first orders to me, "You don't have to feed the dogs until tonight, so you can start that load of towels in the wringer washer."

The wringer washer scares me, because Susie Carenini got her boob caught in her wringer washer last week. She is a little older Italian lady who speaks bad, broken English. She lives on the Hill. She was telling Mama at our kitchen table when she came to visit on Monday, "Ah, Isla, you watch-eh out for dem-eh ringer washers! I caught-eh my boob-eh in-eh one oh my god-eh, hurt awful-eh bad-eh." I was so frightened listening to her, trying to picture Susie stuck to a washer with her boob in the rollers. It scared me good. I don't have boobs yet. Still, something else might get caught in it. Who knows what!

So, I protest. "No, it's Dee's job, not mine!" Right then Dee comes in the door. Dee is older than me, and she is Daddy's "favorite." She always does what she is told. She will do anything just so Daddy likes her best. As she is walking in the door, she hears me protest to Daddy that I am not doing the wash.

"You little spoiled twit! You think I need you? I don't need you! Just do me a favor and get lost!"

Daddy's cheerful mood just changed. He is not happy with the ensuing argument between Dee and me. He yanks me by my arm, hard, and pulls me onto the back porch. "You got out of it again!" He is disappointed in me. "You will go to the company store for us just for that!"

Stifling a giggle, I am thinking, "Oh my, what a punishment! I love the company store! Make me go, please do!" I don't dare say it out loud. The storm has passed and I can see a beautiful rainbow out our front door, which makes the store trip even more fun. I'll look for the pot of gold at the end of the rainbow.

Daddy badly scribbles a list of what he wants me to buy at the company store. It says one chicken, 4 lb. flour, 4 lb. sugar. The word candy isn't on there. I am sure he forgot to list it. I take the list, skipping past Dee, and out the door letting the screen door bounce twice, a little louder this time just to annoy her. I happily trek down the hill and across the street to my favorite place, the company store.

The name above the door says "VALLEY SUPPLY CO." Since the coal company owns it, everyone just calls it, 'The Company Store'. It is two stories high, and the paint is falling off the window frames. The only phone in town is here in this store. If we get a call from relatives out of town, someone comes to our house to get us and we run here to the company store to take the call or to call them back.

I skip past the logs out front and around the carriages that are parked, and up the front stairs. I can smell the oiled floors as I enter. Five men are smoking in the corner. The cloud that surrounds them stinks of tobacco. Most of them are greasy-looking. Their clothes are dirty. As I get close to them, I am sure I smell alcohol too. Of course, I do. Most men in this town drink a lot. Can't say I blame them, though. They probably need to wash the coal dust out of their throats. The ones that work the all-night shift in the coal mine go directly to the bar when they finish their shift at 8 am to start their alcohol dance.

These men are looking at me and I am wondering if they are Blackhands. What does a Blackhand look like? They keep glaring at me and not in a nice way. I move along and away from them. I can hear one say to the other, "That's Malcolm's girl. You know Malcolm, he lives up on the back street!" I don't like that they know who I am, because I don't know who they are. If they are Blackhands, now they know where I live. I'm a little scared.

I try to forget about it as I run upstairs to the furniture department! I hop from chair to chair. Mr. Conti comes out of the back office hollering at me. "What the heck-eh! What-eh are ya' doin', Patsy?" Mr. Conti is very Italian, and runs the furniture department. He is not very tall, and his mustache is huge! He walks around with a clipboard in his hand. "You don't act-eh like-eh that here! You get-eh yourself down-eh them stairs-eh now and don't-eh you come-eh back up-eh. I mean-eh it, Patsy, cah-PEESH?" He doesn't have to holler it at me like that! His bark is big, but he doesn't scare me.

"Sorry, Mr. Conti!" But, I'm really not sorry. I hop down off the chair and run to the stairway to quickly get out of his disapproving gaze. Then I jump down two stairs at a time.

The company store has a butcher shop; a dry goods department; a candy and cigarette department; and sporting goods department with rifles, pistols, fishing equipment and hunting clothes. The coal company owns it all. There are no shelves to shop from, only counters with shelves behind. I will have to ask the clerks for what I want. There is a grocery counter, a shoe department, a men's suit department, women's and kids' shoes, and some clothing.

I am at the counter to get the flour and sugar Daddy told me to get. The lady behind the counter, Lena Kowalsky, looks mean. She is Polish and is as round as she is tall. She has the worst perm ever. It looks like she got a real bad shock that sizzled her hair. I ask her for 4 lb. of flour and 4 lb. of sugar. Lena gets me the flour and sugar and manages to smile, "Leetel gil run errands for her mada and fada, no?" She writes the charge on Daddy's slip, flour ten cents, sugar ten cents

"Thank you, Lena." I can be pretty polite when I want to be. Now to the butcher shop for a chicken. A guy everyone calls Bumblebee works at the meat counter. He is German. His face is round like a pumpkin and his cheeks and nose are always red. His white apron is always covered with blood and there is blood under his fingernails.

"One chicken please, Bumblebee." He hands me a small but plump chicken.

He always smiles at me. "How's zings going?"

"Good, Bumblebee." In a big jar on his counter are hard-boiled eggs in beet juice. They look interesting. "You sell those?"

He picks up the jar proudly. "Zee eggs, Vee make it."

"Next time!" as I turn around to head to the candy counter.

Mrs. Macina behind the counter looks at me sternly. I don't think Mrs. Macina likes kids. People say she is married to one of the Italian Blackhands.

I pick a red, sugary candy coiled like a wire. She hands it to me, "Don't-eh eat too much-eh sugar."

"Yeah, okay." What I eat is no business of hers. I sure hope Daddy doesn't notice the candy on his slip.

As I turn to leave…… swoosh!!…… and all I see are flowers in my face. I run into the bright multi-colored, flowered skirt of Mrs. Lombardi. She is a very Italian, older woman. With her gray hair and rolled down cotton stockings, she is like a sweet old grandma. "Hey-eh, Patsy girl!" She exclaims as she pinches both my cheeks very hard. I hate when she does that! It even makes me wince a little, and sometimes a wee little squeal comes out because it hurts bad.

She is too sweet to get mad at. "Hello, Mrs. Lombardi."

"You gonna come-eh to my-eh house-eh some-eh day-eh and-eh see me?"

I break away from her, "Sure thing, Mrs. Lombardi!" I rush out the door and up the hill. I like her and I would visit her, if she would just quit pinching my cheeks!

I have my purchases in three bags. I think this is the punishment part. This stuff is heavy! What I bought today will come out of Daddy's paycheck. Also coming out of Daddy's paycheck is 50 cents for the town doctor and 50 cents for the church. The coal company takes care of paying the doctor, the priest, and the preacher with that money. When Daddy gets his "slip" at the end of each month, if he has any money left after all these things come out of it, he gets it in cash. If he spent it all, they draw a line through it and write *You drew a snake this pay*.

I drop off my purchases to Daddy. I hope my candy didn't cause him to draw a "snake". He is happy that it has been accomplished correctly and he doesn't seem to notice the candy on his slip. "So how did it feel carrying that heavy stuff up that hill?" He is smiling like the cat that ate the mouse.

I knew it! That was my punishment. He sure is a sly one! "Wasn't hard at all!" I lie.

He isn't done with me. "I'm tired of you being nasty with your sister, Patsy. If you continue to be so naughty, there will be consequences!" I am just quiet. I know that now is a good time to keep my mouth shut. "Get out onto the front porch! Stay out of Dee's way! We'll talk about this again later!"

Sure, I'm thinking. I will stay out of her way, gladly! I grab a glass of iced tea from the pitcher in the fridge and run to the front porch to just sit on the big porch swing that I love. The air is damp, but the rain is done. The birds are chirping. A gray squirrel is scurrying up the big tree in our front yard. The swing squeaks with every movement. The chains are a little rusty and that makes the squeak even louder. If I swing high enough, it hits the back banister with a bang again and again. That annoys Dee in the house. Out she comes to tell me to stop swinging. I stop and stare at her, she stares back squinting her yes, "You just can't behave, can you, Patsy?"

"Guess not!" I proudly exclaim.

She turns on her heel, "One of these days, Patsy! One of these days!"

"One of these days." I whisper mocking her. I start to swing even higher, banging the banister louder.

My best friend, Ethel, just showed up. We are bosom buddies. She can see my house from hers, so she always comes when I'm out. We swing and laugh.

Bella is coming on to the porch now with Gibs. Bella is always with Gibs. Where Bella is, Gibs is. They are best friends. Bella, is loud and obnoxious sometimes. She gets into a lot of trouble with Mama and Daddy, even more trouble than me! She and Gibs have this very loud, infectious laugh that makes everyone else laugh. They hop onto the swing with me. "Heard you got in trouble already today!" Bella grins.

"S'pose so!" I swing higher.

Bella just chuckles, "Will you never learn? What was the problem?"

I'm glad to tell her. "Daddy wanted me to use the wringer washer again when he knows I'm afraid of it!"

"Why you afraid?"

"Because Susie Carenini got her boob caught in one last week!" Bella and Gibs start that crazy laughing they do. That then makes Ethel and me laugh too.

Dee starts screaming from inside, "Keep it down out there!" We laugh harder.

Now, I think I hear the honey dippers coming around the bend. Honey dippers are men in ugly green pickup trucks with big rusty barrels on the back. They clean out our outhouses. We all have outhouses in Yatesboro. The outhouse is our bathroom. To go to it, we walk out our backdoor and up the backyard past the gardens. Most houses have gardens on both sides of the walk that goes to the outhouse. In our yard we have a shed too, bedside the outhouse. The outhouse is made of rough wood with a little shingled roof. There is a half-moon carved in the door so we have a little bit of light for doing our business. Most have just one hole, but bigger families have two holes. The Sears-Roebuck catalog is there for us to use the pages for wipes. The outhouse is steaming hot in the summer and freezing cold in the winter. Regardless of the season, it always stinks.

We don't use the outhouse during the night. We all use the chamber pot that sits in the upstairs hallway as our toilet. In the morning, we empty it. I get that job a lot. Boy, do I hate it! The outhouses must be emptied once a month. If they aren't emptied, the neighborhood would smell so nasty, we could not go outdoors. The honey dippers, the men in the green trucks, go house to house. They hook up their hoses to the outhouse hole and suck all the poop and pee into their rusty, nasty barrels.

The kids in town love to run after the honey dippers. Mildred and Pee Pee are running by my porch hollering, "Come on girls, honey dippers!" Mildred is a year younger than me and she has way too much energy. She always wants to play with me, but she seems like a baby. She wears her hair up in silly little ribbons and she is always silly-happy. Pee Pee, meanwhile, is Mildred's shadow. She is poor as a church mouse, and skinny as a rail. Pee Pee doesn't act like a baby as much as Mildred. We all love following the honey-dippers.

We all four hop off the swing at once. It hits the banister hard. If I get down the stairs fast enough, I'll be out of sight before Dee can holler at me. I scurry down the stairs, two at a time, and I hop onto the gravel road. Bella, Gibs, Ethel, Mildred, Pee Pee and I start to run, but I can still hear Dee screaming at me from the porch, "This isn't over, Patsy! You gotta come home sometime!"

We start to follow the men in the big green truck. The number of kids grow. Utz and Ike just showed up. They are friends of mine. Ike likes baseball like me and he doesn't take crap from no one. He is skinny as a beanpole and slicks his dark hair back with some kind of goop. Around the corner comes Dwight Moore. I don't like that kid. He has a big nose that turns down at the end like a hook. His lips are unusually thin and his eyes are set too close together. Dwight is ugly and mean, and he has a lisp. He teases me. He is a bully.

We follow the truck to the Enterline house, the Smouse house, the Hilliard house, then the Hockenberry house, skipping and singing and just having fun. The sound of the hose sucking out the outhouses is disgusting and we count trying to decide how many minutes it takes to empty this one, then the next one. This will tell us what family has the most poop and pee. The truck is at Mrs. Hockenberry's now, and we count as the hose is sucking in the crap 1 - 2 – 3 – 4 – 5 – 6 – 7 – 8 – and plop! Unexpectedly, the hose falls off and poop flies everywhere. We squeal like a bunch of newborn puppies being fed and run out of there, onto the road, and let the men in the big, green truck deal with that mess!

Dwight Moore won't stay away from me; he keeps trying to push me off the road, but I push him right back. He starts to lose his balance, but puts his arms out like he is flying to get himself straight again. He is laughing at me, "Wath your mama thleeping when you got drethed today, 'cauth your dreth ith ugly!" He is bent over laughing, "Did your mama'th horth not need it'th blanket anymore?"

"Did my mama's horse not need it's blanket anymore? Is that what you said? You idiot!" I feel the blood rising up my cheeks into my head. I'm going to kill him! This makes me so furious, as Mama makes all my clothes. Mama has to use what is given to her. Nothing matches. The mismatched dress doesn't bother me. It obviously bothers Dwight. I will not let him make fun of my dress that Mama made.

I haul off and smack him one right in the mouth. He goes flying into the ditch that runs along the road. I scream at him, "Even if my dress is ugly, I can fix it. But your face is ugly, CAN'T FIX AN UGLY FACE!" Bella tries to hold me back as I'm moving towards taking another swing at him.

All the kids are laughing and Pee Pee hollers with a rhyme, "Dwight, Dwight took to flight!" How she got the nickname Pee Pee no one knows. So many of my friends have strange nicknames. Clearly, Pee Pee is on my side. I am thinking about my Mama and how long it took her to make this dress. I remember how embarrassed Mama gets when Daddy isn't working and we go on "relief." Ashamed about her situation, Mama has to put her hat on and hang her head when she goes to the company store to get our rations of flour, cheese, and maybe some salami if we are lucky.

I can feel my face turning from soft pink to bright red as Dwight slowly crawls out of the ditch. Before he can stand the whole way up, I kick him in his belly and down he goes again. His lip is bleeding and he is crying. I don't care. I don't care at all!

I am a little scared though. Daddy won't like that I did this to Dwight. He always tells me no matter what, turn the other cheek. I just can't seem to do that. He will find out for sure.

Dwight's mother will tell him. I will maybe get a whooping. Daddy uses a skinny flat board that has a little hole at the end just so it will hurt worse. He only swings once though, so I can take it. I will know it was worth it.

We girls take off from the boys and scurry up to the edge of the woods to walk back towards our house. We take our good, old, time picking some blackberries along the way. We eat all that we pick. There is an old baseball field in the middle of the woods. We walk through some thick brush and come upon it. We play baseball here sometimes. Ike's daddy keeps the grass mowed. It is the best kept secret of the woods.

We sit in the middle of the outfield pulling up tall grass and trying to whistle through the blades. Bella always wins at that. After an hour or more we head home. We walk down from the ridge line of the woods back onto the gravel road in front of our houses. I see Dwight's mother on my porch. Daddy hollers, "Patsy, get yourself up here!" Oh boy, I've had it.

Bella laughs. "Don't forget, Patsy. It was worth it!"

Tragedy

I t got really cold last night. I left my window open, so my room is pretty chilly. When I turned ten in October, Mama told me I could make my own decision about my windows. I don't always make the right one. I shut them quickly and hop down the stairs, missing every other step. Mama is in the kitchen preparing pancakes. Daddy is already at work. Today she put whole kernel corn in them. I love corn in my pancakes!

I have a friend on Yatesboro Hill, Tubby. I want to see him today, but I fear Mama won't let me go. He has a mean daddy. Tubby got that nickname because he is a little chubby. His freckled face is round with dimples on both cheeks. His pumpkin pie orange hair is fussy and wild. He has to work hard to please his daddy. No one seems to care much about him. When his work is done, he can run around all day and no one even looks for him.

"Can I go to Tubby's house today, Mama?"

Mama looks at me, worried. "Best not! You know how his daddy is, Patsy"

"But I really want to go. I won't ask him to play if his daddy says no. I promise, Mama!"

Reluctantly, she gives me permission to go. Pleased with my success, I eat my pancakes pretty fast and run to get dressed. I don't want to give Mama a chance to change her mind. I jolt out the screen door letting it bounce twice, as I always do.

Tubby lives on Yatesboro Hill near the Flats. I can walk there in ten minutes. Sometimes I go to the Catholic Cemetery in Yatesboro where I can look over onto the hill at all the houses. There are a lot! The coal miners were on strike last week and I went to the cemetery to look over at the hill to watch hundreds of the striking miners marching from the hill onto Main Street.

Today, I go down past the church and across the black road. Hopping down an embankment, I cross the railroad tracks to the hill side of town. It is a short distance. I walk up the dirt lane to his front door, passing an old rusty red, tireless truck sitting up on cement blocks. A beagle in a pen is barking at me. It looks neglected. It is skinny and the pen is falling in all around the poor critter. The grass around it is knee high. I wish I had some water to give it. I walk up the beaten broken wooden stairs to the front door. Knock! Knock! Knock! Tubby's daddy comes to the door with a scowl on his face and a beer in his hand.

Tubby's daddy scares me. Once I gain courage, I speak. "Is Tubby home?"

He mumbles something then points to the barn. "He's out 'der in the barn, and tell that worthless sack o' shit, ain't nothin' gettin' done 'round here! Tell him to take 'dem buckets of slop out to 'dem damn hogs and rid up dat barn! Now, ya hear?"

He makes me quake in my shoes. He is so frightening. I am happy to quickly escape. As I go running across the lawn to the barn, I think how much that poor dog and Tubby have in common.

Tubby is in the loft hiding. Tubby often has bruises on him. He is covered with bruises inside too. When I ask about his bruises, he always has an answer that I never believe. "I fell in the barn" or "I tripped on a pipe out back and hit the shed".

I know better. I am no fool. "Tubby, you there?"

The barn smells of hay and horse poop. He crawls out from behind a bale of hay. I can tell he's been crying. He is trying to hide it. "Sure, I'm here. Where'd do you think I'd be?" He wipes the tears from his face. He thinks I don't see.

To save his dignity, I play along. "Well how would I know? When you are done with your chores, come with me up to the Rearick Bus Line and we'll ride up to Sagamore. Okay, Tubby?"

"Patsy, I ain't goin' nowhere! Besides, you know how much trouble ya'all would be in with your daddy if we did that? You lost your senses?" He puts his head down. "That ain't the worst of it. What'd ya think would happen to me? I gotta feed the hogs yet and he told me I gots to rid up this barn too."

I knew he couldn't go when I asked it. Not sure why I did. I just wanted to say something happy, I think. His daddy already barked the orders to me too. I saw the look in his face and I know whatever we do, we cannot leave here, at least not right now. "I'll help you, Tubby. It will be something to do!" We sit down on a bale of hay.

"Why Sagamore anyways, Patsy?"

I twist pieces of hay as we talk. "Well, they got so much stuff there. They got the Sagamore Hotel and the restaurant where all the kids hang out. It would be fun, just something to do. Did you know Sagamore has the biggest tipple in the world? In the WORLD Tubby. Isn't that something?"

Tubby manages a smile, "Not today. Daddy has his pants in an uproar! Changing topics, he asks, "Mama bought me a hoagie at Palilla's Market this morning, didjaeatyet? Wanna split it?"

Come to think of it, it is lunchtime. "Sure thing, I'm getting hungry."

"Deal!" He treks across the yard. I watch him sneak in the back door and out again with the hoagie in a brown paper bag. He opens the brown paper onto the hay bale and splits the hoagie in two with his hands. The hoagie tastes really good.

"Thanks, Tubby. I was hungry!" I have mayonnaise at the side of my mouth he wipes away with his hand.

"Ain't nobody gonna take it from ya, Patsy!" He laughs. It is good to hear him laugh.

He devours his and crumples up the brown paper. "Been out here for a while. Musta fell asleep I reckon."

He is lying again. We both know he is just hiding from his daddy. Tubby will never admit that. I will pretend to not know the truth.

I help him rid up the barn and take the slop to the hogs. After that we settle for a game of kick the can. Normally Tubby has more freedom than me because no one cares about him. But when his daddy is home with a bottle in his hand, Tubby walks on egg shells all day long. His mama spends her days cooking and cleaning and trying to keep peace. She walks on egg shells too. Neither has a way to escape. Tubby stays outside as long as possible. I'm happy when our game of kick the can is over. It is exhausting to play that with Tubby. He is way faster than me. Before leaving, I give him a little hug before heading out. For a brief second, he relaxes and cuddles in. Then he shoves me off, "What the heck, Patsy?"

I have embarrassed him. "It's just a hug from a friend, Tubby, nothing wrong with that!" I don't care if he is embarrassed. He needs a hug. He doesn't get any of those at his house. I feel good about the hug I have given him, as I head for home. I wave bye to the scrawny dog as I leave. I will come again soon. Tubby needs my company.

As I walk down the hill to the Flats, I smell the boney dump. It burns day and night. I have to cross in front of the railroad cars loaded with coal. The boney dump is long and high. Smoke comes from underneath and from the top. It intrigues me. Daddy told me it is red dog, with coal burning underneath. I go by it now on my way home. I like to run around it. I make up stories in my mind that something lives inside. Perhaps the devil? Or better yet, maybe the Blackhands? I want to touch it, but I dare not. It is hot!

I see Ike now up along the road riding his bike. He is hollering something at me. I can't make it out. "What?" I holler back at him.

This time he cups his hands to make his voice louder. "Ballgame at the stadium tomorrow, wanna go?"

"Sure!" I run to get to where he is. "I want to go, Ike! Do you want me to meet you there?"

Ike is a nice boy. He is very tall with blonde hair and blue eyes. He wears pants held up by suspenders. He rides his bike most of the day and delivers newspapers. We are good friends, and we both love baseball. "Sure, Patsy. I will be there at noon. Gotta go, papers to deliver!"

Thoughts of going to the game tomorrow is exciting, but I still am wondering about the Blackhands. I picture them all in black clothes with black hats, black gloves, black boots, maybe even black teeth. Pondering these things, I head to the post office. It sits beside the Valley Hotel at the beginning of Swede Alley. There is a candy store in the post office too! The mail comes from Kittanning about 4:00 every day. Twenty or so kids around my age wait there for it to arrive. Whew, I'm just in time.

Utz is flirting with Jenny. The other boys are making fun of him. Rumbly tumbly Utz has jet black hair sleeked back. He likes the girls. They like him too. Jenny is timid and shy. She dresses well though, always in her little black shoes with the strap and a different dress on every day. Her hair is a sandy brown color, tied up in a pretty colorful ribbon. Utz is always flirting with Jenny. Utz is getting mad at the other guys teasing him about Jenny, "You guys keep your noses in your own business! I didn't ask any of yinz for your opinions now, did I?"

Blitz is here now with his little sister in tow. Blitz mows grass for people in town. Every day he finishes by 3:30, so he can pick up his little sister and get to the post office for their mail. Blitz is a one of those 'good ole' country boys. He gives it to Utz, "Leave 'er alone Utz. Cain't you see she is outta yer league? What ya need is a girl that cain't see yer face!" Utz pushes Blitz to the ground. We all roar in laughter.

The postmaster, old man Burt, doesn't like the noise we are making. "You kids need to be quiet out here!" He slams his door and locks it to keep us out. It doesn't matter. We just sit at the door until he opens it again, making the same amount of noise. I will never understand how old man Burt doesn't get that. Blitz and Utz will be friends again at the end of the day and Jenny will still be up for grabs.

I am going to bed early tonight. I want to have lots of energy for the ballgame that Ike asked me about.

When I am excited about something, I have a hard time falling asleep. I had a dream that I overslept and missed the game. I was so happy when I woke up and knew it was just morning. It is sunny outside. Great for a ballgame!

I get to the ballfield plenty early, and Ike is here early too. "Glad you came, Patsy!"

Our team is the Yatesboro Miners. They are playing Lumsted today. Our team is good. Lumsted has some good players too. James Patterson, their team slugger, hits them out of the ballpark every time at bat. Today may be a challenge. One time the Homestead Grays came here and played. That was a big deal. The Homestead Grays is a Negro League. In 1931 they called it the greatest team of all time. When they played us, their pitcher, Josh Gibson, pitched a no hitter. We lost terribly. We will win today, though. I feel it in my bones.

Ike and I walk through people chatting and drinking root beer. There are six kids on the merry-go-round. I think it is strange that a ballfield has a merry-go-round and the school playground has nothing but a swing.

We reach the little concession stand and Ike buys us each a nickel bag of popcorn. "We've got some good players in this town! Do you think any will make the majors?"

I know my baseball. "Of course, I hear the big leagues are after Souchok already!" We move through the crowd, heading to find our seats in the stands. Baseball is very serious stuff to the coal company and to Yatesboro. These guys who play ball get soft jobs in the tipple, or in the car garage in town. The coal company takes care of their baseball players. They don't want them getting hurt working in a coal mine.

The ballfield has a big grandstand. The grandstand is mostly made of wood with some steel. The roof is tin. Ike is heading up the stairs, "Let's go to the top bleacher." That suits me, I like being high.

We settle in on the top bleacher and anxiously wait for the start of the game as we eat our popcorn. Ike is occupied looking behind him through the black steel rails of the grandstand. He looks puzzled and concerned. "Wonder what those guys over there are talking about?" Since we are so high, we can see into a wooded area beyond the stadium behind us. Two men are standing with the umps, mostly camouflaged by the trees.

"I never saw those two men before." I whisper cautiously in case anyone can hear us. I can't help but wonder if they are Blackhands. The men have scruffy beards. One is wearing a flat cap made of leather. The other has also a flat cap with a little brim on the front. It is brown plaid wool. The men are out of the sight of most spectators. No one has seemed to notice, besides us. The conversation between the men seems deep. One ump is kicking the dirt while they talk. The other just stands with his arms folded. The one man with the flat plaid hat hands the ump a small brown envelope. The ump quickly folds it in four folds to make it small and puts it in his back pocket. The two men in the flat caps then shake the hands of the umps and meander off. I am thinking to myself, "I bet they are Blackhands! If so, they are making deals for the end game result maybe?" My mind is wondering. I look at Ike. "What do you think, Ike? Are they Blackhands?"

"Keep your mouth shut, Patsy. We didn't see a thing!" He answers in a troubled tone.

To be honest, I am troubled too. "But, Ike, what if they paid off the umps?"

Ike looks at me with glaring frightened eyes I've never seen before. "Patsy, you just forget what you saw. No good would come of us telling anyone. You tell no one, you got that?"

I told him I got it but I don't get it. I am glad when the game finally starts. I can temporarily forget about those men in the woods with the flat hats.

The Yatesboro Miners are in the outfield to start the game. The team added some new players in the last couple of years. We are sitting on first base side, and the guy on first looks familiar. "Where did I see him before?" I ask myself. He is young, good-looking for sure. I've seen him somewhere. The first inning ends. "When he gets up to bat, maybe I'll recognize him," I tell myself. No luck there, the batting helmet still hides his head. Maybe if I see him without his ballcap, I'd know him. I no sooner think this when the second inning starts. This same good-looking guy is back on first in the outfield. The batter connects with the ball and it goes straight down first base line. He scoops it up. The batter is out. With that he takes off his cap to wipe the sweat from his forehead. Now I see his sandy brown hair swept to the side. I know him! He lives on our street. I see him often sitting on his porch, across the street from my house and four houses over. Mr. Brinkley is sitting beside me on the bleacher two seats over; he never misses a game. I lean over. "Hey, Mr. Brinkley, who is that guy on first?"

"Oh, that's Sam Kaminsky. He's new, started last year. He's a pretty good ball player, aye?"

"Sure is!" To me, he has just become more than a handsome face. I'm thinking I'm going to have to figure this Sam Kaminsky out.

Just as I am ruminating about Sam, three of the young boys in town are here. They are the same age as me. Yet, they act like they are two-years old. As usual, the three boys, Judd, Charlie and Arnie, are causing devilment. Judd and Charlie are nice looking boys. Not Arnie. Arnie 's nose is kind of flat. His brown hair is rarely combed and his clothes always seem disheveled. What he lacks though in attractiveness he makes up for in energy. He stutters when he talks and never sits still. Arnie has always liked me, but I don't like him. I am near the end of the top bleacher. That makes it easy for him to tap my head and run.

The umpire yells, "Strike one!"

I try to ignore the boys. Arnie comes up again. He smacks me on the head a little harder this time. "P-Patsy h-has a-a b-boyfriend!" He says laughing like a child. He turns to run and trips on the bleacher.

I am ready to swing, when Ike scolds them, "Hey guys, back off! We're watching the game!"

Arnie flicks the tip of my ear, taunting, "P-Patsy P-Patsy!"

In response, I push him hard, so he loses his balance. Arnie falls sideways and lands on Mr. Brinkley.

I am furious. "Back off stupid! Your nose looks like your momma hit you in the face with a fry pan!" I don't care if that hurts his feelings. I am sick of him. "I am so sorry, Mr. Brinkley. I didn't mean for that to happen."

Mr. Brinkley just laughs. "Kids will be kids!"

That finally got Arnie away from me, but the boys move only two bleachers down to tease Margaret and Norma Jean, who are friends of mine and serious about their baseball, same as me. I hear Norma Jean holler at Arnie. "Go fly a kite, and take Charlie and Judd with you!"

The boys finally give up on annoying the girls. Despite the heat of the day, the three of them climb to the top of the stadium roof and run along the tin to make lots of noise to annoy everyone. Once in a while they will sit for a few minutes to fool everyone that they have stopped, but up they pop again. The trio start their running, trying to bang the tin roof harder than they did before. They know everyone is annoyed. That is what they want.

It is the 7th inning. James Patterson for Lumsted is up to bat. The score is 4-3. The Yatesboro Miners are ahead by one. Tension is high. Ike and I concentrate on the next pitch being thrown. We lean into it, holding our breath. All of a sudden, there is loud THUD and screams.

People rise to their feet. The screaming becomes louder. Some start to run down the stairs and away from the stadium to our right. We go too; not knowing what this is all about. When we reach the gravel area, we can now see Arnie on the ground in a pool of blood. He has fallen off the roof. His skin is white. His one leg is bent back underneath him. Blood is pouring from his nose and ears. As his mother screams and tries to get to him, people hold her back. Arnie's daddy is at his side. He has him by his shirt shaking him, "Arnie, ARNIE!" He puts his cheek against Arnie's mouth, trying to hear him breathe. Arnie's eyes are open, but just blankly staring. His daddy takes his hand and closes his eyes as he bends down and kisses him. He is crying, hard. Then his daddy stands up to get to Arnie's mama. He grabs her, throwing his arms around her. I can hear him say to her, "He's gone, Lucy! He's gone!" Arnie's mama is collapsing and people are running to help. Some of the men are running for something with which they can cover Arnie. The players grab their towels from the dugout and throw them at the men leaning over Arnie. Arnie is only ten years old. It took only two towels to cover him.

I don't know what to do. I have never seen a person, a human being, die before. I am flooded with guilt and grief.

I can't breathe. How can this be? Arnie was just hitting me on the head! I don't understand. Now he is dead? Ike puts his arm around me as I start to cry. "Arnie is dead!" I mutter. I can't help wishing I had not told Arnie his nose was flat. The tears now are dripping off my chin. Ike's tears form wet spots on his knickers. Neither of us can move. Time is frozen. My guilt, unlike time, grows like a life-killing alga sucking the oxygen out of the air, causing a red tide in my soul. "How could I have been so mean to him?" I say it to myself over and over. "If I had been nice to him, let him sit with us, would he be alive?"

Just as I feel I will never be able to breathe again, Ike squeezes my hand in an awkward unexpected move of compassion, caring, and camaraderie. He says to me softly as if reading my mind, "Not your fault, Patsy. Not your fault at all! God's will." He paused to let that sink in. He stands and practically lifts me off my feet in one fluid movement as he murmurs, "Let's go home!" He walks me the whole way home, something he normally wouldn't do. As if my ears have just heard an explosion at close range, all sounds are muffled in my head as Ike tells my mama about the tragedy we just saw. I hear "bang," "Arnie," "fell," "roof," "blood," "gone." My mama gently puts her arm around me and leads me to my room, murmuring to me. Vomiting all over the floor, I am cold to the core and yet sweaty. I hear the screen door shut as mama puts me in bed, lays blankets over me, pulls a chair up next to the bed, and sits there, singing softly to me like she did when I was little. I fall asleep.

Two days later is Arnie's funeral. His body is laid out in his house as all bodies are. There is a big oval mirror in the living room. Where the couch used to sit is a casket with Arnie inside. The house is quiet except for the crying. Arnie's mama is being consoled by several women. Arnie's daddy is on a chair by the casket. His head is down. Daddy holds my hand tight as we enter. I don't want to go up to the coffin, but Daddy squeezes my hand extra tight and says, "Come on. It will be okay."

It wasn't okay though. I don't understand death. How can he be alive one minute and not the next? Where is he now? Is he in heaven? Is there a heaven? Is he a ghost standing in this room with us right now? I have so many questions. He looks like plastic. I really wish he would just open is eyes. I'd even let him slap me on the head again if he wanted. Arnie won't be waking up though, I know that.

My heart feels like there is sand in it. My head wants to explode. "Daddy, take me home." He does. Many of the fathers at this very moment are at the stadium, building barriers, so kids can't get to the roof again. I hear the hammers banging against wood as we pass through town. In my mind I hear them say, "Too late for Arnie"

four
Childhood Fun

M any people in Yatesboro speak bad English. Some speak none at all. Five doors down; Mrs. Shevencko is on her porch swing today, and the smell of simmering soup flows out her beaten wooden screen door. She is Ukrainian. Her blue flowered babushka hugs her head. She lives here with her husband and one son, Joe. Like many local immigrants, she speaks very little English. As I pass her doorway, I holler. "Hello, Mrs. Shevencko!" Her withered, thin rolled-down cotton socked legs push her back and forth on her porch swing. She hollers back at me. "Pry 'vit!" I think that means hello.

I wave back at her and she tries her English, "I villy like yu ddress!"

She is very proud of herself.

I spit out, "dobry." Mama told me that means "thank you." I made a bandana headband for my hair today also. It holds in all the wild curls. I point to my bandana and to hers. "See?" Meaning I have one and you have one.

She gets it. She laughs. "Ya, ya, Patsy!" and I move on.

Most of these people had come here in the bilges of ships into New York. Their passage was classified as steerage. This is the same classification for the animals they had on board. Daddy told me in the early 1900's, work was slow, so these people had no money to pay the rent. Consequently, the company sent the company wagon and horses to their rentals and moved everything the people owned to farms on sectors of land outside of town. Then they dropped the people and their belongings off on a farmer's property. These sectors came to be called "Shanty Towns" where the people cooked on their stoves outside the barn, and slept in the barn. Once they got back to work, the company moved them back into their house which had sat empty all that time. That didn't make much sense to me, but my Daddy knows his history. I am mesmerized by his stories about the past.

Franklin D. Roosevelt won a third term this year and Daddy isn't happy. Daddy said gas went to eleven cents a gallon and sugar now costs twenty-five cents for 4 lb. and it is Franklin's fault. He even blames him for our house rent going from $25 a month to $30 a month. I am pretty sure that one should be blamed on the coal company.

I saw that Sam guy on his porch today. I waved and he waved back. Someday I will get brave enough to say hello. Today is whittling away pretty fast. Maybe tomorrow I will be braver.

I get to bed at a decent time and wake up to mama shaking me. "Wake up, Patsy. You are going to learn how to bake bread this morning!"

I could care less about baking, but Mama says I have to learn these things. I drag myself out of bed, throwing on some clothes, I get downstairs. She has started, but lets me eat my breakfast first. At my last bite she is like a turkey vulture ready to pounce on her prey. "Get your apron on, start mixing the flour in this bowl as I add to it." I try to learn without scowling, but it is hard. I don't know why we have to do this. I would gladly walk to the company store to buy bread. I struggle my way through it. I have flour in my hair and everywhere else. I am finally done and it is raising. I want to get outside.

Blowing the flour off my pants that Mama now allows me to wear, I tie up my hair with one of daddy's blue bandanas. Mama is in the garden now so I'm going to get out before she gives me another chore. Bella and Gibs are on the front porch swinging. I go out the front door. "Where you goin'?" asks Bella.

"Gonna pick up some kids for a baseball game. Wanna go?" The two of them hop off that swing with one swoop.

"Git down the stairs quick before Mama sees us!" Bella laughingly exclaims.

We start to walk from house to house, skipping and laughing. I pick up Ethel first. I never have to ask her twice; she is always ready to join me. At Slick's house, I yell to his Dad in the garden, "Hey, is Slick home?" Slick is a good player. He is tall and lean and runs fast.

"Yeah!" he replies. "He's under the front porch fixing his bike!"

I run to the side of the porch where there is just a hole made in the cement big enough to get into. I stick my head in. I startle Slick." Holy crap, Patsy, you scared me!"

I laugh. "Come on, Slick! Baseball game?"

Slick throws down the wrench he is holding. He jumps onto the porch, "Give me time to grab my bat!"

The next house is Loretta's and she loves sports. She is like me, not all girl, a little bit boy. Today she is reading on the back porch as Slick and I come around the side. "Hey, Loretta, baseball game?" Throwing down her book, she grabs her glove from under the ladder leaning on the porch and races towards us.

At the next house, we tell Jake to quit shoveling in the garden and grab his glove. Jake wears big thick glasses and squints when he talks, but boy, can he can play ball! Ike is at his house mowing and stops his mower to join in. By then Tubby shows up. I swing by Uncle Frederick's house and pick-up Dickie and Billy, my cousins. Uncle Frederick is Daddy's brother. His boys, Dickie and Billy, are only a year apart. They are younger than us, but they can play baseball really good!

We pass the Catholic Church on our way. Slick has strong opinions about religion. "You know that Catholics are the only ones goin' to heaven!"

Loretta seems insulted, "Shut up, Slick! You don't know what you are talking about!"

"You think?" He retorts, "Well my mama said she heard Mrs. Moretti tell Arnie's Mom at the funeral that it was a lucky thing Arnie was Catholic, 'cause at least he'd be in heaven."

Loretta is disgusted, "Slick, you are more than stupid, listen to yourself!" "You think for a minute I ain't goin' to heaven 'cause I'm Presbyterian? You are as dumb as the rest of the people in this town!"

I let them argue. I am not getting into this fight. As far as I can see, people make way too much about religion around here. Sometimes I think it would be best to have no religion at all, then people wouldn't argue about it.

We keep walking down the hill until we reach Tipple Alley. The tipple is to our left, for which Tipple Alley was named. It is on the south side of Yatesboro. The railroad cars are loaded with coal again. It comes in from No. 4 mine. Just off to the side of Tipple Alley is a grassy field where we can play baseball.

Slick is giving orders. "No cheating today, we are picking these teams fair and square!"

That was meant for me. I always figure out how to get the best players on my team. "Whatever, Slick!"

We manage to split the good players evenly. Still, my team wins. With the last out we feel we don't want our day to end. I have a proposal. "Leave your stuff here! Let's go to The Devil's Washbasin!"

The Devil's Washbasin is a large pond in the middle of the woods. It is a 3-acre pond and right at the end of the four mile stretch of the Great Shamokin Indian Path. Lots of fishing gets done there, but we swim there too. Shedding our shoes, we jump in the dirty water, clothes and all. Slick comes up with a giant turtle to tease us with. Ethel swims hurriedly to get away from him. Trying to get up onto the embankment she slides on the mud and slithers back into the water. Bella and Gibs do that obnoxious laugh they do.

Once the squealing and teasing all stops, we venture home, picking up our stuff first at the ballfield. I walk home carrying my shoes. My clothes are all muddy as well as my face. My hair is wet and wild. That guy, Sam is on his porch. I am embarrassed. Hope he doesn't see me. He does. He waves. I wave back. I am humiliated he saw me like this. Today is not the day I want to be brave and meet him. Gonna do that when I'm clean!

five
Swede Alley

I t is Wednesday, middle of the week. A good day to go to No. 4 Dam to swim. At the end of Swede Alley is the Yatesboro No. 4 dam. Ethel, Ike, Margaret and Norma Jean want to go with me.

Swede Alley was named that because mostly Swedes live there. It is just a dirt road with several houses lined all on one side. First house is Mrs. Benson's, a nice little Swedish lady who just sits on her porch. She always greets us with a hearty, "Hello!"

Ethel sees her first, "How you doing, Mrs. Benson?"

"Jist fine, darleengs." She stands up to lean over her banister. "You keeds vatch out for dat bear down by zee dam. Don't vant him to eat you now!" Her face is round like the moon, and her rosy cheeks light up as she smiles. I love her accent; it has a little lilting and song in it.

We pass the Kulick house, Brochetti house, then the Gosetti house. Mrs. Gosetti is out hanging clothes. "Hey kids!" She hollers.

"Hey, Mrs. Gosetti!"

Passing a couple more houses, Mr. Catardy is cutting his grass. At the next to the last house, we see Mrs. Pelligrini picking apples. We know she will give us each one. She does. She is a sweet lady, "You kids-eh be safe-eh at de dam-eh, okay?" She is always happy. Ethel laughs and gives her a thumbs up as she devours her apple.

We reach Mr. Johnson's house last. Slick teases him a bit as he is cleaning out his shed. "It is a great day to clean out a shed! Surely wish I could help, but ya see, I got business at the dam!"

Mr. Johnson likes Slick. He laughs. "Well, ven you are done vis your business at ze dam, ze vork vill be vaiting for you!" As he chuckles, we meander along. We round the corner, and there on the right, is No. 4 dam. I love the dam. All the kids swim there. We don't know what is in it. It is wet, which is all we need to swim. We climb to the cement wall from where we will dive into the murky water. Today we are going to swim all day. We will go home only when we hear the cow bell ring or when we hear our daddy bellowing to get home.

Margaret didn't have to babysit her younger sisters today. She is so happy to be along. Margaret is poor. She never has ribbons in her hair or nice clothes and shoes. She is pretty though, with her soft brown hair and brown eyes. Norma Jean, meanwhile, is an only child and she is spoiled. She is always dressed with everything matching. Her blonde hair is combed precisely into a ponytail with a pretty ribbon. She often steals her mother's lipstick to adorn her lips and she makes her cheeks rosy with the same lipstick. She looks ridiculous! When she makes herself look like that, I think she is just after the boys. I think she might be a loose goose.

Ethel and I sun ourselves for a little while, then let Slick and Ike push us into the water until they tire of it. I can dive deeper and swim faster than all of them. I never get tired or let them think they bug me. That takes away their purpose. After all the pushing, shoving and swimming, we all spread our towels on the cement to sunbathe which ultimately turns into napping. I am watching and waiting for them all to fall asleep. Finally, I see they are all sleeping. Slick is even snoring. I am able to sneak away.

I pick up my shoes very quietly and tiptoe over Margaret, over Norma Jean, over Ethel, and I jump off the wall into the grass to the wooded area. Quickly putting my shoes on, I make my way to the red brick building where daddy says the Blackhands hang out. There is a path through the woods. It is somewhat overgrown. I take my time, parting the bushes and getting pricked now and then from a wild rose bush. When I run onto huckleberries, I eat a few first before moving on.

Finally, the red brick building appears. The brick is weathered and old, and there are many cracks in it. I look up to see smoke coming from a chimney. "Jackpot!" I take a moment for a little prayer that daddy never finds out I came here. I creep around to the back, stumbling on a stump. I let out a slight squeal, then I just stop, hold my breath, and wait. No one has heard me. I peek through a crack in the brick. There I see five men standing around the flame of a fire. It is midday. The building has no windows. It is dark inside. Their weathered faces are lit only by a firelight, smoke billowing across their foreheads from their cigarettes and cigars. Each man has a flask or bottle of booze which each pause often to guzzle. In the corner is an old, beaten, wooden desk where a man sits, leaning back in a chair sleeping. His feet are up on the desk and empty booze bottles surround him. He is wearing the wool plaid hat like the guy at the ballfield!

Through the darkness I can see four men playing cards. I think it is Uncle Frederick sitting there in a dark corner handing money to another man. I must surely be wrong; this could not be Uncle Frederick that I see. Suddenly, I hear the cowbell that daddy rings when it is time to come home. I scurry out of there without having been seen. Norma Jean asks me where I have been. I just smile at her. "Nature called, silly!" She is too dumb to think any different.

We decide to go home up Tarzan Hill. That is a shortcut through the woods from Swede Alley up to the high school. When walking towards home, I think about Uncle Frederick. He is daddy's younger brother. He works at the Blacksmith Shop. I hear daddy and mama talking about Uncle Frederick sometimes. They say there are rumors that he does bad things. I don't believe that though. Uncle Frederick always plays with all us kids, tickling, throwing balls, or just chasing us around the yard. He loves kids. Uncle Frederick lives two streets down, with his wife, my Aunt Nora, and my cousins Dickie and Billy. No, Uncle Frederick could never be a Blackhand. Not my Uncle Frederick I deduce. I decide to forget what I saw.

Daddy's older brother is Uncle Tip. He is nothing like my daddy or Uncle Frederick. He is a burly guy with a loud voice. He and his wife, my Aunt Jane, live near the Catholic Church. They never had any kids. I don't think they can. Uncle Tip is our town cop, and when he isn't doing that, he works at the Blacksmith Shop with Uncle Frederick. As a cop, most days his job is boring. Nothing much happens in Yatesboro. Uncle Tip walks around town carrying his leather braided club, his pistol in his belt, and a cigar in his mouth. Much of his day is spent just chatting with people. I like Uncle Tip. When he is in his police uniform, he sometimes teases us that he is taking us to jail. We have a lot of laughs with Uncle Tip.

As bedtime approaches, I am still thinking about the red brick building and what I saw. It takes me longer to fall asleep than usual. My dreams take me back there to the red brick building. Soon, my dream turns into a nightmare of a man dressed in black chasing me. He is just ready to grab me when I scream. Daddy is shaking me. "Patsy, wake up! What are you dreaming about?"

It takes me a minute to gather myself. "Can't remember, daddy. Just know it was scary." I can remember though, but I can't say. I could never tell him what I did today.

six

Loss and Mystery

E thel and I have wasted many days doing a lot of nothing together. We talk a lot about stuff. We gossip too. We think we have everyone figured out pretty good.

We stop by Mrs. Shevencko's porch for a short visit. We don't know everything she says to us, but we always get a cookie and milk. From her porch I watch Sam come onto his porch, go back in, come back out. Seems like a boring life he has, to me. I have never gotten brave enough to meet him, and lots of time has passed since I first saw him. Going home for dinner, I wave to him. He waves back. Just that little wave he does.

Mama's dinner is delicious as usual. She has added buttered bread to our meal of meatloaf and mashed potatoes, my favorite! Now time for dessert! Mama is going into the kitchen to get the delicious cherry pie she made. The front door flies open, hitting the wall hard with a loud bang. Dickie runs through, trying to catch his breath, "Uncle Malcolm! My Daddy! We don't know where he is!"

Mama grabs him. "Dickie, calm down! What do you mean?"

Dickie tries to catch his breath, "He left last night and never came home. HE NEVER CAME HOME!" he cries hysterically.

Daddy is grabbing his hat from the hook on the wall. He looks at Mama, "Get the kids and come on!" Mama quickly takes the cherry pie to the kitchen, covers it with a towel, and grabs her shawl.

We all scurry down to Uncle Frederick's house to find Aunt Nora in despair. Uncle Frederick has been gone now since last night. No one knows where he is. Dickie and Billy are distraught as we try to comfort them, but where is Uncle Frederick? Flip Skerkovich from next door comes to the door. Flip got his nickname because he flipped his wagon over many years ago. He limps because of it. He is from the Czech Republic. Uncle Tip and Daddy invited him onto the porch. I listened from the open living room window. Flip told them in his strong Czech accent, "I suw Frederick wulk down da strit just ufter suppa lust nat."

Uncle Tip has many questions, "Which way did he go? Did he look troubled?"

"He wunt dat way!" Flip pointed his shaking finger towards Swede Alley and No. 4 dam. "He dun't look no deeferunt dan any oder time, Tip. Frederick ulways had a luuk of daturminaton yu knuw." He shifted his feet and took a puff of his cigarette, "Yu knuw vat's down dere, Tip, nut'in gud. People say dey seen Frederick goin' into dat red brick bulding duwn dere."

Daddy steps in at this point, "Let's not get ahead of ourselves, Flip. Let's take this one step at a time. What was he wearing?"

Flip thought for a minute. "He hud his green jackut on and dat flut cap he wures. Malcolm, dere wus sometin in his belt, a gun I tink."

Daddy and Uncle Tip were quiet. I feel like the air could be cut with a knife, it is so thick. Flip continues, "I've seen hum with dose Bluckhunds, but Tip, dun't tell no one I tuld yu dat."

At this news, Uncle Tip was starting to look sick. "Thanks, Flip. We'll take it from here."

Uncle Tip and Daddy know a lot about the Blackhands. Uncle Tip told me about them one day when daddy wasn't around. Daddy would have been mad. Uncle Tip said the Blackhands are sneaky and evil. They will entice people to gamble on things that are not legitimate. The Blackhands got poor Mr. Snyder to gamble his savings on horse races that never took place. His money was gone. Mr. Snyder dare not fight them to get it back. Mr. Snyder had six kids and needed to keep living. He would not have lived, had he gone after his money.

Blackhands show up when they know people are in dire straits. They loan them money and people take it, because they are desperate. When the person goes to start paying it back, they find out they owe five times more than they borrowed. Of course, it is impossible to pay. The Blackhands will take them down to that red brick building and torture them. He said some don't come home at all. It scared me really bad, what Uncle Tip told me.

We are in fear that Uncle Frederick has met his fate at the red brick building. Neighbors are starting to gather. Daddy, Uncle Tip and several of the neighborhood men walk down the hill to Swede Alley and the red brick building. It is empty. They go throughout the woods, then walk through town knocking on doors, asking if anyone saw Uncle Frederick. Several men dove into the dam to look The search continues for days, and days. Days soon passed into weeks and weeks passed into months. Uncle Tip does not give up. His normal boring job became something much more after Uncle Frederick disappeared. Uncle Tip visited houses again and again, asking questions, walking to the backs of houses, searching old sheds and even looking in outhouses. He walked through the woods often, trying to find clues. He often went back to the red brick building.

It is months later now. We never found Uncle Frederick. Life has gone on. Mama helps Aunt Nora the best she can.

Tonight, is a calm summer night. A knock just came to our door. Daddy answers the door. Mr. Johnson is here with several other men. "I've gut bad news Malcolm. It's your broder, Tip. He's gone. He gut shot down by ze dam, at ze red brick buildin'." Daddy's legs seem to give out.

Mama gets him to the couch and sits him down. "What do you know? How did it happen? Who shot him?" She is firing questions at the men.

Mr. Johnson does all the talking. "Ve don't know much, ma'am. Some keeds seen him layin' dere in da dirt. Nut no one around. Dere will be an investigation, ya know. Maybe ve ceen find the one who dun dis."

Daddy is crying. He looks sick. Uncle Frederick is gone and now Uncle Tip. Everyone knows the Blackhands are responsible, yet nothing can be done. Everyone is afraid for their families.

Mama takes Daddy upstairs. I am worried about him. I am sad too. I loved Uncle Tip. I sit at the end of the couch curled up. I cry.

Two days later we must bury Uncle Tip. The whole town comes out for Uncle Tip's funeral. He was well liked.

After Uncle Tip's funeral, men in the town gathered in front of the company store. Mr. Neal from over on the hill is the ring leader. He stands on the landing of the store to be above everyone, talking loud to the men. " No more fear, you hear me men? We are done being afraid of these evil Blackhands!

DONE, YOU HEAR ME?" Now, let's form into groups. Jed, Shin, Ben and Shy; you guys head to the left of the red brick building. Dick, Norb, Geno and Ed, you go to the right. You've all brought your weapons, have them drawn! Let's go!"

Carefully and with fear, they all walked through the woods to the red brick building. But it seemed as though the Blackhands had gotten wind of it. Seems as though they disappeared off the face of the earth. With shovels the search party overturned every inch of dirt inside and upended every table and chair. They found many empty bottles and cigarette butts. They found a flat hat that looked like one Uncle Frederick used to wear. They found a few coins and an empty flask, but that was all. They found no answers to anything.

I never told anybody that I saw Uncle Frederick in the red brick building. I couldn't. Daddy would have killed me for going there.

S everal days pass. The sadness overtook me. I know I have to
move on. Uncle Tip would want me to. My tears won't bring
him back.

It is Saturday. I am awakened today to a rain storm. Winter
is coming, and the breeze is frigid. I had left my window open
only a crack. Big mistake. Jumping up to slam the window shut,
I think about going back to bed, but my belly starts to growl. I
can smell something cooking. Mama has made me pancakes
again, this time with blueberries. I run down the stairs.
"Morning, Mama!"

"Good to see you smile, Patsy!"

"I know." Her pancakes with blueberries fill my tummy. I
can see the storm has passed. The sun is coming out bright. I
look out the back door and there is a colorful rainbow forming.
I love to go out after a rainstorm and just walk down the street
to skip through puddles, even when it's cold.

I head out the door wearing my raincoat. I am going to
be brave today. I am going to meet Sam, the baseball player.
I have now been to many games where I've watched him play.
Today, he will be sitting on his porch swing four houses over.
His tattered house is the same as mine. Both have paint falling
off the windows with cracks in some of the glass. The old porch
swing is in need of some repair but the faded cushion makes it

a welcoming place to land. He looks lonely. I am curious about his life's story. He maybe is only in his very early twenties. Being eleven now, I don't think he'd think of me as a snotty little kid. I'm going to break the ice. I move toward him, leaving the road to walk up his sidewalk. Reaching the porch, I stop on the top step. "Hi, I'm Patsy. Patsy McDonald."

I am noticing everything I can about him. I give him a quick scan. I notice he is wearing the same red and black flannel shirt I see him in every day. My mama wouldn't approve of someone wearing the same clothes every day. I wonder if that is because he is poor, or just lazy. Now I look closer. His hair is light brown, full and swept to the side, which makes him look handsome. Oh my! He has blue eyes! I like blue eyes. His eyes are sad. Why? I wonder. His hands are still dirty from the greasy cars he worked on yesterday. I know he works at the car garage. I saw him there last Monday.

"Hello, Patsy McDonald." He volunteers. "You Malcolm's girl?"

I study him. He seems normal, "Yep, that's my Daddy. I just live just four houses over across the street." He is quiet, struggling to converse. I decide to ask him something to help him out. "You work at the car garage?"

He just keeps looking away from me as he talks. "Yeah, Passerini Car Garage. I got that job a couple years back because I play baseball for the coal company."

"I know you play ball, silly. I go to your ballgames all the time. You got a name?" I ask.

"Sam. Sam Kaminsky."

"Well how do you do, Sam Kaminsky. Do you live here alone?"

He hesitates, "I been alone for a while now, but maybe not forever. We'll see. How old are you?"

"Eleven. How old are you?"

"You're pretty nosey!" He laughs. "I'm twenty-one."

He scratches his chin. "Eleven huh? You ask a lot of questions for eleven!"

He laughs and I laugh with him. I like this Sam guy. "You want to talk awhile?"

"If you quit asking questions, Patsy McDonald!" He laughs again.

I see an old wooden stool beside his swing. It has 3 legs and it swivels. I hop onto it.

"Got any pets, Sam?"

I can see he is still amused at my silly questions. "My dog out back, Spankey. He and I are buddies. Hey, you are still asking questions!"

He is funny. "Okay, I won't ask anymore. Who do you think will win the World Series this year?"

"That is a question, Patsy! The Pittsburgh Pirates, of course!"

He starts to talk a little, about gardening and how he had the first red tomato last spring.

The rain has stopped and the sun has come out bright. He stops and looks at me. "Do you want to meet Spankey?"

"Sure!" I love dogs.

Spankey is a pretty female beagle. She is well kept and friendly. We sit in the grass and play with her. She loves licking my face. "You got family, Sam?"

"You are looking at it! Spankey is my family."

I find that odd. "That's too bad, Sam. You are alone here."

"It's okay," he smiles. "I'm expecting something to show up one of these days, and it will have a red ribbon on it. Then things will be better."

I thought that was an odd thing to say. "What is it?" I have to know.

He grins and I can see there is a little space between his two front teeth. It is kind of cute. He picks at the grass as he talks. "Maybe not a package as such, but something big. It's a surprise. Don't know when it's coming. Maybe soon. Maybe not real soon, but I know it's coming."

I figure I better not ask any more questions. There is something else, I think. Not sure what, but something.

An hour passes in no time when Daddy starts bellowing for me to come in for dinner. "Maybe I'll stop tomorrow, if that's okay, Sam!"

"Suit yourself!"

He is a nice fellow, and I feel like he needs company. I'm going to come back here, for sure. "See you tomorrow, Sam Kaminsky!"

"If the good Lord's willin' and the creek don't rise!" He answers chuckling. I think that is a strange thing to say.

At dinner I ask Daddy about Sam. "I visited that Sam guy across the street today, Daddy. What is his story? He seems to be so alone over there. He seemed to like chatting with me. I think I should visit him again, to give him some company."

Daddy smiles. "A man's story is his own to tell. He will tell you when he is ready. He is a nice young man, that I know for sure. I worked with his daddy. Sam was good to his parents in every way, even as a young boy. When he was a teenager, he would be at the mine entrance with water for us all when we finished our shift. Now that was a nice kid! I talked with him a lot there. I kind of took him under my wing when his daddy got sick. He and his mama moved from the Hill over to this side after his daddy died. He works at the car garage."

I told him I knew; I saw him there one day.

"Good baseball player too!" Daddy seems to really like him. "It is okay to visit him, Patsy. He may like having company. I know he is lonely. He's had some hard luck in his life. But, Patsy, please don't make a pest of yourself. And don't forget I can watch you from here!" He walks to the front screen door. "Come here, Patsy."

I obey, as he pulls me close to the door. "You look out there, four houses over, I've got a good view of you. You see that?"

"I see it Daddy, gheez!"

Mama chimes in. "I think it would be nice if she visits him, Malcolm. Sam is a good person. He used to come cut our church lawn of his own free will. He wasn't even getting paid! Rev. Murphy really liked him. Go ahead, Patsy, be his friend if he is open to it. But, don't overstep your boundaries. And, Daddy is right. We will be watching you!"

The next day I go up Sam's porch steps again. He isn't on his swing yet. Noticing yesterday that he is very thin, I thought maybe he'd like something homemade. I holler in the screen door, "Hello, Sam! You in there?"

He comes to the door holding a dishtowel and cup he is washing. I hand him the homemade cookies I made last night. He smiles. "Wow, homemade!"

He sits the cup and dishtowel on his kitchen counter. "We might as well sit awhile, Patsy. Patsy who asks too many questions!" He laughs and meanders out to his porch swing. I go to the beaten wooden stool that swivels.

He seems deep in thought today, as he eats his cookie.

"What's wrong, Sam? Something wrong?"

"Nothing is wrong, Patsy. Just trying to get through another day. That's all."

He puzzles me, "Things can't be that bad, Sam. The sun is shining and you have a friend now, me! Doesn't that make you happy?"

He looks at me and manages another smile, "Oh, you're a friend, is that what you are? I thought you was just the cookie fairy!" He laughs. "We can be friends if you want. Then maybe you'll be around to see what comes here with that red ribbon on!"

I am thinking what the heck is this thing with the red ribbon that is so darn important? I suppose he'll eventually tell me. I like Sam a lot. I am going to visit him often! I have to say goodbye since dinnertime is approaching. I jump down his stairs, my gleeful self. "See ya later, alligator!"

Sam replies, "If the good Lord's willin' and the creek don't rise!"

There that is again! I need to ask him what that means.

eight
Conflict and Emotions

A unt Sara came to dinner tonight with her son, my cousin James. James has a brother Rich. Rich is working at his auto body shop tonight. Rich is good at fixing cars. Aunt Sara is mama's sister, and she looks a little like mama. She Is even roly-poly like mama. James is eighteen. He is a clown. During the entire dinner, he makes us laugh. He can tell the most stupid jokes and make them funny. Once in a while he uses a swear word in his jokes. Aunt Sara scolds him. We all just laugh. We love James. The dinner ends and the adults play cards while Bella, Ina and I sit on the porch with James. We have to wear our winter coats, since it is cold outside. We sit on the swing listening to more of his jokes. James is popular with the girls. He is handsome. Henrietta is walking past the house with her girlfriend, Lillian. They are his age. James stops his joke-telling to lean over the banister and flirt with the girls. I am jealous. I know he is just my cousin, but I want his attention right now. The girls move on.

"Do you like those girls, James?" I want to know.

"I like all girls!" He laughs. "Hey, did you hear the one about the actor who fell through the floorboards?"

"Let's go, James!" Aunt Sara orders as she comes out the door and down the steps. "We've got church tomorrow!" James knows how important Sunday morning church is to his mama.

As he gets up to leave, he laughs and bends down to us. "He was just going through a stage!" Oh, James!

Sunday morning is a simple wintry day. It is December 7, 1941. It had snowed a little during the night, and as the sun comes up the snow glistens on the trees. After breakfast mama chases us to the upstairs to prepare for church. Faking a sore throat, I try to get out of it. Mama knows better and tells me to get dressed. Daddy just stays out of the way of the arguing as it is simply part of our Sunday morning ritual. At the church we will fill up the back pew. Mama will pinch the fleshy parts of our arms every single time we are mischievous to get us to settle down. Daddy will let me sit next to him. He tries to save me. I do not look forward to going to church. After our usual arguing and hair-pulling, dressed and ready to head out the door, down the stairs we go and off to church.

Sunday is family day. Nothing is open. No one goes nowhere. Sunday is for our family meal and being together. We are all helping Mama prepare our supper in late afternoon when she realizes she is out of butter. "Go to Uncle Joe's, Patsy, and see if he has any butter."

I'm glad to get away from them all chatting in the kitchen. It is like a beehive in there!

I run out the screen door. I stop. There are people gathered on the street. Mr. Johnson is here, he is screaming, "Da Japanese haz attacked Pearl Harbor!" He is gasping for air. He has run all the way here from Swede Alley.

"MAMA!" I scream. Mama hurries out with Daddy behind her.

"What's wrong, Patsy?" In the same moment she sees all the people and hears Mr. Johnson. She runs down the wooden steps. She grabs Mr. Johnson's arm. "Where did you hear this? Is it true?"

"It is true. I heard it on ze radio!"

Mr. Schmidt is hollering from his porch, "I've gut the radio un!" On any normal day Mr. Schmidt is an unfriendly German. Today he welcomes everyone to his porch. We all run to his porch. There is static, but we can hear, "The United States of America was suddenly and deliberately attacked by naval and air forces of the Empire of Japan. Eighteen ships have been sunk or damaged in Pearl Harbor, and the death toll could be in the thousands!"

Mama crumbles onto the top step with her face in her hands, "My boys, we will be at war! My boys will be going to war! God help us all!" Daddy tries to calm her. Mama knows though, she is well-read and smart. She knows. I am scared.

Not knowing what to do, I run to Sam's in tears. He had been listening to the radio from his neighbor's porch. "Sam, they say there's going to be a war! Will you have to go off to war? Will you have to go?"

"No, unfortunately I won't be going to war." He stares across the yards. "I wish I could. I'd go and fight. But Uncle Sam doesn't want me. I have a heart murmur. It is not a bad one at all. But Uncle Sam doesn't want someone with a defect. I'm just worth nothin', just nothin.'"

"That's not so, Sam. You are a good man. It's meant to be. You are meant to be right here when your package comes. The one with the red ribbon!" Then he smiles.

The Selective Service System requires all U. S. male citizens and immigrants ages 17 through 25 to register with the government to serve for at least one year. Married men have to go too, if they have less than three children. My brothers are registered. Mama is afraid. The United States will now enter the Second World War, and my brothers will have to fight.

The very next day, December 8, 1941, President Roosevelt declares war. My poor brothers! In the next few months many boys in town are drafted. If they are seventeen, they are called. They do not get to finish high school. Sid just turned nineteen and Doug is eighteen. I wish they were twelve. They both receive their draft notice a day apart. They are scared. We are scared. It is hard to see so many go off to war. Sid and Doug are to report Friday to the company store. A bus will pick them up to take them to Camp Lejeune in Jacksonville, North Carolina. They will have eight weeks of training and then be shipped off to fight. Mama and Daddy are sad and troubled. We spend the week preparing for Friday.

Friday comes and we all walk to the bus station with Sid and Doug. Doug teases with me. "Stay away from boys, Patsy. They are nothing but trouble!"

Sid is quick to chime in, "Who would want her? A boy would have to be afraid she'd beat him up!" I give Sid a push and we all laugh. It is good to keep the mood light.

The bus is on time, noon sharp. Daddy gives them each a small wooden cross. "Keep this in your pocket. It will keep you safe. Now bring that back to me."

Mama gave them each a picture with all of us in it. She tries to manage a smile. "Just so you won't forget us!" She is struggling to hold back her tears. She hands them each a brown bag with the sandwich she made them.

I am so troubled. I want to take their hands and say "RUN!" I know I can't do that. I try to soak in their faces. The fear of never seeing them again is consuming me.

Doug can read me pretty good, "We'll be home before you know it, Patsy!" He grabs me, picks me up and swings me around. Once he puts my feet back on the ground he smiles. "Try to stay the size you are. I don't want to get home and you are too big for me to pick up!" We all laugh.

Sid and Doug get onto the bus and each take a window seat so they can wave at us as the bus pulls out. We all try to smile as we wave goodbye. The minute they are out of sight we are in a family-huddle, crying our eyes out.

My cousin James had to go. Even Mrs. Shevencko's only son, Joe, went off to war.

Everything is different now. There are no boys left in grades eleven and twelve. Factories start producing tanks, cannons, bullets and armor for the troops. No cars are being built.

I am scared a lot. When I get really scared, I go sit with Sam. Somehow, he calms me down. "Everything's going to be okay, Patsy. We are safe here in Yatesboro. I promise!"

"You make me see things in a different way, Sam."

"Well, someone has to, Patsy! You are stubborn and you think too much!" Somehow, he seems to take some of my burden onto himself when I am with him. It gives me a break from carrying such a heavy load.

Living with all the unknowns of loved ones at war is hard on families. Everyone tries to live a normal life, but nothing is normal. Every day is stressful for Mama and Daddy. Our life is different. We all worry so much about Sid and Doug being at war. I picture them with their guns pointed, waiting for the enemy to come out of the shadows and shoot. They must be scared. Are they cold? Are they hungry? Daddy finally got a radio and we all huddle around it, hanging onto every word of news of the war. Mama is determined to know what is going on every minute of every day. She is so sad sometimes. We are all scared. I am afraid when I hear a knock at the door. I don't want to look. I am afraid it is a man in a uniform, or two or three, coming to tell us bad news. I wish I could crawl into a cave and hide until the war is over, so I wouldn't have to think anymore.

Eight weeks after they left, Sid was stationed in the South Pacific, and Doug in Europe.

During WWII the whole country changed. Our little town changed a lot. Life became hard. There are blackout drills. When the sirens start, we turn out all of the lights and pull black material down over our windows. Every time the sirens go off, I shake and cry. I feel like at any moment a bomb is going to hit me. I put my hands over my head. I doubt that would save me anyways. Mama says I'm like a dog afraid of a storm.

Ration books are issued to families. The ration books contain removable stamps, good for certain rationed items: like sugar, meat, cooking oil, and canned goods.

Many homes took in "boarders" to bring in more income. Mama took in boarders too. I don't like having strangers in the house, but I don't complain.

I spend every day worrying. We don't play baseball games anymore. There are no games at the stadium either. The girls in town are sad. Their friends, boyfriends or brothers, are off at war. When the school holds their annual prom, it is attended only by girls. There are no boys that age left in town. The little kids in town play war games in their yards instead of just "kick the can" or "hide n' seek" like they used to play. People say things like, "I thought for sure we would be bombed." When adults say things like that, I get so scared. I go to Sam's porch and he tries to calm me, "Patsy, you must try to relax. There is no amount of worrying that makes anything better. Don't keep thinking the worst things. Think only good things." But I just cannot do that. I don't even answer him. I just sit on the stool with the three legs and spin back and forth, back and forth. "Come out back!" He grabs my hand. He leads me to Spankey. He knows Spankey makes me happy. He gives me love that is pure. We sit in the grass and play with Spankey long enough that I forget my worries. Sam knows this. I could sit here forever, but daddy hollers for me to come home.

"I'm okay, Sam, I will try to think good thoughts like you said." I pet Spankey one last time and kiss Spankey's nose. "See ya later, Sam!"

"If the good Lord's willin' and the creek don't rise you will!" He laughs as he cuddles Spankey to his cheek.

I stop and turn around, "By the way, Sam, what does that mean?"

He smiles that deep smile where his blue eyes glisten. "It means if the good Lord is willing and he doesn't let the creek rise, he will bring you back to me."

My heart feels warm. "I'll be back, Sam. No matter what!"

I arrive just in time for dinner. After the delicious meal of pork chops and fried crisp potatoes, mama has her dessert, as usual. Then she sits back down to knit more socks and mittens for the boys at war. She knits every day. Ina and Dee knit also. Mama tried so hard to teach Bella and me, but we just did not understand how to do it. Actually, Bella and me are not the knitting type. Mama has not heard from my oldest brother, Sid. My brother Doug writes to her often. Doug is safe where he is in Europe, at least for now. I don't want mama to worry. Though, I worry too that we have not heard from Sid. Is he somewhere so deep into the fighting he can't get a letter to us? Is he injured? Then my mind goes to prisoner. Is he a prisoner of war? My mind goes where I wish it would not. I need to think about mama. "You'll get a letter soon, mama. I'm sure of it!"

"I just can't hardly take it, Patsy. If I knew it was him going to wear these mittens, I'd be okay!"

Then I remember something I had heard about how the Red Cross could help locate soldiers. "Mama! Margaret's mama didn't hear from her brother, Rob, for a long time. Her Mama went to the Red Cross and they found him for her. Why don't you do that?"

Mama's head picked up and her eyes twinkled with hope. She put the mittens down and went straight out the door for Margaret's house to find out how to do this. The next day Margaret's mama took her into Kittanning to the Red Cross to fill out the forms. Within days, Mama got a call that Sid was okay. After that Mama seems to brighten up. She starts making mittens even faster than before. She has started to sing her hymns again around the house. I need mama to be happy, for me to be happy.

nine
Grief Beyond Measure

The war brought great sadness to Yatesboro. Years passed. Some boys came home and the town could celebrate. Some came home in coffins and the town would grieve. Mrs. Shevencko lost her only son, Joe. It was a hard day, the day we heard that Joe was killed. They won't even get his body for at least two weeks to have a funeral! The day after we heard Joe died, Mama took me with her to Mrs. Shevencko's house.

Mrs. Shevencko is sitting in her kitchen, staring at the flowered tablecloth. Her husband, Angelo, is in a rocker in the back room, just rocking and crying. He needs a bath. Mama kisses Mrs. Shevencko on her check. Mama goes to Angelo. With her hand on his shoulder, she tells him he needs to eat. He just shakes his head left to right and cries more. Mama pats his shoulders, "It's okay, Angelo."

Mrs. Shevencko looks beaten. Weeping, she shows us pictures of Joe from grade school up until his eighteenth birthday. In her broken English she cries, "Min dosyt' boi!" We know what that means. It means "My pretty boy." My eyes are filling up with tears that I am trying to hold back. My head wants to explode.

When the army officers had come to her door with the news, they gave her a flag to hang in her window. It is square, red on the outside, then white with a gold star in the middle.

It is lying on the table by his pictures, ready to be hung. "Can I help you hang this, Mrs. Shevencko?" Mama asks. She nods yes. In homes whose boys were lost, these same flags hang in their window. This flag tells of their sorrow and loss. I am always so sad when I see these flags.

Mama knows there is nothing we can say. Mama pulls her kitchen chair over to Mrs. Shevencko and wraps her arms around her. Mrs. Shevencko sobs into mama's shoulder.

I am so sad. I can't breathe. I can't talk. I am afraid if I move, a river will run out of my eyes. Mama motions for me to leave and I am glad. I need to cry.

I go straight to Sam's porch. He is on his swing. "Come on up, Patsy."

My legs feel heavy walking up his stairs. I say nothing. "Sit here." He says as he puts his hand beside himself on the wood of the swing. I do. I am silent. He looks at me. Sam's hand comes around my shoulders. He draws me in. His hands are warm, full of compassion. My tears start to flow. I just can't help it. My sadness has taken over. He rubs my back. It feels good. He says nothing at first. He knows why I am crying. Sam is such a kind man.

Finally, I catch my breath and am able to stop crying. "I'm okay, Sam, just needed that little cry I guess." He just smiles. I think his blue eyes are getting bluer as time goes on, is that possible? "I need to get home, Sam."

He kisses my forehead, "You sure you are okay?"

"I'm okay." I assure him, but I'm not really sure. "See you tomorrow, Sam. "

If the good Lord's willin' and the creek don't rise you will." He smiles and it warms my aching heart. "You come back if you need me, Patsy."

I get home and Mama is home now. She is as sad as I am. "Patsy, will you go to the company store for me and get us a chicken?" She hands me her ration book. I don't feel like doing that today, but I know Mama doesn't either. I will do it for her.

I have to pass Sam's house again to get to the company store. He is still on his porch, so I walk up his stairs and lean on his banister, "Thanks for being there for me, Sam. I feel better now."

"I'm always here for you, girl. You know that!"

"Do you think life will ever be normal again, Sam?"

"It will, Patsy. Trust me!" He smiles a soft smile.

I wish I could bottle that smile, put it in a jar, and open it every time I need it. "Thanks, Sam. You are probably right."

We chat for a while but my heart remains heavy. Suddenly, I remember what it was I was supposed to do. "I better get going. Been here too long. Mama needs that chicken you know! See ya later, alligator!"

"Stay away from the candy counter!" He chimes as he smiles that big smile showing that cute little space between his two front teeth.

"That's all you got to say?" I stop to ask.

"Oh yeah, If the good Lord's willin' and the creek don't rise!" We both laugh.

I am not really okay. I am so sad. I walk down the hill to the company store just trying to put one foot in front of the other. My body seems like it is walking in slow motion. The air outside feels thick and I feel there is heavy fog in the air. But mama needs a chicken.

There are several men around the meat counter in the company store. Some are familiar neighbors. They are in their own little group, talking. I ask Bumblebee, who is behind the counter, for a chicken. As he goes into the back to get it, I am listening to the conversation of the men. Italian Gus Forinini, who lives next door to Aunt Sara, is here with Ray Roebuck. They are deep in conversation. They don't even see me. Gus puffs on his cigar. He talks broken English in a loud voice. "Sure is-eh a shame. They say he was-eh a tail-gunner, I guess-eh the plane got shot-eh down. No-eh survivors."

My ears perk up. Who now?

Ray answers Gus, "Too bad for Sara, but lucky she's got the other boy, Rich."

My heart jumps out of my chest and gets stuck in my throat. It's James! James was killed! I drop my ration book and run out the door as fast as I can to home, crying all the way. Sam sees me and hollers, "Patsy, what's wrong?" I just keep running and crying. I feel his steps running behind me. Suddenly he grabs me. I fall into his body as he holds tight.

"It's James!" I am gasping for air. "JAMES IS GONE!" There is nothing he can say. His arms grow tighter around me like a warm blanket. He just lets me cry, holding me tight.

Ray Roebuck is by us now, holding my ration book. "I'm so sorry, Patsy! I wasn't paying attention. I didn't know you were there. I am so sorry you had to find out that way."

Sam assures him he will see after me and walk me home to Mama. Ray retreats. Sam's strong arms hold me close to him and hold me up as we walk. My tears are drenching his shirt.

When we reach my house, it is obvious the entire family has just found out. Bella is crying, and just going out the door, "They have all gone to be with Aunt Sara. Come on, Patsy."

I am sobbing. "I can't go there, not yet."

Bella hesitates, then her heart speaks. "It's okay, Patsy, I'll tell mama you'll come later. Take care of her, Sam." He nods.

Sam keeps me out on the front porch swing. We just swing, in silence. We sit there forever. His feet guide us back and forth, back and forth. He keeps his arms around me as I sob. He is comforting. He is all I want right now. I cannot think beyond this moment. I cannot think of how I will face tomorrow. Right now, I just want to feel Sam's warm arms around me and feel the motion of the swing, back and forth, back and forth.

ten
Life Resumes

T wo months pass by. I don't get less sad, but somehow, I learn how to manage my sadness. Things get a little better as boys start to return home. Not all of them come home. The war isn't over. Some men have simply completed their term of duty. I'm not so scared anymore. Though war still rages, my panic and worry are not so intense.

I am almost twelve now. Mama tells me I'm a cross between a child and a young woman. We visit Aunt Bertha often. Not that I want to, Mama makes me. She is my daddy's sister. Aunt Bertha is an old maid, an old biddy. At least I think she is old, but mama said she is just forty-three. She lives on the next street down. She is an elementary school teacher. To be a teacher, you only go to a "Normal School" for six months. The coal company runs the schools. They don't allow female teachers to get married, so Aunt Bertha never got married. I don't really think anyone would want her anyways. She is mean. Kids going into second grade pray they don't get her. When students are writing left-handed, she hits their left hands with a ruler making them write with their right hand. She shuts kids in the closet in her classroom when they are bad. I think in the Normal School, Aunt Bertha missed the class called, "How to be nice to kids." Her sister lives with her, Aunt Cloris. Aunt Cloris is a kind old soul. She waits on Aunt Bertha day and night. She cooks, cleans, washes clothes, and does anything Aunt Bertha orders her to do. Today Aunt Bertha is giving her orders to me, "Patsy, go to King's Drug Store and buy me Modess." She then spells it, "M-O-D-E-S-S."

I respond quickly, "What? I don't want to! Mama, must I?"

Aunt Bertha talks to me curtly, "Oh for heaven's sake, just go. Listen to what I'm telling you. It is in a blue box with white letters. Listen, it is spelled M-O-D-E-S-S. It's for my monthly 'blessing'."

"I know what the 'blessing' is!" I am mortified, "Let Bella do it!" I spout. "Must I, mama?" I plead. Mama dares not cross up Aunt Bertha.

I know mama is embarrassed for me "It will be fine, Patsy. Just go."

Aunt Bertha hands me one dollar. "Get that frown off your face, Patsy. I'm not asking you to walk to Kittanning or anything!"

I whisper to myself, "old biddy."

"What did you say, Patsy? Isla, did you hear what she said? Did you hear it, Isla?" Aunt Bertha has her girdle in an uproar.

"I didn't hear anything." Mama is defending me. I know she heard what I said. "Patsy, now get going and come right back." Mama is getting me out of here.

I walk the mile to King's Rexall Drugs. It rained last night. The streets of red dog are messy. I walk hard and fast, hopping over the poop from the horses that pull the carriages. I can walk really hard and fast when I'm mad. I finally arrive. Norm, the owner, is behind the counter. Jack, the pharmacist, is with him. Jack sees me first. "Hey, Patsy! What do you need, honey?"

I am embarrassed. My mouth feels like there is sand in it. I cannot say Modess, just cannot. Instead, I say, "Aunt Bertha needs those things in the blue box with white letters."

Jack looks at Norm with raised eyebrows. Norm smiles and points to a top shelf where the blue boxes are. "Is that what it is, Patsy?"

"I suppose so." I reply with my head down.

Jack reaches for the box and puts in a bag for me so no one will see. He takes the dollar bill, returns seventy-five cents to me, and winks. "Tell your Aunt Bertha I said hello." I smile and thank him. Jack is such a nice man.

I return to Aunt Bertha's house and throw them onto the table. "There!"

"Was that so hard, Patsy?" she asks in her normal mean tone.

"Yep, it was. Next time send Bella. I'm not doing it!" Mama pulls me by my arm out onto the porch. She orders me to go home, scolding that we will talk about this later.

Ironically, three days later I get the "blessing" as everyone calls it. I am a little young for it. Mama said my older sisters got it early too. I would not call it a "blessing!" I would call it a "curse!" Mama shows me how to use a sanitary belt. It is a skinny white thing with a small bucket type device on the front and the back. Then she hands me a box of Modess. My very own box, how wonderful! She has me step into the skinny white belt and she pulls it up around my waist. Then she hooks the strip of material from each end of the Modess pad into each little buckle hooking one on the front and one on the back. I want to die. I think to myself that God wasn't very smart when he created us, giving us "the cursed blessing" every month. It is just a miserable thing. Surely God made a mistake.

I have little bumps under my shirt now too. Mama says soon I will need a training bra. "To train me for what?" I ask.

Mama just smiles, "Well, other than training your breasts where to stay, maybe it will train you to be nicer to your Aunt Bertha!" I know she is kidding. Maybe not.

Two weeks pass by. Sid returns home. Mama is so happy. He served his time and is done. I am so happy too, especially because it has always been his job to mash the potatoes for supper. I got stuck with that job when he left. He used to make the oleo too, using lard that was white. He put in a dry packet of orange color. The oleo ended up being yellow. I took his place doing that too, but it was never quite right. Not like when he did it. I'm glad he's home. I'm glad of course for more reasons other than potatoes and oleo.

I spend a couple days celebrating Sid's return. I just want to be home with him. We make oleo together. He shows me what I was doing wrong. Three days after his return he returns to his job in the coalmine.

I'm going to go check on Tubby today. Skipping my way down onto the Main Street, I stop. A big bus is parked at the company store and there is a figure walking towards me. As he comes closer, I can see, it is my brother, Doug! "DOUG!" I scream as I run towards him. He picks me up and I throw my legs around him. We swing around on the sidewalk as Mrs. Blose claps from her front porch.

Doug is half laughing, half crying, "Lucky for me you didn't get too big for me to still pick up!"

Life feels a little better. There are still families waiting for their boys to come home. We still use our ration books and sit around the radio every evening listening for news of the war.

Our Yatesboro Miners start to play baseball again. Sam asks me to go when he plays. In the last game he hit a homerun. When they gave him his homerun ball, he threw it up to me in the stands. I was proud as punch.

People stop talking so much about us getting bombed. I am getting used to the sirens going off. It doesn't scare me so bad now. People talk about things other than the war now.

We miss James terribly. Aunt Sara doesn't come out of the house much. James' brother just goes to work and goes home. We never see him. Mama visits and tries to talk to him, but he always retreats from her. Angelo Shevencko died last month. People say it was from a broken heart. Mrs. Shevencko went back to sitting on her front porch just yesterday. My heart gets heavy as I near her house. I smile at her and wave. "Dobry, Mrs. Shevencko!" She does not wave back or even smile at me. I understand.

eleven
A New Life

Just as we are finishing dinner, there is a knock at the door. I open the door to the cool night air. It is Sal Matteo.

The Matteo's are the last house on the hillside almost in the woods, past the Notto house. They don't come into town much. Sporting a strange tattoo on the side of his face, Sal Matteo, is somewhat of a mystery. He has a wife and eleven kids. People say he doesn't care much about them. He is very tall and thin, he always needs a shave, he never smiles, and they say he is a Blackhand. He scares me.

I am not sure what to do. What does he want? He is looking at me with piercing eyes, "Where's your mama?"

It takes me a second to reply. "She is eating dinner. What do you want?"

Daddy's hand grabs my shoulder and he pulls me back. "Excuse my daughter's rudeness, Sal. What's up?"

"It's my wife. She's having a baby. We need Isla to come!" He says it without emotion.

"Give her time to gather her things. She will be there shortly, Sal."

"Thanks." He simply turns and walks down the steps.

Mama, having heard all this, is already packing her medical bag. "This will make twelve kids for Mrs. Matteo. I haven't seen her in months. I didn't even know she was pregnant!"

Daddy scowls, "All that guy knows is how to make babies. Mrs. Matteo has to take care of all those kids herself, and now another! That guy is no good. I tell you, no damn good!"

Mama scolds him, "Shush, none of our business."

I see Mrs. Matteo at the company store. She is not very tall and she always wears the same flowered house dress. Her matronly shoes fit perfectly with the cotton socks she wears rolled down. On her head is a bandana made into a headband, hiding the wisps of gray forming above her ears. She always looks tired. There is always a child on each hand and two or three in a wooden wagon the older kids are pulling. Her husband never accompanies her. He never comes to town. He doesn't come to drink in the bars either. Daddy says Sal is one of those Blackhands that does all his drinking at the red brick building. Mrs. Matteo seems to live rather poor. Sal works in the coalmine with a good salary, but daddy says he spends all his money on drinking and gambling. He won't give her any more than enough to feed the family. Poor Mrs. Matteo. She's just weak, I think. Demands nothing for herself, nor for her kids.

Sal Matteo has a brother, Bruno Matteo. Bruno seems much different from Sal. He is just a bit younger with a stocky, yet muscular build. He has dark hair and eyes, and he is handsome. His hair is always mussy, but that just makes him more handsome. He has olive skin and always wears a white tee shirt with the sleeves rolled up. It is rumored he is a Blackhand also. That is hard for me to believe. He just doesn't look the part. Bruno will come into town to the bars and the Valley Hotel where he flirts with all the women in town. I haven't seen him for a while now. I heard he moved away. People will soon forget he ever existed, like they do everyone else who leaves our little town.

Daddy walks Mama to the Matteo's. We girls get in a game of rummy and head to bed.

I wake up to birds chirping and the sun shining. Daddy would have left for work already. I head to the kitchen. Perhaps I will be kind and make everyone pancakes today.

As I am putting my scoop into the flour bin, I pause a moment and listen. There are sounds of a baby crying. It is coming from upstairs. I hurry up the stairs to find Mama bathing a teeny-weeny little girl baby. Mama looks at me and smiles. "Meet your new little sister, Ruby. She has come to live with us. We will love her like our own."

This is confusing. I don't know what to think. "What, Mama? What do you mean?"

Mama lays Ruby down on the bed. She sits beside her and pats the bed looking at me, which means sit down, Patsy. I sit down. "Mrs. Matteo couldn't feed another mouth, Patsy. It is that simple." Mama can see my blank face, I have so many questions. She keeps talking. "You know, Patsy, it is not unusual for a parent to give up a child because they can't afford it. It happens often. They want this baby to have a good life, that is all. I told them I could give her that life. Don't you agree?"

"Mama! How can a mother give up her baby? How?"

Mama put her head down, then looks at me, "It is an act of love, Patsy. A mother gives up a child because of love."

This seems confusing to me. I don't understand. "And just like that, they are going to forget about her, when she is just across town with us?"

Mama seems nervous. "Yes, they promised. They promised to never come into her life. When I saw her, I fell in love with her. When they asked me to take her, I took her. That's all."

"This doesn't seem right, Mama. What about the Blackhands and all that business? Someday Sal Matteo will decide he wants her back and he'll be at our door with a gun!"

"No, Patsy, he will not. He clearly, CLEARLY did not want this baby. Heck, we all know he doesn't even want the eleven he already has!

I know this to be true. Mama looks serious, yet troubled. "Patsy, we are never going to tell Ruby she isn't ours. No need for her to know. It will be as if she came from my womb, do you understand?"

I look at the little baby lying on the bed. I put my little finger into her hand. Her tiny fingers wrap around it. She is sleeping but making sweet little motions with her mouth. Her skin is soft and she smells so good. "I guess so. Who named her, Mama?"

"She was already named, Patsy. I like her name, 'Ruby', don't you?"

"I suppose so. But, what about Daddy, what did he say?"

"You worry too much, Patsy! Daddy loves kids too. When he knew the story, he agreed. We will give Ruby a home."

"This is all so strange, Mama. I don't know how to act when I run into Mrs. Matteo now. It is all so strange!"

"Mrs. Matteo is not going to be a problem. She is so busy with all those kids we barely see her now." Mama started to fold diapers onto the bed. "Mrs. Matteo was so happy we are giving Ruby a home. She promised me she will act like it never happened. I trust her, Patsy. Her husband is no good, but Mrs. Matteo is a good woman."

I stroke Ruby's head. It feels like an over ripe peach. "Good woman? A good woman doesn't give up her baby!"

"You need to stop it now, Patsy." We have made this decision. You are Ruby's sister. She is your little sister. Forget everything else and look at her. How could you not love her?"

Ruby is starting to make sucking motions with her lips. "Can I hold her, Mama?"

"Of course. Now be careful of her little head."

I pick her up gently and bring her cheek to mine. Under her long white gown, she is wearing purple booties. I feel her little toes with my hand through the booties. She is warm and soft, and now she is cooing. She is a beautiful little thing. She squirms in my arms and leaves out a whimper. I rock her gently and sing to her. She falls into a deep sleep on my shoulder. I look down at her beautiful little face next to mine. I'm going to forget how this all came about. I'm just going to forget it. I love Ruby.

I do not put Ruby down today, except to change a diaper. I feed her bottles and give her a bath before bedtime.

The next few weeks I take care of Ruby every day when I get home from school. I never complain. I love doing it. She is soon two months old. I am ready to take her out! I wrap her in a quilt and walk over to Sam's. He is on his porch, as if he were waiting for us.

"What you got there?" Sam smiles; he knows it is Ruby. I had told him the story of how we got Ruby. He has been anxious to meet her.

I put her in Sam's arms as he reaches for her. "If she cries, I'll take her back, Sam."

"You think I can't manage a crying baby?" He beams at the sight of her. "There now, Ruby. Show me your pretty smile!" Sam talks to her in baby talk which surprises me. Ruby does not fuss. She smiles back at him and Sam loves it. He puts his finger in her hand and she holds on tight. I visit for two hours. Sam never relinquishes Ruby, nor does she fuss.

We finally have to leave as it is time for Ruby's bottle. Sam reluctantly hands me Ruby. "Will you come back tomorrow with Ruby?"

I am glad she makes him so happy. "Of course, Sam."

Sam seems happier nowadays. He still talks about that package coming with the red ribbon, but not as often as he used to. Seems as though it is never coming anyways! Maybe Ruby will get his mind off that package

We'll be back tomorrow, Sam." He reluctantly hands me Ruby. "See ya later, alligator!"

"If the good Lord's willin' and the creek don't rise! By the way, now the Lord needs to bring two girls back to me, not just one!"

I walk away with Ruby and look back, "He will, Sam."

twelve
Destruction and Loss

T oday is June 23, 1944. I am growing into a young teenager. Franklin Roosevelt is still President, so Daddy still isn't happy. My favorite song is "I'll Walk Alone" by Dinah Shore. There is a verse in that song I love. I sing it to myself, but in my head, I am singing to Sam. "I'll always be near you wherever you are each night in every prayer. If you call, I'll hear you, no matter how far. Just close your eyes and I'll be there." I feel that way about Sam. I am there for him. After all, he has been there for me.

My figure is starting to fill out. My flat butt now has a little bubble. I'm thinking I better quit eating so much. Utz, Blitz and Ethel just came by, "We're going to the movie, Patsy. Wanna go?"

Of course, I do. I run into the kitchen. "Mama, can I go to the movies with my friends?"

She stops rolling her bread dough to look at me. "You can if your sisters go along. I don't trust you!"

"That's not fair!" What did I do?"

"You are always flirting with those boys down by the company store. I keep telling you that ladies don't do that, but you keep doing it!" She seems annoyed with me.

I am angry, but since I want to go to the movie, I know to be kind. "Just so you know, mama, I don't like any of those boys. It isn't flirting. It is just being friendly."

"So be friendly with your sisters, Patsy. Try that one on for a change!"

I can't win. I am giving up. Mama is sending Ina, Bella and Dee along to the movies with me.

We start to walk from Yatesboro the mile up the road to the Liberty Theater. It is a hot day, unusually hot. There is no breeze at all. Approaching Passerini's Auto Garage, I feel sorry for the guys pumping gas. This is where Sam works. He must be inside working on cars today. Reaching Avi's Tavern next, the door is open. "Hey, Patsy!" I hear someone yell. It's just Jake Nelson. He sells popcorn at the ball games.

Ina is annoyed, "How do you know the men at the bar, Patsy?"

"I go out with them after you go to bed every night!" I answer sarcastically. She deserves it. That is a stupid question. She gives me a shove and runs ahead with Dee. I can hear her telling Dee what a twit I am. I never did understand that word. What exactly is a twit? I think a twit is a pregnant goldfish.

As Ina and Dee pass the Lazzeri Bar, the American Legion, then Colo's Bar, Ina goes slow hoping someone will holler out the open doors to her. No one does. Hilarious!

At Palilla's Market, Ina tells us to wait outside. Mama has an outstanding bill and Mama has given her the money to pay it. Lucio and Chuck are the owners, they are brothers. Lucio is behind the counter today. As she pays him, he waves to us all standing outside his store window. Then he hands Ina a lollipop for each of us. Lucio is such a kind man.

Passing Pina's Restaurant, the smell of freshly baked pizza coming out the door is heavenly. I must tell Mama we are due for a Pina's pizza soon. We stop next to peer into McClanahan's jewelry store window. The gold and silver sparkles as the light hits the jewelry. Passing Geno's Barbershop, his inside door is open, so he hollers through his screen door. "Who out there wants a piece of candy?" We all run into his door as he hands us each a little round ball of candy. Geno is a very short Italian man and his barbershop smells of cheap men's cologne and baby powder.

Mr. Bobeck is in his barber chair. "You gonna'eh make a da kids fat'eh!" He laughs.

Geno just laughs. We love Geno, and he loves us.

We keep moving on. Another half mile, and we pass Abe Cohen's clothing store. They see us and wave through the front window that is floor to ceiling. They sell pretty clothes in their store, but Mama doesn't take us there. We can't afford it. Passing the firehall, the big doors are open. The firetruck has gone on a call. Jed Craft is in the doorway talking to Mrs. Barriss from down the street. "What happened?" I want to know, I am nosey.

He laughs, "Mrs. Samson's cat was stuck in her tree!" We all laugh, that is life in a small town. A cat stuck in a tree is a big deal.

We finally reach the Liberty Theater in Rural Valley, to the smell of popcorn and musty wood. The theater is owned by Mr. and Mrs. Nagy. There behind the glass, as we enter, is an older lady. Her gray hair is up in a bun and her glasses are halfway down her nose. We pay her the twenty cents to get into the movie. She shoves a ticket under the half-moon of the glass while glaring at us. "Thank you!" I say softly. She does not respond. From there we walk through the door to Flo sitting on a stool to the right. She takes our tickets and says nothing. She is quiet as a church mouse, at least for today. They say she is a smart woman but eccentric, to say the least.

Next is the candy counter that Mrs. Nagy runs. "Popcorn please." I hand her my ten cents.

The movie today is *Edge of Darkness* with Errol Flynn and Ann Sheridan. It is all about Nazis and war. The boys are looking forward to it. We girls aren't so much. We just love coming to the theater. We will carry on and chatter until Mr. Nagy comes down the aisle shining his flashlight to scold us. The movie begins, but I hardly notice, as I am arguing with my sisters. Blitz just wants to watch the movie, "Can't you girls shut up? I'm watching this!" Utz tries to put his arm around Ina as she throws it off.

I can see Ina is mad. "Back off Utz! Can't you just back off?" Utz retrieves his arm and dives into his ten-cent bag of popcorn. We are all laughing. Bella leans over to Utz, "You don't want her Utz! She's a freak show, trust me!" Ina doesn't respond. It never pays to engage with Bella.

The big rolls of film are spinning from high above us in the balcony. About midway through the movie when the little fishing village is about to revolt against the Nazis, the lights go out and the movie stops. Mr. Nagy quickly comes with his flashlight onto the stage in front of the big screen, "This is simply a power outage. You all need to just sit there and behave until the power comes back on." Behave we do not! This is an opportunity for us to be more mischievous than before. All the teens in the theater are joining in, throwing popcorn, wrestling, calling each other names. We just continue to cut-up and misbehave like children.

Poor Mr. Nagy just cannot get a handle on any of us. Finally, after an hour, he walks onto the stage in front of the big screen waving his flashlight from left to right. "You all go home now, still no power so no movie!"

Disappointed, we all walk towards the doors, chatting a mile a minute. Utz throws open the door and with him goes Ina, Dee, Bella, and Blitz. I am last with Ethel. The others stop dead in their tracks and we run into them. No one can speak. There is debris everywhere. Across the street someone's roof is half off. There are trees down, garbage cans on the street, plus wood and all sorts of debris. House windows are broken. Porch furniture is everywhere. A tornado has hit Rural Valley while we were cutting up in the theater! It was so strong, it was able to projectile pieces of wood and debris into the sides of houses.

We start to run home as fast as we can, jumping over huge tree branches. We have to dodge metal and glass lying in the street. There is a dog house on its side in our path and somebody's wheelbarrow and porch swing. We climb over it. We come upon the Lutheran Church. The tower is the only thing standing. The building is destroyed. The Balaugh family's farm is next. There is a cow lying dead. Their barn is crumbled to a pile of wood, yet Edward's Funeral Home next door to it is intact. The Postlewait house is laying on its side. Ira Schrecengost is with Mrs. Postlewait in the yard, trying to console her. The Judson's garage is lying in a heap. "Run!" I holler to the rest, "Run faster!"

We finally reach Yatesboro. One more hill to go and we are there. As we turn the corner at the top of the street, we can see our houses still standing. Some are tattered a bit, with shutters hanging off. There are willow tree branches and other debris strewn across lawns, but the houses are standing. We are so relieved. I race into the house to Ruby running into my arms.

Mama and Daddy are here and we all hug. They have been so worried about us.

"You all okay?" I cry. "Everyone okay?"

Mama seems calm. "Calm down, Patsy. We are fine. The worst thing we got was our burn barrel coming down from the top of the backyard and hitting the house. It scared us to death!"

There are no casualties, but there is so much destruction. The town is turned tipsy turvy and everyone is out walking about in a daze. I leave Mama and Daddy to run to Sam's house. Sam is not on the porch. "Sam, Sam!" I holler, running around the house. Sam is in the back yard by his dog pen, sitting on the ground. He is holding his beagle, Spankey, in his arms. When the tornado hit the buildings on Main Street, the lumber flew at least a mile wide. A splintered board hit Sam's little Spankey. Sam is pulling the splintered wood out of Spankey's back. Spankey is a small beagle. His injuries are serious. I can see the blood pouring from the top of Spankey's back. Sam is holding his hand firm on it with his handkerchief. I kneel down, "Let me help, Sam."

Sam waves me off, keeping his head down, but I can see the tears falling onto Spankey.

It is too late to help. Sam holds Spankey in his arms as he draws his last breath. My heart aches for Sam. I put my arms around Sam. We both cry. I sit with him until he is able to get up. "Will you stay with him, Patsy, until I get a blanket?"

"Of course, I will, Sam." I take Spankey onto my lap. Sam goes into the house and comes out with a soft blanket with bright squares of every color and a wide satin hem. Together we wrap Spankey in the blanket. I sit with Spankey on my lap, wrapped in the colorful blanket. Sam digs the hole. Together we bury Spankey. After we are done, we stand over the fresh earth, speechless. I take his hand. He is trembling. He looks at me. In his eyes I see his grief. It feels like I am looking into the depth of the sea. His tears have created dirt streaks on his face. I squeeze his hand. I look down at Spankey's grave. "God, this is our friend Spankey. Please take good care of him." Sam puts his arms around me and we stay in a long embrace. We so loved Spankey. I wish I could take Sam's pain away, but I can't. I stay until darkness falls, sitting together in the grass by Spankey's grave.

It seems as though Spankey was all he had. Spankey was his family. He only has me and Ruby now. I am so sad for Sam. "I wish you had family, Sam."

He manages a smile. "I've got you and Ruby, that's enough. And when my package comes with the red ribbon, then I'll be really good. Really good for sure. Don't worry."

As time goes on, he begins to expect our daily visits. If we miss a day, he asks us where we were. Ruby begs for his attention. She makes him smile again. Ruby is becoming a toddler. Sam loves playing with her. He mixes up mud pies with her, laughing at her face covered with mud. When Ruby brings a book, he reads to her. He never wants us to leave, even though he knows we will be back the next day.

Ruby isn't talking yet. I have to tell her, "Wave bye to Sam!" She picks up her little hand and waves. I speak for her. "See you later, alligator!"

Sam always smiles at us, "If the good Lord's willin' and the creek don't rise!"

thirteen
End of Terror

My sister, Ina, acts like she's my mama. She is always telling me what to do. Now that I'm fifteen, Ina thinks all I do is look at boys. The boys like me, sure. She hates that because none of them like her! Little does she know I like no one as a "boyfriend" or even think about that. I just flirt. There is not one of them I consider mature, like Sam is. Maybe someday I will find a boy that acts like Sam. I sure hope so!

We're going to the dam to swim today. A bunch of kids are going. Dee is painting the shed for Daddy today. Dee was the only one that volunteered. She does anything Daddy wants. That is why Daddy likes her best. Ina is coming along to the dam. She will be watching my every move! She says Blitz and Utz are too fresh with me. Maybe I'll give her something to get worked up about! I got a new bathing suit. It is pink with tiny black polka dots. The strap comes up around my neck and the bottom of it is straight across. I look pretty good in it. I'd have to say. The boys think so too. Sam hasn't seen it, but I'm sure he would say it is nice, though I think Sam would say it doesn't cover enough skin.

We start down the street and pick-up Ethel, Margaret, Norma Jean, Blitz, Utz, Slick, and Ike. Today we decide to take a different path than just walking up Swede Alley. If we go up behind my house, we will hit the railroad tracks. We can follow the tracks, then go through some woods, and come out at the

97   THE CREEK DON'T RISE

dam. The train doesn't use this track anymore. Each railroad tie peeks through the grass. I balance myself on the steel rails as I walk. We soon arrive at the empty train boxcars. A door is missing on one so I hop in. The wood inside is old and smells of oil. There is a broken coffee cup here, pieces of an old newspaper and some hay. I have to wonder if someone hasn't slept in here. After a short while, we get back to our path to the dam.

It is a pretty day and the birds make music in the trees. I am enjoying all this wondrous nature when I notice that Blitz has sectioned me off by myself. Blitz plays football for the school now, so he is pretty full of himself. He gave me his wrist watch to keep for him after the last game. I like Blitz as a friend, but that is all.

Just as I am ruminating about Blitz, I feel Ina behind me. I look at Blitz. "Hitler is here!" He laughs.

We pass an opening to an old coal mine that has been abandoned. We peek inside. Slick starts to venture inside the opening. As he starts to disappear in the darkness, Ina hollers, "No! Don't go in there! Get out of there, Slick!

Slick emerges running and hollering, "Run, the bats are coming!" We believe him. So, squealing and screaming, we start to run. I am way ahead of everyone else. I look to see if they are coming. Bang! I run smack dab into what feels like a wall. It is a tall dark man in a dirty jacket and pants, crumpled hat and dirty face. He grabs me by my arm. I can see his filthy hand with all the black dirt under his nails.

"What you doin' here, girl?" He seems angry. I can see his rotten teeth. His breath is foul. I instantly freeze in fear. Just then the other kids come through the trees. They all stop and stare. The man releases me. "Just wantin' to know what she was doin' here, that's all!" I sprint around him like my life depends on it. The rest follow me, taking a path just above the man to avoid him. He is scary and I wonder, is he a Blackhand? Is he the one that is sleeping in the boxcar?

We eventually reach the dam and jump onto the cement wall, gathering to discuss our strange encounter. None of us have ever seen this man before, but Blitz surmises, "I'd say for sure he is a Blackhand, 'cause that red brick building is right through those trees there!" He points south. I know very well where it is, I remember when I had visited it.

"I just want to forget about it. Can we just swim?" I plead. Nothing we can do now but get on with our day.

The dam is over 20' deep in the middle with an overflow called "the chute". We like to dive from the chute. The coal company had built the dam to make power for the mines. It didn't work like they planned. The power is often off. At least it is good for swimming. Ike and Blitz waste no time in trying to push us all off the wall. There is a lot of squealing going on. I am a good swimmer. I challenge Blitz and Ike to a race. They accept readily. We all jump into the water to do three laps which will take a few minutes. Everyone knows I will win.

Suddenly we hear the horns of cars, many horns. Pickup trucks pull up to the dam and the drivers' doors fly open. Mr. Johnson stands on his running board and is yelling, "Git in da truck keeds, da vwar is over! Da vwar is over!"

We climb onto the cement wall and try to understand what is happening. Blitz is quickly rubbing his towel on his hair. "I think he said that the war is over!"

"Holy crap!" I holler. We all grab our towels and run to the trucks. We ride all over town waving our towels as we scream. "THE WAR IS OVER! THE WAR IS OVER!"

Everyone in town is out on the street waving flags and cheering. The celebration goes on into the night. The bars are giving away free drinks. People are playing music and dancing in the streets. This is a very good day, May 8, 1945. Any boy from town still at war will come home now. There will be no more sirens blowing. No more drills. No more ration books. No more tears.

Daddy is happy about the war ending, very happy. He still isn't happy about our President though. Franklin Roosevelt died on April 12th this year and Harry Truman took over. Still a democrat, of course. Daddy desperately needs a republican to take office.

I laugh at him. "Daddy, it doesn't really matter. Does it? Our little town is going to be normal again, no matter what!"

He scowls. "Won't never be normal with a democrat in office!"

fourteen
Sad Larry

Y atesboro is happy again! Everything seems to have gotten
  back to how it used to me.

Two months after the war ended, the carnival came to town.
The carnival is a big deal here in Yatesboro. The anticipation of
the start of the carnival goes on for weeks. The carnival company
starts to set it all up in a big grassy field. As each tent rises, the
excitement rises also. The rides come in one at a time and the
whole town watches as it is all put together. The opening night
is Friday night. I can't wait!

Friday finally arrives. It is a moonlit night with lots of
stars, and the lights of the carnival seems to glow in the sky.
The smell of the caramel corn and greasy French fries fill the
night air. As usual, I have Ruby at my side. I hold her hand
tight as we navigate the long rows of rides and games. Ruby is
too small to ride, but she squeals with delight when I buy her
a cotton candy and lift her up for her pony ride. "Win me a
stuffed animal, Patsy!" Ruby is always begging to play games.
I love to play games, so we head straight to the stands where
men coax us in with promises of winning the biggest stuffed
animal. I want to win one of these for Ruby. I try for a long
time and finally I win a stuffed monkey. Ruby is thrilled. "I'm
going to name him Jocco!"

The carnival guys are a breed of their own. Most have dirty faces, and wrinkled dirty hats, with a cigarette hanging out of their mouths. Their lives could not be pleasant for sure. The guy that runs the penny pitch is Larry. I like his game the best. His brown hat is all crumpled and tilted to the side of his head. He always has on the same brown plaid shirt. His eyes are sad. He has a big old chew of tobacco in his mouth with a little of the brown juice running down his chin. He needs a shave. I think of how sad his life must be. Seems like he has no one. I try to kid with him to make him smile, "What's happening, Larry? You having a good day?" I ask as I try to get a penny to land on a plate I like.

Larry grumbles, "Nothin' good 'bout nothin.'" That is what he always says every time I ask.

I return daily to pitch pennies at his stand, but I cannot make Larry smile. It is the fifth day of the festival and I'm going without Ruby. Mama insists I need a day without her. Maybe I do, but Ina comes along. I would rather have a three-year-old along. We ride our bikes down to the carnival just after lunch. I hurry to Larry's stand to pitch pennies. The stand is closed. There is a sign hanging on the post that says, "Help look for Larry."

"What's happening? Where is Larry?" I ask the guy at the next stand, the one where you pitch darts at balloons.

When he talks, I see his rotten teeth. "Don't know where he is. He just didn't show up this morning and that ain't like him."

Suddenly I hear someone screaming, "THE DAM!" People are jumping in their cars. Everyone is rushing to No. 4 dam. I jump on my bike along with Ina and we ride as fast as we can. We pass the row of houses on Swede Alley and race around the corner until we reach the dam. On the cement wall is Larry's crumpled, dirty brown hat, just sitting there. The men are staring at it, with sullen faces, talking in low voices.

Tubby, Ike and Slick rode their bikes here too. They shed their shirts and shoes and dive in. Ina and I shiver as we watch. What seems like an eternity passes when suddenly up comes Slick from the dirty water, then Ike, but no Tubby. Ike is out of breath. "CAN'T FIND HIM!"

I wait for Tubby as I shiver and cry. I don't know why it is taking Tubby so long to come up! Finally, Tubby emerges. I can see Larry's brown plaid shirt as his body emerges. Tubby has his arm around Larry's neck, dragging him and trying to stay afloat. Larry isn't moving. He is dead weight. Tubby is struggling.

Slick jumps into the water and hollers to Tubby, "Grab my hand!" He is able to pull him close enough to pull him over to the edge where Tubby can touch. Tubby never lets Larry go. The other boys grabbed onto Tubby's shirt to help get him onto the cement. The two older men grab hold of Larry by his belt to pull him up and lay Larry down. We all stare in horror. Mr. Johnson starts pounding Larry's chest and then turns him on his side, but nothing. Larry is covered with dirt and moss. He is blue. Tubby is sitting at the end of the cement crying, and trying to get his breath.

I go to him to comfort him. He pulls away, "Leave me alone!"

I just rub his shoulders. "It's going to be alright, Tubby. You are a hero today."

That didn't change the fact that Larry is dead. Larry has drowned. He committed suicide. Ina and I cry. I want to be strong for Tubby, but I can't. I wish I could have made Larry smile more. I wish I would have asked him why he was so sad. I wish I could have said something to make him want to be here. I wish, I wish.

fifteen
Dancing the Night Away

've overheard people tell Mama I'm becoming pretty. I heard mama talking to Mrs. Shaffer across the street. "She'll be even prettier once she learns how to not talk back to her mama!" I don't know what she means by that! I am way better than Bella is. Bella gives Mama a hard time all day, every day.

Later, I tell Sam what Mama said. "Maybe just be careful how you talk to your mama, Patsy. And she is right. You are pretty." He is embarrassed when he says it. I see him blush.

I laugh. "I'm not a little girl anymore, am I, Sam?"

He just frowns, "Time's moving way too fast for me!" Then he gets quiet. "I'm beginning to think my package with the red ribbon isn't coming, Patsy. Not coming at all!"

There it is! That package again! I will not discourage him though. "I'm sure it will come, Sam." I think I'll change the subject. "Hey, did you ever go to the Valley Hotel, Sam?"

"Yes, I've been there. Why do you ask?"

"Just wondering, that's all!" I am lying. I am going there. I don't want him to know.

The Valley Hotel in Yatesboro sits right where Swede Alley begins. That is where things are happening. The hotel is large and has hotel rooms, a dining room, bar room, barber shop and dance floor. Beside the hotel is a barn for the horses. Bella and Gibs go to the hotel a lot and sneak onto the staircase to watch people. They never get caught. I had asked Bella to take me and Ethel tonight. She finally gives in. First, she gives me instructions. "Now, Mama thinks we are going to Slick's house to play cards. That's our story."

It is dark out as we make our way down the hill. Slick is there to meet us. He opens the old wooden door that leads to the back staircase. I can hear the music.

The staircase goes up the back of the building, across a hallway, then the stairs go down onto the dance floor. We sit at the top two steps where it starts down, just above the people dancing. There are men everywhere, smoking and drinking. Many of them have pretty ladies around. Some of the women are not so ladylike. The women have such pretty dresses on and the dance floor is full. Some women are smoking long cigarettes dangling from their fingers with their long red painted nails. My mama and daddy had an apartment here long ago where my first two brothers were born. Mama and Daddy cleaned the hotel to make money. I feel bad for them. I know they never had fun like these people are!

The night ends and we don't get caught. We sneak back down the staircase to the back. I go to bed tonight dreaming of being one of those ladies swinging around the dance floor. Even the ones not so ladylike, smoking the long cigarettes.

I decide to tell Sam I went to the hotel. He doesn't like it. "Not my business, but that's not a place for a young girl like you." I shouldn't have told him. I don't know why I care what he thinks.

"Well, it was only once, Sam. It's no big deal!"

"It would be a big deal if you got tangled with some of the not-so-nice people and Blackhands that hang out there, Patsy!"

He is not my boss, though I find it endearing that he cares about me, "Okay, Sammy. I won't go again! But teenagers can go to Sgro's Sunset Grove, and I'm going there!"

"That's okay, Patsy. People are your age there. Go have fun!"

Sgro's Sunset Grove is five miles up Route 85. It is a long low building of wood with a large muddy parking lot. One side of the dance floor has old wooden booths where all the teens sit who want to just neck. Some great bands come in and out of Sunset Grove. When there isn't a dance, we can roller skate on their shiny wooden floor. I am old enough to go now. I ask Ethel to go. She is all in. I know I have to ask my sisters to go along too, or I won't be allowed to go. Bella, Ina and Dee are all three going with us, and of course Gibs. Bella never goes anywhere without Gibs.

We get onto the coal miners' bus at Liberty Theater to get there and arrive fairly early. Dom is here. He is from one of the richer Italian families in town, though people say they make their money illegally. He is handsome and tall, with thick black hair slicked back perfectly against his head. His eyes are dark brown and his olive skin is evident against his starched white shirt. He thinks he is God's gift to women. He dresses sharp and thinks he sweats gold. His three, also rich friends surround him. He is flirting with Dee. Ina pulls her aside. "He likes all the women, not just you. You know that, right?"

Dee pulls away, "Mind your own business!" I am actually quite surprised that Dee stood up for herself. As much as I fight with Dee, I have to admit she is the kindest of all my sisters. I would even call her timid. She is only mean with me sometimes, but I ask for it.

We all have to constantly argue with Ina. She is so bossy. This turns into a sisterly argument, until the band begins.

Tonight, the band is Lawrence Welk. The place is packed. We girls are all dancing together, singing and spinning. Many boys admire us from the sidelines. As I dance, I keep spinning to see which ones are watching me. Dom walks onto the floor to ask Dee to dance. She accepts. Ethel and I are having fun dancing. Ina, Bella and Gibs dance beside us. Ina is watching Dee. Dee continues to dance with Dom. They dance to "Paper Doll" by the Mills Brothers. When the song, "You'll Never Know" begins, Ina sees Dom reach his hand around Dee and lay it on her butt. It takes Ina two seconds to get across the dance floor. She gives him a push that knocks him badly off balance. He is shocked. "Keep your filthy hands where they belong! You no good SOB!"

He glares at her. His buddies chuckle a little under their breath at his defeat. Dee says nothing. Dee is a little laid back and shy. She is definitely the prettiest of my sisters, with her dark hair swept into finger waves that hug her head. She has big eyes and ivory skin. But what Dee lacks in forwardness, Bella makes up for. Bella is boisterous and foul-mouthed and everyone laughs at her and with her. She bellows to Dom. "How'd you like that, you rich bastard!" Her and Gibs then start that obnoxious laugh that they do.

Dee is mortified. "Bella! Stop! That is not ladylike!"

Bella takes a drag of her cigarette, "Well I'm not a lady!" That shuts Dee up, as she is well aware this is true.

The evening ends and we all go home on the same coal miners' bus which brought us. I fall asleep quickly. This evening of dancing wore me out! I hope I dream of dancing with some handsome dreamy man, kind of like Sam. I hope I dream that.

sixteen
Sorrow on Second Street

R uby tags along with me most times. She is almost four. She is bright. Yet, she is not talking in sentences. I talk to Sam about it and Sam says, "It's okay, Patsy. It's not like she doesn't talk. She'll put it all together soon." Daddy is very upset about it. He is trying so hard to help Ruby to speak in sentences. Ruby will just not cooperate.

I tell him, "Don't worry, Daddy. All kids don't talk at the same age. She talks a lot! She is just too lazy to make sentences!" Yet, he insists this is a worry about Ruby.

He is persistent. "She should be talking in sentences!"

As Ruby and I visit Sam, I complain about Monday coming because I have to go back to school. I don't like school. He always tries to tell me different. "You like school, Patsy. You just don't know it!" I don't and never will. I go to Sagamore to school now. I am in grade nine. The bus picks me up at the company store. My music teacher, Mr. Colonna, taught us a lot of songs and how to sing them with no breaks in between songs. We sing them the whole way there and the whole way back. Our bus driver, Anthony, looks frustrated listening to us, but doesn't complain. I like Anthony. I like Sagamore. I just don't like school.

"I was here yesterday afternoon and you weren't here, Sam. Where were you?"

THE CREEK DON'T RISE

"Sorry I missed you, Patsy. I stopped down at Maffei's Service Station for a root beer and got talking to some guys."

"Maffei's? Where is that, Sam?"

"Don't you ever go outside of Yatesboro, Patsy? It is just down there in Rose Valley. It is a gas station, and they've got the best root beer in there!"

"So, bring me a root beer sometime! Or better yet, take me with you!"

He laughs. "Next time for sure!"

Time to get home. School starts tomorrow!

Monday comes and I go to school, reluctantly. At the end of my day, the bus drops us off at the company store. My sisters stay there and talk to friends. I like to get home. Daddy was night shift last night, so is upstairs sleeping. I will have to be quiet until he wakes up later to go back to work. My snack, the popcorn Mama always has in the big glass jar with the red lid, is sitting on the counter waiting for me. Mama is in the garden gathering vegetables for supper. Ruby is beside her.

As I munch my popcorn, I watch out the screen door at the garden. Just as I am replacing the big red lid, I hear a loud and heavy THUD. Very heavy. It seems to have come from the upstairs.

I rush up the stairs looking in every bedroom, daddy's bed is empty. I rush to the end of the hallway where the bathroom is. The door is open just a couple inches. Daddy is on the floor!

"Daddy!" I push the door hard. I can't get it open. "MAMA! MAMA!" She comes running with Ruby behind her. Together we force the door open enough for her to squeeze in, then me. Mama gets down by his face. She puts her ear to his mouth.

There is no movement, no sign of him breathing. He is turning blue. I cannot comprehend what I am seeing. Mama shakes him and hollers at him. "Malcolm, MALCOLM!"

I am screaming, "Daddy, wake up, Daddy!" Mama puts her finger on his neck then leans very close as if to kiss him but just stays there listening, turning her head slightly. She then pulls me back and holds me tight, "Shush, baby, Daddy is in heaven."

I pull away from her. "NO, NO, NO!" Ruby is crying too. Mama gets her arms around us both as we cry into her feed sack apron. Daddy is dead at age fifty-two.

Mama weeps quietly but is trying to hold herself together. She takes us downstairs to the kitchen. "You girls stay right here until I go get Uncle Joe, I'll be right back."

Uncle Joe came quickly. Mama came back to us and let us cry more tears into her apron, as she cried with us. Uncle Joe called my sisters and brothers and Edwards funeral home. When Mr. Edwards came to take daddy, Mama took us to the back porch. She didn't want us to see.

One by one, my sisters and brothers arrive home. We all spend a lot of time crying. Mama cries with us as each of us embrace her, sharing our tears. The sadness is suffocating. We all realize that Mama has been left destitute. There are no pensions or money set aside for a rainy day.

Dee gets up to make coffee, "No more time for crying all of you! We have much to do. Buckle up now!""

My brothers and sisters quickly gather themselves up and get to work making plans to help Mama. We all assure Mama it will be okay; but she is not worried. She is a strong woman. She wipes her eyes and talks in a whisper. "Daddy is in heaven now with our Thomas. Daddy will be happy to see Thomas."

Thomas, my older brother, who I never knew. He has been in heaven over twenty years now. She smiles. "He'll have Thomas and James, too! I'll bet James is telling him jokes already!" It felt good to think that. Mama knew that.

Daddy's funeral is incredibly sad. I cannot breathe. Daddy's casket lies in the living room as we stand and stare, trying to realize life without him. People are flowing in and saying they are sorry. Their voices are a blur as I try to remember to thank them politely.

I stand by the dining room table in the next room where I can gaze into the living room at Daddy in the casket. I am in charge of Ruby at this moment and she wants to stand on the dining room table beside me. I hold onto her legs. Ruby just stares into the living room at the casket. I can feel her legs tremble in my arms. The tears are falling down my cheeks. After a couple minutes, Ruby takes her hands and wipes my cheeks. Then she asks, "Daddy?"

"Yes, Ruby. Daddy is in heaven now." I smile at her and softly kiss her cheek.

Then Ruby replies, "I wanna go to Sam's house." That was a full-blown sentence! Daddy had willed her to talk! Little did I know that Ruby would never shut up after this day.

Hours turn into days, the days into months. Sadly, life must go on and somehow it does. We all rally to make everything work. My brothers and sisters who are working will pitch in money to pay the bills. I will help Mama best I can.

Our house is different without daddy. Ruby and I spend more time than ever at Sam's house. I've been noticing Sam does not seem so thin. He just looks healthier. He dresses nice nowadays too. I can't quite figure out what has changed in Sam's face, but he is even more handsome than he was when I first saw him. He has a tiny line on the side of his eye. An old injury from baseball, he says. I like his scar. I pride myself on the cookies and sweets I bring him that have helped fatten him up a little. I know he loves when Ruby and I visit. He always laughs at Ruby running across the wooden porch to get to the stool beside him. Yet, he carries a sadness in his eyes. It is something I think only I can see. But what is it?

seventeen
High School Fun

I t is almost Christmas. Today I am taking Ruby to the William Penn to sit on Santa's lap. When we arrive, she clings to me and hides behind my legs. I get down to her eye level. "Really, Ruby? This is the girl who seems so brave any other time? Don't you want to tell Santa what you want for Christmas? You are almost five now. You are a big girl! But if you can't go see Santa, we'll just go home."

Ruby wipes her eyes and straightens up. To my surprise, when I take her hand, she lets me lead her to Santa. She is like me. If someone tells me I can't, I be sure that I do! She timidly allows me to pick her up onto his lap and I step back. She tells him about the doll she wants. Santa hands her a brown paper bag with a popcorn ball, an orange and a candy bar inside. She runs back to me. I praise her. "You did good, Ruby!"

As she opens her bag and unwraps the candy bar, she looks at me. "Santa is wearing Uncle Joe's shoes!"

Not being sure how to get out of this one I simply reply, "How nice. Santa has the same taste in shoes as Uncle Joe!" I will tell Uncle Joe about this when he gets home. He'll get a kick out of it. He almost gave himself away with his shoes!

I made Sam a tin of cookies for Christmas and did a homemade card for him. I draw pretty good so he loves the decorated tree I drew. I made him a pretty book mark too. I painted a red ribbon on it. I've seen him reading books so I know he'll use it. I made him a tin of homemade candy too. He stands the tree card up on his end table to display. "There, I'm decorated! It is beautiful!" He holds the bookmark staring at the red ribbon. He seems sad. "It's perfect, Patsy. Thank you."

He then gave Ruby and I a pretty little wrapped package. We open them together. Inside is a Christmas ornament with our name on. It is a shiny metal and surrounding our name is a wreath of red berries. "That is so sweet of you, Sam. I love it!" He just smiles.

Winter goes fast and it is spring before I know it. It is the end of my sophomore year. I want to go to the prom. I don't really want a date. My cousin Dick has a car now. Ethel's cousin, Jack, is his best friend. So together we decide that Bella, Gibs, Ethel and I will go to the prom with Jack and Dick. None of us are interested in dates.

We arrive at the school and enter just behind Wally Sheldon and Susan Bauer. This is an odd match. He is rough and rugged and she is quiet, simple and sweet. I saw her parents drop her off. She would never be allowed to get into a car with any boy. Especially Wally! I am sure they will pick her up too. Wally turns and sees us, "Hey gang, prom goers now, are ya?" We all laugh.

I compliment them. "You are maybe the handsomest couple at the prom. No?"

"Thank you." Susan sheepishly answers. Maybe she'll be good for him. Maybe she'll tame him down.

We don't take a seat right away, though most do. We stand with each other drinking punch and making small talk. The goodie-two-shoes sitting at the tables are staring at us. I just smile back. Bella sticks out her tongue at them. "Stop it, Bella!" I scold. She blows me off.

Blitz is here with Jenny. He has been dating her for a while now. Over in the corner is that stupid Dwight. He brought his cousin Darlene to the prom. Too funny!

Jack is bored. "Let's go outside. I've got cigarettes!" I don't think I want a cigarette, but going outside sounds good.

We are quick to hit the long bar on the door and get out of there. Jack lights one cigarette after another and passes them to us. "Take a drag, Patsy!"

"No thanks, Jack, I'm good."

He won't take no for an answer and lights me one. Bella is a pro at smoking, Gibs seems to be, too. The smoke billows as they puff away, giggling about the corny prom. Ethel takes a drag and after coughing just once, goes on to smoke the whole thing. I can't do it. They all laugh at me, and coax me to take a drag. I get sick of listening to them. Finally, I hold my breath and let the cigarette just faintly touch my lips. I breath in oh so little, and immediately, I am sick. "I told you I didn't want it, Jack!"

"Ah, relax Patsy, you'll be fine!"

Bella and Gibs are doing that awful laugh they do. Sometimes I just want to slap them when they do that.

Johnny Boyer comes out with his date, Lillian Reefer. They are bored with the prom too. "Got one for me?" Johnny asks.

"Sure thing," Jack hands him the pack. "Help yourself! What's going on in there? Are they crowning the king and queen yet?"

"In about fifteen minutes." Lillian offers. "If it is who we think it is, we need a smoke first!" We all laugh. Finally, we walk back into the school for the crowning of the king and queen. Mr. Colonna has the microphone and Mr. Bernardi will crown them. "Your king and queen of the Shannock Valley High School prom are Dwight Schmidt and Jenny Fischer!" Now I know what Lillian meant! Go figure, ugly Dwight! Must be something everyone likes about him, but I sure don't see it. Even now, at this age, I would still like to push him into the nasty tanks of the honeydippers! Dwight and Jenny are smiling up there on the stage like they are something big. I would love to go ask Dwight if it is an ugly contest he just won, but I won't.

"I'm done with all this," Jack chimes. "Let's go for a drive!" We are all up for that!

There is a narrow dirt road that winds around the Roundtop which allows us to drive to the water tank at the top, where the teens hang out. The Round Top is in the middle of Rural Valley, and it is just a big hill. When I was young, I thought it was a mountain. There is a campfire built. Slick and Utz are here. They have beer. Eventually, cars start pulling in. It is kids from the prom. Wally is first to show up, "Whew, glad that is over!" he exclaims.

"Where's your hot date, Wally?" I want to know.

"Home with her mama and daddy. They picked her up. Thank goodness! She was boring! I couldn't wait to get out of there and get here!" He lights a cigarette.

"Why did you take her then, Wally?"

"My parents made me. I dented daddy's car in March and I got grounded with a big sermon. They said if I ask a nice girl to the prom, I'll get the car back. Got the car back, but had to suffer through the prom!" He laughs. We all laugh with him. We spend the rest of the evening talking about all the kids at the prom.

Wally is drinking too much beer. "Slow down on the brews, Wally." I plead nicely.

He just laughs. "I deserve to drink tonight, Patsy, I earned it!"

I stay until midnight and ask Dick to take me home. It has been a long night. Before I leave, I walk over to Wally. "Slow down on those beers, Wally. You gotta drive home."

He just laughs, and I get in Dick's car and head home.

eighteen
Strolling Through Rural Valley

" I am sleeping in, at least I think so. Ruby is pulling on my sheet, "I wanna go to Rural Valley!"

"Awe, Ruby, can't you wait a little?" I turn over and pull my sheet up.

She jumps on top of me. "Come on, Patsy!" Who can resist Ruby?

Yatesboro runs right into Rural Valley at Avi's Tavern. We can have one foot in Yatesboro and the other in Rural Valley at the same time. The Main Street is nicknamed Macaroni Street. Some people say it is named that because it is long and narrow, like a noodle. Other people say it is named that because so many Italians live on Main Street. No one knows for sure. Cars can park only on one side. It is not unusual for the parked cars to be sideswiped by cars trying to navigate the narrow street.

We pass Shy Bosick's Barbershop on our way. He is the barber across the street from Avi's. The company barn is right next to Shy's. Often a stumbling coal miner will take a break from his afternoon dance of drinking to stop in for Shy to cut his hair. I like to stop by to say hello to Shy. We walk up the stairs and I peek in. Shy has no customers right now.

He is sweeping up hair from his last customer. "There's Patsy and Ruby! Come sit down and visit!"

Shy likes to talk about everybody in town and to gather new information. He quizzes me about people, "What do you know about that woman at the end of your street? Seems as though she has a new boyfriend!"

I just laugh at him. "Heck I don't know, Shy. I don't even know her!"

Norb Peters walks in the door. He has been the town prankster for many years. He drinks a lot. Sometimes his humor is unacceptable. He is hard to tolerate. Other times he is funny. He is wearing his normal white button-down collar shirt that is now gray. He tucks it into his pants which are way below his waist in order to make room for his big belly. I think he is not a dumb man. He is just an opinionated, loud-mouthed racist. People in town refrain from engaging him in conversation.

Today he walks into Shy's for a haircut. He smells of booze and his speech is slurred. "Hey Shy, how 'bout gettin' some of this mop trimmed up?" Then he looks at us, "Hey there, girls!" He is always nice to me, but always drunk.

Shy answers him, "Sure Norb, if you can sit still long enough!" Norb wiggles himself into the barber chair. Ruby and I should probably leave, but I'm thinking maybe I'll stay awhile to listen to Norb blunder.

Next enters Shin Rearick. He is a family man with five kids. He works hard in the coal mines. When he isn't doing that, he is around delivering ice. The little kids in town follow his ice truck trying to get chips of ice. Shin is a nice, polite man with sandy hair and a small beard and mustache. He says hello to us and sits in the corner where there are two chairs. He picks up the newspaper as he sits, hoping to not engage in conversation with Norb.

Then Ben Pelligrino comes in and sits next to Shin. Ben was a friend of Daddy's. He is older but distinguished. His hair is gray and with his tanned skin and glasses, he is somewhat striking for his age. His children are grown now and he is a grandpa four times over. He sees us first, "Patsy and Ruby! How you girls doing?"

"We're doing swell. See how big Ruby is getting?" I proudly show her off.

Ben looks at Ruby sizing her up. "Is this the little lady that turns six this year?"

Ruby giggles, "Three more days!"

"How did you get so old?" Ben tussles the hair on the top of her head.

Ben looks at Norb, then turns and leans down to Shin. "Oh boy!" Meaning he hoped they did not have to deal with Norb being stupid today.

Shy gets done with Norb. He powders his neck and removes the cape. Shin will be the next one in the chair and begins to stand up, putting his newspaper down. As Norb is getting out of the barber chair, he reaches into his deep pants pocket. He brings out something made of white material. He puts it over his head. It is cone shaped with eyes cut out. Shy hollers at him, "Take that damn thing off, Norb! What the hell is wrong with you?"

"Ah, just kiddin'! Cain't you take a joke?" Norb defends himself.

Shy is upset, "That's no joke to me! Don't you ever bring that into town again. You hear me?"

Norb is annoyed, "Ah, you guys ain't no fun!"

"FUN?" exclaimed Ben. "We all know what that thing is and what it means! We ought to burn it with your head inside it!"

With that Norb slithers out the door, after paying Shy for the haircut. He shoves the white hood back into his pocket. He lets the door bang hard to let us know he is mad. He heads straight for Avi's bar.

Ruby is curious. "What was that?"

She is too young to understand what it means, "It is an evil thing honey, nothing you need to worry about. Norb was wrong in bringing that in here." I think now we better leave, who knows what will happen next at Shy's! We head out the door and up Macaroni Street.

As we pass Lavosky's Store, Mr. Lavosky is loading a washing machine on his truck for someone. "Hello there, girls!"

"Hey there, Mr. Lavosky!" We keep moving along.

Rural Valley always has had one individual that is the town legend. Like Old Jessop. He walks the streets in his drunken stupor, mumbling to himself and handing children pennies to go to the local candy store. He is bent over. His pants hang on him like old drapes. His shoes have holes and most times are not tied. His white stained shirt smells of sweat. His face is drawn and dried like the earth. When he gets too drunk, his sister, with whom he lives, will banish him to the outdoor shed to sleep. The next morning, he will awaken and start his trek again to local bars. Everyone welcomes him and loves him in their own way. No one ever stops old Jessop from drinking. It is just what he does and how he lives. Handing her his pennies, Ruby admires him and looks forward to seeing him.

I am walking Ruby to King's Drug Store where I'll buy her my favorite thing, a Mexican Hot Tin Roof Sundae. It is vanilla ice cream, chocolate topping and red-skin peanuts. She can sit at the counter with me. Macaroni Street is no longer just red dog. It is brick now, with a thin sidewalk alongside. On our walk we come upon old Jessop. He jumps in front of her like a rabbit and stops. He sways a little. A little spit is dripping down his chin. He proclaims in his slurred speech, "Ruubi, Ruubi", as he hands her three pennies.

"Thank you, Jessop!" Ruby beams.

"Can we go to Arduini's, Patsy?" Of course, I am glad to take her.

Mr. and Mrs. Arduini own the candy store that sits atop the first hill. It is an old building with dark burgundy shingles that look like sandpaper. The beaten wooden door opens to counters full of glass jars of candy of every kind. Mr. and Mrs. Arduini are glad to see her. Mr. Arduini reaches his wrinkled hand into the big candy jar. He gives her the three pieces of candy for her three pennies. They are a sweet old couple. "Thank you!" Ruby chirps.

Mrs. Arduini is always happy. "No eat-eh too much-eh sugar, honey!" Ruby just giggles.

The sugar from her sweet candy is all over her lips. Her hands are sticky. She skips down the sidewalk. I'll be darned if she doesn't run into old Jessop again. We see him before he sees us. He is ahead of us, with his back to us. Ruby sits down on the sidewalk to watch him. Jessop is at the alley at the Brewer house. He is studying the fire hydrant. He sways as he studies it, getting down on his hunkers looking at it like he is measuring the putt, as if he is going to hit his golf ball. He then stands up and tips his hat as if he is greeting a lovely lady. He takes a little run, a hop, and he has accomplished jumping the hydrant. He lands on his feet, though he nearly loses his balance. He puts his arms out to balance himself. He then just politely tips his hat, puts his hands in his pockets, and meanders along. Ruby giggles.

At King's Drug Store she sits up at the counter with me on the padded stools that go around. It is hard keeping her still as she eats her Mexican Hot Tin Roof Sundae. Thelma, behind the counter, asks her how old she is. Ruby is never shy. "Almost six!"

You're awful pretty for six!"

Ruby just beams and keeps licking her ice cream.

Jack comes in the door and to the counter where we are. "Where you been, Patsy?"

"I've been walking the town with Ruby, why?"

"Didn't you hear? Wally wrecked last night. He's hurt bad. He is paralyzed!"

I jump off my stool. "Oh no! We were just with him. What happened?"

"He ran off the road and hit a tree. Thank goodness Susan wasn't with him!"

I feel numb. "Jack, he wasn't drunk, was he?"

Jack hesitates, "No one seems to know."

I don't feel like finishing my sundae. I wish I would have taken that beer bottle out of Wally's hand last night. I wish, I wish. I'm always wishing for something I could have done. "Keep me up on how he is, Jack. Surely there is hope he will walk again, surely! That makes me sick. Find out when he can have visitors and let's visit him, okay?"

Jack assured me he would.

I can't get Wally out of my mind. I am so sad for him. He is not like a close friend or anything, but I like Wally. Seems sometimes that I just like the "bad" boys.

On our way home, we stop at Sam's. He is on the porch looking at his newspaper. "Hey, Sam, what cha' doin'?" Ruby quizzes.

Sam laughs, "I'm mowing the grass, can't you see?" She jumps onto her stool as I sit down on the swing beside Sam.

He turns to me. "How was the prom, Patsy?"

He can see I am troubled. "It was okay, I guess. But do you know Wally Sheldon? He wrecked last night. Hit a tree. He is in bad shape. Jack says he is paralyzed!"

"Paralyzed? That's awful, Patsy! That is going to be so hard on his family." He pauses as he looks at his porch floor. "They say that God never gives us more than what we can deal with. But still, I can't imagine."

He puts his arm around me and I lean my head on his shoulder. He is always so comforting.

But yet, why didn't I take that bottle out of Wally's hand last night. Why? Why?

ninteen
Teenage Shenanigans

O n our way home from the company store, we stop on Sam's porch for a minute. Ruby is still months from starting first grade but it is all she talks about. She is anxious to tell him. "I'm going to elementary school pretty soon, Sam, you know!"

"NO!" Sam grins, "You can't be that old?"

"I am! What you gonna do without me, Sam?"

Sam's face is sad. "Don't know, girl. Don't like to think about it! Will you still come to visit me?"

"Heck yeah! I'll be over, Sam!"

Sam leaves out a sigh. "Thank goodness, Ruby. If I didn't have you and Patsy, I'd have no one you know."

"Well, you got me, Sam! There's me, Patsy, you and the sky is blue, Sam!"

Sam laughs, kisses her on her forehead. "Not as blue as your blue eyes!"

Ruby hops down the stairs. "Gotta go! Mama's fixing supper. Hey Sam, did your package get here yet? The one with the red ribbon?"

"No." Sam pretends he is smoking a big cigar. "But I ain't losin' faith darlin'." (He talks in a redneck drawl). He is so endearing when he does that.

Ruby laughs, "Hope I'm here when it comes! See ya tomorrow, Sam!"

Sam chuckles at her, "If the good Lord's willin' and the creek don't rise!"

We arrive home to the phone ringing. I pick it up. "Hello?"

It is old maid Matilda Robinson. "Just wanted to tell your mama they are selling sweet corn down at the company store."

I thank her. Matilda Robinson is the phone operator. To make a call, we pick up the phone and tell her who we want to dial. She dials, but she then stays on the line and listens. Mama says she repeats everything she hears backwards and frontwards. People in town get mad at Matilda. It scares me that she is listening. I try not to use the phone too much. Our phone number is 14R2 and Uncle Joe's is 14R1. Uncle Joe can pick up and listen to us and we can pick up and listen to him! We don't, though.

After dinner Ruby runs to the garden. It is June now and there is a judging going on for gardens! The judges are here. Daddy always won the blue ribbon. He was so proud of his garden. It is not the same since he is gone. Mama plants the garden best she can. It doesn't look anything like Daddy's. Ruby is always in the garden with mama. She is hoping for a blue ribbon. The judges walk around the garden, whispering to each other, looking at Ruby. They whisper to each other again. Finally, one hands Ruby a red ribbon, which means good effort. Ruby is thrilled, jumping up and down and waving her red ribbon in the air. She doesn't know it isn't first place and it doesn't matter.

I congratulate Ruby. She is excited. "Let's go show Sam!"

She runs up his stairs and into his kitchen. He is just finishing dishes, "Here's your red ribbon, Sam!"

Sam laughs. "This is a beautiful red ribbon! It is not quite the one I have been waiting for, but I love it just as much as that one! Now you keep it, and when my red ribbon comes, we will both have our own! I'm so proud of you, Ruby!"

Ruby just smiles. She hears a car coming and looks towards home. "Uncle Joe got a new car!" She jumps down off the porch and starts to run.

Uncle Joe, across the street, has just bought himself a Chevrolet Special Deluxe. Ina and Dee are crossing the street to see. Uncle Joe is proud as punch. "Wanna go for a ride?" he asks proudly.

Ruby is quick with the response, "Yes, yes, yes!" Ina sits in front. Ruby, Dee and I take the back seat. With the windows down and our hair flying in the wind, we drive through Yatesboro, then Rural Valley, then up Dayton Road. As we arrive back to Yatesboro, he takes us by the Company Store. Across from there, the Yatesboro Sons of Tirolo Band is practicing on the 3rd floor of the Collins house. The Sons of Tirolo Band is comprised of immigrants or descendants of the Province of Tyrol in the mountains of Northern Italy. These band members represent the majority of Italians that settled in this area. They are always practicing on the third floor that they call the "lodge."

Uncle Joe pulls into the Company Store parking lot, so we can listen to the music. There are other people around listening too. Ruby is breaking into a little dance in the back seat.

After listening to three songs, we see several cops pulling in, which is unusual. The town only has one cop of its own. Others come from other areas only when big trouble arises. The cops get out of the three cars they came in. They talk for a minute, then start going house to house, knocking on doors.

The band seems to have stopped. Mr. Corolla comes out of the house where the band is playing. He is a drummer for the band. He leans on our driver's door, "Did ya hear about the raid today, Joe? They're looking for Blackhands!"

Uncle Joe chuckles. "Well their efforts are useless. Blackhands always get tipped off about the raids, everybody knows that."

We stay and watch the cops. All three come back to their cars, get in and pull out. Once again, they found no Blackhands. I see a curtain move in the Shields house. It is rumored Vinny Shields is a Blackhand. The cops missed him! He was in there! He was watching them from behind the curtains! Will we ever be safe in this town?

As we head home, Uncle Joe takes us up the hill past the Catholic Church. Next is my high school. It used to be called Cowanshannock High School. Last year they changed the name to Shannock Valley High School. For my eleventh and twelfth grades I get to come back to Yatesboro to school. I am a junior at Shannock Valley High School. Uncle Joe drops us off at the school to let Ruby swing awhile on the swings. Our house is only seven houses over from here, so Uncle Joe asks, "You girls okay to get home on your own?"

"Heck yeah, Uncle Joe. You go ahead home. Thanks for the ride!"

Ethel runs down the hill to where I am at the high school. Bella, Gibs, Ethel and I are a foursome. Today though, Gibs wants Bella to go back to her house with her, so they leave to go there. My sisters go home, taking Ruby with them.

I get bored quickly. I start throwing rocks at a little window in the peak of the school. Finally, one hits the window and it cracks. Ethel is laughing, but stops quickly when she sees Mr. Nelson coming towards me. "What are you girls doing? You owe someone for that window, Patsy!"

We see Father Berto coming towards us. "What's going on, Mr. Nelson?"

Mr. Nelson is talking mean, "These brats threw a rock at the window up there. They cracked it!"

Ethel is offended, "Not me, I didn't do it!" Thanks Ethel, good friend you are!

The priest is calm, "Patsy, this isn't like you."

I am embarrassed, "I know it isn't. I don't know what got into me. I am so sorry."

He turns to Mr. Nelson, "I actually have a window in the basement of the church just that size. I can replace it. How about we forget about this, Mr. Nelson?"

He isn't happy but he concedes, "Very well. But, Patsy, next time I'm telling your mama!" He slithers back down the hill from whence he came. I love Father Berto. Maybe I should turn Catholic.

After we thank Father Berto, Ethel and I walk to Gibs' house. When we call each other, we make this sound I-O-UT! We reach Gibs' front porch and together Ethel and I cup our hands. As loud as we can we holler, "I-O-UT!" Out comes Bella and Gibs.

We walk a few houses over to Ike's house. He is in the back yard with Slick. Slick is talking about old man Peters. "He hollered at me yesterday for cutting through his yard!"

I jump in on the conversation. "Really? I know a way to get even. You in?"

Everyone replies, "Yes, we're in."

It is getting dusk now and the six of us cut down through the yards to old man Peters. In the backyard are two empty garbage cans. I get in one and Slick in the other. Ethel and Gibs put the lids on for us. They run and hide. Bella is just standing behind the garage smoking. Once Ethel and Gibs are out of sight, Ike knocks hard on the back door of the house and runs to hide. Mr. Peters comes to the door and opens it. Slick and I start making all kinds of noise inside the garbage cans, scaring the crap out of Mr. Peters. He slams the door and runs into his house. Slick and I force the cans on their side by swinging our bodies, then worm our way out of the can. I am laughing so hard; I almost pee my pants. The six of us run as fast as we can up the hill and don't get caught. Got even with old man Peters for sure! But what is wrong with me? I'm too old to be acting like this! I just got out of one predicament and moved into another. I might have to start thinking about growing up soon. Don't want to, but might have to.

twenty
Ghosts and Potatoes

E thel wants me to sleep on her front porch tonight. I have to coax Mama a little. She isn't sure, "You girls can sleep here in the living room."

"Ah, Mama, please? We'll be good!"

She looks at me with the look of distrust. "If I find out you left that porch, Patsy, you have me to answer to!"

"I won't, I promise!" She doesn't know I'm lying. I look over to Ruby. She is pouting.

Just then, I hear farmer Wilson ringing his bell. He comes on our street in his horse drawn wagon with ice cream. "Grab your bowl, Ruby!" I holler. We have to take our own bowl out and he scoops the ice cream in our bowls for us. Since Ruby isn't happy that I'm leaving, maybe this will make her happy.

I gulp my ice cream and kiss her goodnight. I head over to Ethel's. Bella and Gibs come too. After laying our blankets and pillows on the floor of her porch, we lie on our backs.

Ethel likes telling ghost stories. "If we walk the street in the middle of the night, dark figures will come out from behind the houses and chase us!"

I am scared but don't want to show it. "What do they look like?"

"They have little heads with eyes that light up, and long bodies. Their arms go all the way down to their knees. Smoke comes out of their ears, and they can run really fast!" She cups her hands on her mouth and whispers. "Now, once Mama and Daddy are asleep, we'll go out and find them!"

I'm frightened, but don't want to be a baby. Once her parents are fast asleep, we jump down off the porch and start up the street. I'm trying to be brave and fearless. The street is quiet, and dark. Up one street and down the other we go, whispering and laughing. Bella and Gibs hook their arms together. Gibs then hooks her arm to mine. We walk crossing over each other's feet. We keep walking that way, crossing our feet across each other's, laughing. Bella starts singing a song I've never heard before. **"My sweet little Alice blue gown, the first time he rolled into town. She was bashful and shy, when he opened his fly, the first time she saw it, she thought she would die!"**

"BELLA!" I scold, "That's a dirty song!"

She laughs like a hyena and starts into another song, **"There once was an Indian maid, who took to the whoring trade. For two cents a crack, she'd lay on her back and let those cowboys…."**

Just then "BOO!!" Ethel comes up behind us and scares the heck out of us. We all scream.

I am scared and mad. "That was rotten, Ethel! You scared the crap out of me!"

Ethel is bent in half laughing. "You don't really believe in those creatures I told you about, do you?"

"Of course not!" I am lying. "But you didn't need to scare me like that!"

"Come on, Patsy. You believed it!" Ethel loops her hands into ours. We all start crossing our feet again, walking and singing. **"Who threw the whiskey in the well (in the well). Who threw the whiskey in the well (in the well)? Deacon Jones knelt down to pray. All he said was, 'Hey, Hey,' so who threw the whiskey in the well (in the well). Now who threw the whiskey in the well (in the well)."**

We are rounding the corner by the church. The priest hears us. He lives in a house beside the church. He is out on his porch. "You girls need to wrap it up and get to bed!" We run back to Ethel's porch. I hope he doesn't tell Mama!

In the morning Ethel's mama cooks us breakfast. Bella and Gibs go home, but I tell Bella to tell Mama I'll be just a little while yet. Ethel and I spend an hour in her bedroom getting all dolled up. It is Saturday and the boys will be hanging out at the company store. They lean on the big log outside. We love to flirt with them.

Ethel puts makeup on me. "A little more rouge than usual and some lipstick today, Patsy!"

I borrow her green scarf for around my neck, which brings out my green eyes. My dark hair is down to my shoulders now and turns under in what we call a Page Boy.

We trek down the hill to the company store. Here is where we act like we have no interest at all in the boys. We walk past them like we don't even see them. There are five of them there this morning, Utz greets us as we pass. "Patsy and Ethel, what's up girls?"

"Oh, didn't see you there!" I lie. "Nothing is up. Need some things from the company store, that's all." I know I look pretty good and they are looking. I've learned how to wiggle my butt just a little. I love to tease the boys. Though we've been friends for a long time, I still love the thrill of flirting. Blitz has become more appealing as he grew some height and muscles along the way. I go into the company store and buy a candy bar for me and a loaf of bread for mama. As we come out of the company store, they are waiting.

Blitz is following me with his eyes. "Wanna come to our potato bake this afternoon at the dam?"

Slick chimes in, "Yeah girls, come along!"

"Maybe, maybe not." I answer, swinging my head so my hair sways. I walk slowly away from them but once out of their eyesight, I hurry home to my chores, so I can leave the house and go to their potato bake.

When we arrive at the dam, the boys have a fire built with potatoes wrapped in foil. They are already in the fire. Blitz wants me to take a drink of his beer, but I don't. I'd be afraid mama could smell it on me. Ethel and I just flirt and eat their potatoes, though they are black and hard. Blitz keeps staring at me, "How 'bout going to the movies with me, Patsy?"

"Maybe, we'll see." Don't want to be too forward, and don't want to go with him.

The potato bake is fun, but I know when to get home. What Mama doesn't know, doesn't hurt her.

Next day, Ruby and I stop on Sam's porch. He just got home from work and is coming out to his swing. "Where you girls been?"

"Riding in Uncle Joe's new car yesterday!" I don't tell him about the bad stuff I do.

"That sounds like fun, Patsy!"

"It was! He took us up Dayton Road. When we got back, we were sitting listening to music down across from the Company Store. The band was playing across the street on the third floor of the Collins house. We saw the cops doing a raid, looking for Blackhands!"

Sam's face grows sullen and he seems deep in thought. "Did they find any?"

"No, Uncle Joe says the Blackhands are always tipped off when there is a raid coming."

"There is no good in any Blackhand, Patsy. No good at all! Too bad they didn't find any. They should wipe those bastards off the face of the earth!" He then apologizes. "Sorry for my language."

"It's okay!" I am amused at his embarrassment. "My Daddy always told me too that they are not good men. He told me to never go near one."

"Your daddy was right. You are smart enough, Patsy, to stay away from them."

It frightens me to think about them. "Sam, you ever had any dealings with the Blackhands?"

He still seems like he is thinking about something. "Not any of your concern, girl." I know not to ask more, but I know he isn't telling me something.

I really need to lighten his mood. "Did your package with the red ribbon come yet, Sam?"

A slight frown came on his face. "No, let's talk about something else."

He is losing faith that it is coming. I am sad for him. "It will come, Sam. It will!" I try to sound hopeful, but I am pretty sure this package doesn't exist, except in Sam's head.

Ruby is jumping rope on the sidewalk below reciting rhymes. "Cinderella dressed in yellow, went upstairs to kiss her fellow, made a mistake and kissed a snake. How many doctors did it take? 1...2...3...4....5. Oops, her foot tangles in the rope. She throws the jump rope into the yard in a fit. Ruby has a bit of a temper.

"Giving it up, girl?" Sam chuckles.

"Quit laughing at me!" She scolds.

"Awe, come on, Ruby! Come up here to your stool beside me."

She comes up the porch stairs with a long face. She plops herself onto the stool.

"Well, Ruby. Tell me. Do you have a boyfriend?" Sam smiles. I know he is trying to lighten her nasty mood.

Her face turns red. "Kind of, yeah."

I am shocked. "Who, Ruby?"

"Jimmy."

"Jimmy who?" I want to know.

Her nasty frown has turned into a grin. "He lives on Swede Alley. Frankie and him are friends. There's Frankie's house then skip two and that is where Jimmy lives."

I have taken her many times to play on Swede Alley with kids. These two boys were part of the group. I had no idea she was smitten with one. It is kind of cute.

Sam is interested. "Jimmy, huh?"

Ruby is all smiles now. "Jimmy just moved there last year. I was playing with Frankie and his sisters the day they moved in. That was the day we started to play with him too."

"That so?" Sam smiles as he cups his chin in his hand. "You best be bringing this Jimmy here. I have to approve of him, you know!"

"Stop it, Sam!" Ruby laughs.

It is sweet how Sam interacts with Ruby. He knows how to snap her out of her grouchiness.

I've noticed lately that Sam has bought some new shirts. Today he has on a plaid shirt with a button-down collar. He has put on more weight too, and he smells good. He looks healthy. He must be happier these days. I hope it is Ruby and me that make him happy!

Ruby is in a hurry to get home. "Bye, Sam!" She hollers as she is running across the yards.

Sam always laughs when he has to holler his goodbye. "You bring Jimmy next time, Ruby!"

She sticks her tongue out at him. Oh, Ruby!

twenty-one
Ruby, Ruby

O ur summers are so lazy. The streets are filled with gossip and laughter. Now and then a heated healthy argument starts. There is always the sound of dogs barking and the smell of garlic cooking. Ruby likes to play and do simple things like dissecting crabs in the local creek. She loves to fish, and she is good at it. She is so much like me.

Today, I tell Ruby, "No Swede Alley today, we are going fishing!" She doesn't complain. I will take her to Cowanshannock Creek. The word Cowanshannock is of Indian origin. It is the largest creek in Armstrong County. We know exactly where to go where the stream is very shallow and the fish will bite.

"Can Jimmy come?" She looks at me with those blue eyes of hers.

"Not today, Ruby. Just me and you, okay?" I don't want to keep her from her puppy love, but it won't be long she won't want to spend time with me at all. Time is going so fast, and Ruby is getting so big. She is seven years old now. I have grown too. Four inches in the last two years. At eighteen I have caught up to the height of other girls my age. I look pretty good in my rolled up blue jeans. I roll them up three times to mid-calf. I usually wear a white blouse with a pretty chiffon scarf tied around my neck. I top that all off with my white socks and saddle shoes. Boys my age roll up their blue jeans too, but they leave them at ankle length. Most wear just a white t-shirt with the sleeves rolled up, a pack of cigarettes in the fold.

We head up Main Street to get to the creek. The bars that speckle the town are never empty. We are now passing Avi's Tavern. The door is hanging open. Many of the men inside are from our street, so they know Ruby and me. "Ruby, Ruby!" Mr. Moore hollers, and all the guys laugh. We can see Mr. Kanerski sitting his daughter Celia onto the bar. We stop to watch and listen. Celia is only three, and a very odd child. People in town talk about Celia, not knowing what is wrong with her, but something is for sure. Her eyes don't seem to stay focused. She makes unusual movements with her hands and head. Today, as her daddy sits her on the bar, he hands her a newspaper. She begins to read, "At Kittanning, our county seat, there will be a folk festival in August. It will be called Armstrong Folk Festival." The men in the bar are speechless. I am speechless.

I whisper to Ruby, "Yep, I know now what's wrong with Celia. She is a genius. She is so smart she is going down the other side of the hill!"

"What?" Ruby says loudly. "What's that mean?" Now everyone at the bar has heard us. I take her hand and run. After word got around town that Celia could read at age three, everyone was talking about it. I am happy I am not a genius, because at least I am normal. Well, at least what I call normal.

Ruby never shuts up. She engages everyone she passes. It is late afternoon. She stops now and then to jump through someone's hopscotch drawn on the sidewalk with stone. She always chirps as she walks. "Step on a crack, break your mother's back. Step on a nail, put your dad in jail." She enjoys visiting so many of the old people sitting on their porch swings that are covered with old quilts. Everybody in town likes Ruby. Mrs. Pina is on her porch today. Ruby jumps up holding onto the banister. "Hello, Mrs. Pina!"

Mrs. Pino likes Ruby and asks, "You want a whiskey and coffee, Ruby, Ruby?"

I think it's funny how many people talking to Ruby say her name twice.

Ruby looks puzzled when Ruby says, "You know I'm just a kid, right?" Mrs. Pina and I laugh.

Then Mrs. Pina hands us both a biscotti she made this morning. It is vanilla with chocolate icing drizzled on the top. It is delicious! Ruby shoves it in her mouth as she starts skipping away. "Thanks, Mrs. Pina!"

After leaving Mrs. Pina's porch, I tell Ruby to stop talking to people. "If you want time fishing, you have to keep walking, Ruby!" She obliges. We finally reach the creek and she quickly throws her line in. It takes her an hour, but she finally catches one. When she takes the hook out of its mouth, she gives it a kiss and throws it back in. She looks at me laughing.

"Why did you do that, Ruby?"

"So, it will be there when I bring Jimmy fishing. Him and me can catch it again!" She sticks her tongue out at me.

"Oh Ruby, Ruby!"

twenty-two
Picnics and Grapes

Jack and I made a plan to visit Wally today. He was in the hospital a very long time. I am nervous as we walk across the yard and up to his back door. His mama welcomes us. She looks tired. The smell of medicine fills my nose. She leads us to the living room. It is no longer a living room. It has a hospital bed and equipment of all kinds. There are pulleys to help move him, I presume. He has tubes in his arms, and a bag hanging on the side with pee in it. Wally can't walk. Wally can't do anything but move his head. I don't know where to begin. "How you feeling, Wally?"

"Don't feel nothin', literally!" He laughs.

I know what he means by that. Yet he laughs. His television is near the ceiling so he can see it. He has one window that looks out onto the street. He stares out the window.

Jack pipes in. "You look good, buddy!"

Wally chuckles. "Yeah, I won a weight lifting contest yesterday!" I want to cry but he won't let me. "Don't be sheddin' no tears for me, Patsy. I don't want no tears!"

I understand and admire him. I try to pull myself together. "Did you hear, Julia Bellotto and Paul Dixon are getting married!"

Wally laughs. "Now that's a strange mix! Didn't hear, but maybe she'll straighten him out. He's been a wildcat his whole life. But she is Catholic and he is Presbyterian, wonder how they'll work that out!"

I'm feeling a little better as we talk. "He will have to be a Catholic, period. That is how that goes!"

"Yep, you are right, though I never understood it." He turns his head to look out the window again. "Is it warm out?"

I am getting weepy again. Jack answers for us. "Not bad out right now, Wally. A storm coming this afternoon."

I want him to forget about outside. "I'll bet you didn't hear this one, Wally. Pia Schmidt is pregnant to Philip Beckley! Can you believe it?"

Wally looks at me and frowns. "Really? They are pretty young. Do you think they just didn't know how babies are made?" We all laugh. He still has his hearty laugh.

He stops laughing as he continues to stare out the window. "When you are at the Roundtop, guys, drink a beer for me, okay?"

My heart breaks for him. "Don't worry, Wally. We'll find a way to take you with us to the Roundtop. You just keep the faith!" Though I know he won't be going there.

I try to relax and enjoy the rest of our visit. He is funny like he always was. He seems tired and is nodding off to sleep. "Gotta go, Wally. We'll be back!" I give him a kiss on his cheek. Jack pats his leg. Wally wouldn't feel that.

As we leave and pass through the kitchen, Jack rushes out the door. I think he is crying. Wally's mama is at the sink. She looks at me with tears in her eyes. I put my arms around her. "I'm so sorry." I don't know what else to say.

She just hugs me back, takes my hand in hers and pats it. She nods her head up and down. "Thank you, Patsy."

I wish I could do more. "I'll visit him often, Mrs. Sheldon."

She is still nodding up and down. "Thank you, honey. He will need his friends."

I get home and sit on my front porch swing trying to wrap my head around the life Wally will now have. Why didn't I take that beer bottle out of his hand? Why?

I don't have a lot of time to think. Ruby comes out the screen door letting it bounce twice. "Take me to the Roundtop, Patsy!"

"Did you do your chores, Ruby?"

"Just did! Can we go?"

"Give me a minute to make us a lunch." I hop off my swing and she hops on to wait for me. In minutes we head out. The Roundtop is bordered by the Kroh farm. Ruby loves to go past the farm with all the animals and the smell of horse poop. Passing the barn, Mr. Kroh is feeding his pigs and greets us, "Hey girls. Going to the Roundtop?"

Ruby, runs over to pet his smallest goat. "Yep, we got a picnic lunch!"

Mr. Kroh likes to kid with us. "I hear there's some thieves in them there woods, and they make their bed on the Roundtop!"

Ruby's eyes get big. "Thieves? In the woods?"

I laugh but scold Mr. Kroh. "She doesn't know you are kidding; she'll have nightmares tonight!" Ruby laughs. I guess she does know he is kidding.

We go straight up the hill. It is steep. We pass through some high grass and prickly bushes. It is a beautiful day. There are many chirping birds and squirrels running up trees. We climb to the top and look down over the valley. It is like being in heaven. The top of the Roundtop is fairly bare. Trees are sparce at the top. I come here often with Ethel. It is peaceful. Our best friends are the rabbits, squirrels and an occasional white tail deer. The large water tank that supplies the entire town sits at the top. We climb up the ladder on the side of it and look in. So many things floating on the water. It amuses us. We don't think about the water being the water that we drink every day in our homes. It is just fun to climb up and see if there is anything new floating in the water. The skinny road that a car can drive to the Roundtop ends right here at the water tank. This is the road that brought Wally here on prom night. I can't think about that.

Ruby and I enjoy the day, eating our lunch and hiking. We head back down the hill, leaving ourselves enough time to visit Sam.

A thing called a frisbee came out this year. Sam bought one. "Want to play frisbee?" He asked before we even get up his porch stairs.

"Sure thing, Sam." The three of us head to the back where the yard is big. He loves throwing it back and forth to Ruby and me. I can't figure out how to throw it. When it leaves my hand, it hits the ground. Sam comes behind me. He gets very close. His chest is against my back. The frisbee is in my hand and he puts his right hand on my wrist. "Now watch, Patsy. Put your hand up across from your chest, bring it in like this, then come back out again and let it go!" I don't want to "come back out" because when he brings my arm into my chest, he is close. Very close. He feels like my favorite blanket wrapped around me on a cold winter's night. I quiver at his touch. I have to bring my arm out again to let the frisbee go. It flies across the yard and Ruby is there to catch it.

"Let's do that again, Sam, until I get it!" I'm lying, I just want him close.

We do the same dance five times. Ruby is getting bored. "Come on, Sam, let's get going on that grape arbor you want to build!"

Ruby spoiled my moment.

Sam laughs, grabbing his hammer from under the steps, "You girls are slave drivers!" We are happy to help, carrying the boards and helping string wire across to hold firm the grape vines as they grow.

I watch him and Ruby working in perfect unison. He pounds the nail. She brings the wire to the nail, uncoiling it as she walks. "You making wine with these grapes, Sam?"

"I suppose I might. Maybe some jelly. What do you want me to make?"

Ruby loves her sugar. "Jelly, Sam, Jelly!"

"Then jelly it will be, pretty lady!" Ruby is getting so tall now, and what words she didn't say before she started to talk, she is making up for now. "I am going to be the best kid in school and everyone will like me!"

He is amused at her confidence. "For sure they will! Who wouldn't like a pretty girl like you!"

Her face melts into a scowl. "Well, Patsy says I don't need to worry about being pretty, just need to worry about being smart!"

He is trying not to laugh. "You are already a smart, girl! Patsy is smart too. She is just telling you pretty isn't everything. But you are going to be pretty AND smart, like Patsy!"

I like that he said that.

She ties up the last wire and we all stand back to look at our masterpiece. Now we need to plant the grape vine plants. Sam has the roots of the grape vines in six little pots. He digs a hole at each post. Ruby brings the pot to him and helps. She picks the root up out of the pot and he puts it into the ground. Both of them pat the new dirt around it.

They stand together admiring their work. Ruby hugs Sam's leg. "I can't wait to see them grow, Sam." He strokes her hair. I so enjoy watching the love he has for her.

Mama is hollering dinner is ready.

"See ya tomorrow, Sam!" Ruby chimes as she runs across the lawn.

Sam laughs, as he hollers, "If the good Lord's willin' and the creek don't rise!"

Mama's supper is delicious as usual. She did deep fried chicken, mashed potatoes and green beans. There is always dessert. Today it is fresh apple pie. She cuts all of us a piece. Mama cuts herself a big slice also. We all worry about her sweets. She just won't listen. She loves her sweets. I can't let it go. "Mama, you shouldn't be eating that! Do you forget you have diabetes?"

She points at me, makes a motion across her lips like she is closing a zipper, and I know what that means. She wants me to shut-up. Ina, Bella and I look at each other and say nothing, as usual, but we worry.

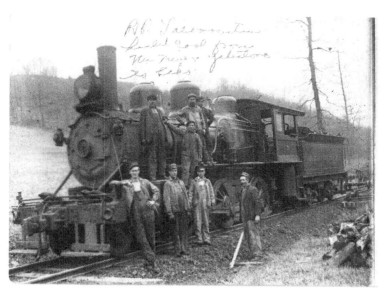

The railroad was built in 1899 from Echo to Rural Valley to transport coal and passengers. It was a branch of the R & P RR and serviced all five mines of the Cowanshannock Coal and Coke Company.

Coal Miners striking, marching from the "Hill" onto Main Street.

THE CREEK DON'T RISE

The Cowanshannock Coal & Coke Mine No. 1 in 1900. The larger boiler house provided electricity for the mines. The loading tipple is in the center with the red dog pile at left (boney dump). Red Dog is reddish, slate-like material shale baked hard by the coal burring inside the piles. Company houses are pictured in the background.

Sons of Tirolo Band was comprised of immigrants or descendants of the Province of Tyrol in Northern Italy.

Lauster Flour Mill was constructed in 1904 by W.P. and H.F. Lauster and was known as Yatesboro Flour and Feed Mill on Line Street. In 1935 the name changed to Lausters Flour Mill. In 1959, the America Legion purchased it. The Stack from the Mill still stands.

Coal Miners at the start of their shift

Valley Supply Co. (The company store) built in 1900, it was the largest outlet of this type in the area. The fire destroyed it in 1953. It sat where the present Yatesboro Post Office sits.

R & P Baseball Champions 1929

Avi's Tavern in Yatesboro. The next building, Lazzeri's Bar, is in Rural Valley, next to it is American Legion, Colo's Bar, Palilla's Market, Pina's Resturant.

No. 5 Yatesboro Coal Tipple

The Valley Hotel was built in 1899 and housed many immigrants until their company home was built. In this picture you can see St. Mary's Catholic Church on the right. To the left of the church is the Cowanshannock High School

Yatesboro Baseball Stadium with the tin roof, where Arnie fell to his death.

Rural Valley Elementary School where Ruby went to school.

*A view of the company houses on the "Hill"
taken from St. Mary's Cemetary.*

Caught In Machinery—

Boy, 4, Killed In Farm Mishap

DAYTON — Four-year-old Loren Dale Stewart, son of Mr. and Mrs. Dale Stewart of Dayton R. D. 2, was fatally injured at 1 p.m. Monday when he became entangled in a corn loading elevator's drive shaft while helping his father on the farm.

According to reports, the little boy was helping his father toss corn cobs into a loading elevator operated by a power takeoff device. As corn was taken up the elevator, some spilled over onto the ground.

The power takeoff drive shaft, connected to the tractor, supplied power to operate the elevator loading corn into a corn crib.

With the father less than two feet away, the little boy's clothing became entangled in t h e drive shaft and the powerful machine started to hurl the boy over and over. The father raced for the power shutoff switch but the few seconds were enough for the machine to take its' toll.

The parents rushed the boy to Armstrong C o u n t y Memorial Hospital at Kittanning, but he was pronounced dead on arrival.

Armstrong C o u n t y Coroner, Jack Kennedy, attributed death

to multiple fractures of the skull and entire body.

In addition to his parents, the little victim is survived by three sisters.

A complete obituary appears on page two of today's editions of the Gazette.

LOREN DALE STEWART
... fatally injured

Leader-Times Newspaper article of Loren Stewart, killed in a farm mishap.

The tower of the Rural Valley Lutheran church standing after tornado of 1944. Chevrolet Special Deluxe in front.

Destruction from tornado of 1944, girl unidentified.

Tornado of 1944, house destroyed.

THE CREEK DON'T RISE

Maffei's Service Station and Store in Rose Valley.

*Passerini's Service Station and
car garage on Main Street Yatesboro.*

King's Rexall Drugs. Norm King and Jack Arbuckle. Jack won this car by writing in 25 words or less how to display "Modess".

Mr. and Mrs. Arduini inside their candy store after decorating for Christmas.

Arduini's Candy Store front with Mr. and Mrs. Arduini. Main Street, Rural Valley.

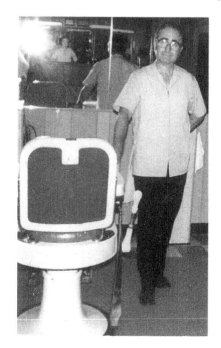

Geno Cicchiani, Barber, in his shop on Main Street, Rural Valley.

THE CREEK DON'T RISE

A wedding at the altar of
St. Mary's Roman Catholic Church.

The Enterline Blacksmith Shop. The shop was located
on Swede Alley just beyond No. 4 Dam.

THE CREEK DON'T RISE

The Liberty Theater in Rural Valley.

Dotsy Enterline (Patsy's sister Dee) painting the family shed.

Palilla Brother's Market on Main Street.

Sagamore Tipple, the largest tipple in the world

View of Yatesboro from the roundtop

Sgro's Sunset Grove.

Yatesboro No. 4 dam.

The Arcade by L.H. Nevins & Co.

Sagamore Hotel

Jack Nagy and his mother Ann in front of The Liberty Theater.

Yatesboro Presbyterian Church.

twenty-three
Sorrow Times Two

It is late evening. I love listening to the crickets through our open screen door. There is a slight breeze blowing the sheer curtains at the open window. I think about crickets and how simple their life is. Their only job is making evening music for us. I smile to myself at the simplicity of it all, as I look at the Sears-Roebuck Catalog. Suddenly, the screen door opens. Uncle Joe enters. He looks sad. He talks in a low voice. "Hi, Patsy. Is your mama home? I've got something to tell you all." This is strange. What does he have to tell us?

Mama comes out of the kitchen. "Hi, Joe! Just in time for dessert!"

He looks troubled. "Can we sit?"

Mama sees the concern in his face. "Come on in the dining room, Joe. I've made a delicious apple pie."

We all pick a chair, staring at Uncle Joe. He feels us staring and looks down at his hands as he turns them around and around each other. He swallows hard. "I'm having a hard time saying this."

Mama lays her hand on his hands to stop them from moving. "Just say it, Joe. It will be okay."

He looks at Mama, then down to his hands again. "Alice has consumption."

I don't know what he means. "Consumption? What is that, Uncle Joe?"

Uncle Joe wipes the tear that is trickling down his cheek. "Just a pretty word for cancer, Patsy. Your Aunt Alice has cancer."

I don't know what to say. I know about cancer. Mama's best friend, Madge, died of cancer last year. Mama sat with Madge for days as she slipped away, in pain. I remember how hard it was on Mama, and how she cried.

I think of how I had to see Arnie and Daddy laying in the casket. Now I will have to see Aunt Alice in the casket. I just can't think about that. Mama is standing now. She gives Uncle Joe a hug. "Now, Joe, let's think positive. Some cancers can be cured. You have to think positive. After all, you know it ain't over 'til the fat lady sings!"

Ruby is puzzled. "What? What fat lady?"

"It's just a saying, honey." Mama releases her hug.

Uncle Joe wipes his eyes. "Thanks, Isla."

She turns to cut him a piece of pie. "Keep your faith, Joe. Faith does amazing things you know! Now tell me how this all came about, and how she is feeling right now."

Uncle Joe timidly takes a bite. "She had a pain between her shoulders. We thought maybe she twisted the wrong way or something. It got so bad I took her for tests. There is a tumor in her lung causing the pain. They've given her pills for the pain. She is feeling okay right now. We are going Wednesday to discuss options." He lays down his fork. "I can't imagine life without her, Isla. I just can't!" He starts to cry.

Mama always knows what to say. She puts her arms around him. "Don't put the cart in front of the horse, Joe. Keep faith that they can help her. She is going to need you. She is a strong woman. She will fight this. Cancer is not always a death sentence. Let's all stay positive, and help her fight!"

He seemed to calm down. "Thanks, Isla. I'll try not to think the worst."

As soon as he leaves, Mama starts to make Aunt Alice her own apple pie to take across the street. Mama treats every ailment with food. Food cannot, however, fix how upset I am. I cannot think. I run out the door to Sam's.

He is always comforting, no matter what is happening. Now when I sit on the swing beside him, we are almost at eye level. Seems like yesterday I sat on the stool and looked up at him. Now I look across at him. I tell him about Aunt Alice. He takes my hand. "There is always hope, Patsy. You must never give up hope. I'm sure your Aunt Alice is staying positive. She will win this battle. I know she will." My mouth, until now, had the bitter taste of vinegar in it. Sam has just washed it away. He has a way of doing that.

He smiles at me and wipes a tear off my cheek. "You need to go visit her tomorrow. You will see, you will feel better."

I stay on his porch until darkness falls. He walks me across the yards to home.

Sleep doesn't come easily. I suspect I fell asleep in the early morning hours. I awaken to beams of sunshine through my window. I lay a minute watching the dust dance in the sunlight that beams from the window to my bed. I make up my mind to pick myself up. I am going to make this a good day. After breakfast, I will visit Aunt Alice. Mama baked two loaves of banana bread this morning. She is glad I am going across the street to visit Aunt Alice. "Take her a loaf of banana bread, Patsy."

It is still warm. I wrap it in a towel and walk across the street. Aunt Alice looks normal. She seems her normal self. I'm trying to smile more vigorously than usual. "How you doing, Aunt Alice?"

"Better since you are here, Patsy!" Her smile is infectious.

She loves to chat. We sit and chat until almost lunch time. Aunt Alice is full of love. I wish she could have had children. She would have made a great mother. We don't talk about her illness. As I leave to go home for lunch, I feel better about Aunt Alice.

Returning home, I walk in my door to cheesy bread for lunch. I love cheesy bread! Ruby gobbles hers before I even take my first bite. I laugh at Ruby. "Quit laughing at me!" She is always scolding me.

"A little testy today, are we?"

She takes the last piece of cheesy bread in her hand and runs out the door.

I am just finishing my lemonade when mama asks me to go get field corn for fall decorating from the Stewart farm. I'm not taking Ruby along. She is crabby today.

The Stewart farm is on the outskirts of town. Mr. Stewart, Dale, works hard on his big farm machinery planting all the crops. In the fall, he harvests corn. It is field corn. It is meant for feed for the animals, but Mama loves to use some to hang on our doors for fall. I head out the door for the mile trek through the woods. It is October 21. The leaves on the trees are bright yellow, red, and orange. The sun shining through the trees creates a beautiful hew of colors. I turn my face up to soak in the sun's rays and enjoy the colors, basking in the beauty of fall.

Through the shadows of the trees, I can see someone coming toward me. It is Bud Cherney. He lives next to the Stewart farm. He is running fast. He looks terrified. He reaches me and grabs my shoulders as if to balance himself. I can see he is lathered with sweat. His face is soiled with tears. "What's wrong, Bud?"

He tries to catch his breath. "It's Loren Stewart, I think he's dead!"

My heart stops.

Loren is four years old. He is the youngest child of Mr. and Mrs. Stewart. He is the only boy. He has three older sisters. I always play with him when I go to the farm. He is a happy child, always laughing.

I feel like I am going to throw up. "NO! It can't be! How do you know, Bud? You have to be wrong!"

I can't breathe. The air is thick and still. The sun I was enjoying has turned to gray fog in my eyes and the colors of the trees are gone. My heart is going to explode, I am sure of it. I feel a chill run through my body like a cold winter wind. This can't be! "Bud, it can't be true. It just CAN'T!" He is sobbing and shaking. I see his distress and try to calm us both. "Let's not get ahead of ourselves, Bud. What happened?"

Bud wipes his eyes with the back of his dirty shirt sleeve. "Loren was helping his daddy put ears of corn on the elevator going up to the corn crib. I was near there chopping some wood. You know that big motor that runs under that corn elevator? It is under there going around all the time! A corn cob fell on the ground. Loren went to pick it up and the motor caught his little coveralls. Oh my God, Patsy! It was awful! Just awful! His daddy was screaming and his mama came running. I can't, I can't............"

I grab Bud. I can see he can't catch his breath. I hold him in an embrace. "Breathe, Bud. Just breathe." I feel his body relax a little. "Then what happened?

"Bruce Harkleroad was working there. Him and Mr. Stewart got to the motor to stop it. Bruce helped get Loren into the car. They took off for the hospital. I just started to run! Just run! I don't know where I'm goin', Patsy!"

My hearts breaks for him. "Okay, Bud, you are okay. You are here with me. Now listen, since they took him to the hospital, that means Loren is alive."

Bud shakes his head as he weeps. "I don't see how, Patsy."

I throw my arms around him. "But he is, or they wouldn't have taken him." He needs my hug. "Come to my house with me, Bud. We need to gather ourselves together and tell everyone what happened. Can you walk?

He nodded yes, though the tears still run down his cheeks. As we walk, he keeps talking. "Mrs. Stewart had wanted Loren to take a nap. I heard her hollering to Mr. Stewart that he needs his nap. She said they had to go to the Grange tonight. Loren fussed that he wanted to help his daddy. I heard his daddy tell Mrs. Stewart to let him help, and he'd bring him in for his nap in a few minutes. Oh, Patsy, if he had only just gone for the nap!"

I grab his hand. "But he didn't go for his nap, Bud. He wasn't supposed to. We don't decide what takes place. God does." We walked the rest of the way to my house in silence.

Mama was in the living room. We told her what we knew. Mama's face is white as a ghost. She melts into a chair and covers her face with her feed sack apron and weeps.

Bella, Ina and Ruby hear the commotion and come down the stairs. I explain it again. I feel myself talking, but it is like my voice is in a tunnel.

Bud has managed to gather himself together. "Need to get home to my family, Patsy."

I manage a smile for him. "It's going to be okay, Bud. Pray, just pray."

Mama stops crying and stands up. She knows she needs to be strong right now. "They'll need food at their house when they get home from the hospital. Loren will probably be in the hospital for a good while, so let's do what we can to help them." Mama seems sure Loren is alive. I feel a little better.

I will help, but I feel like I am walking in a fog. The fog is thick. It is like being in water and I can't go fast. Mama shakes me. "Patsy, you can do this! We have to help. Pull yourself together!" She hands me a knife and a cutting board. "Cut those tomatoes in slices and put them in this container." I wipe my eyes with the back of my hands as she ties an apron around my waist. Mama hurriedly starts to fry pork chops that she had in the refrigerator. Ina is peeling potatoes.

We are all worked up. No one is talking. We are all just working. I suddenly feel pain. "Ouch!!" I sliced my finger pretty good. I don't know what part of the red on the cutting board is my blood and what part is tomatoes. Mama runs over with her dishtowel and grabs my finger to stop the bleeding. She takes me to the sink to wash it and puts a bandage on for me. I grab the sink as my head feels like it is floating. Mama catches me. She gives me water. My head stops floating.

She hollers up the stairs, "Bella, get down here and take over slicing tomatoes! Patsy cut her finger! We need to get done!"

Bella comes down the stairs like a bull in heat. "You did that on purpose, Patsy, so you wouldn't have to do it!"

I want to hit her. "Who in their right mind wants to cut their finger with a knife, you idiot!"

Mama is upset with us. "Get upstairs, Patsy, I am not putting up with this right now. Get out of my sight!" She starts to cry. "There is a family right now trying to deal with the worst tragedy a parent can imagine, and you two selfish girls fighting makes me sick!"

I am ashamed of myself. "I'm sorry, Mama." I scurry to my room.

Once everything is ready, Mama calls Uncle Joe to take her to the Stewart farm. Mrs. Stewart's mama lives there. She will leave the food with her. I don't have to go. I don't know if I could stand seeing this family. I've seen enough death. I got through Arnie dying and Daddy dying. I just don't think I can take anymore. And Loren, such a sweet boy. He can't die, he just can't! I curl on my bed. My body is trembling and I am cold. Tears fall onto my pillow.

Mama left Ruby with me. She comes into my room and lies on my bed beside me. "It will be okay, Patsy." She strokes my hair, "Let's walk over to Sam's."

I manage to gather myself together. "I suppose so, Ruby."

Sam is sad too. He has heard. Who wouldn't be sad? I sit on the swing beside him. Ruby hops onto the stool. We can't talk. She swivels the stool. She does that when she is nervous. Swivel to the left, swivel to the right. Left and right, left and right, staring at the floor. Sam reaches over and grabs her hand. He firmly pushes her hand down onto her lap so she stops turning. He doesn't let go. He says nothing. He just squeezes her hand.

THE CREEK DON'T RISE

With his other hand he grabs mine. I look at him. His chin is quivering. He is a man with a huge heart. He doesn't even know Loren, but he feels the pain of this. We both start to cry. He holds our hands tight. "Darn that God of ours, giving you and me these big hearts! Darn him!" We both cry-laugh.

Sam named that a long time ago, a cry-laugh. He said it is when we cry about something sad, but try to come out of it by laughing also. "There's our cry-laugh again, Patsy!

I cry-laugh, gasping air between each breath as tears run down my face. He does not let go of our hands. Ruby and I are able to calm down.

I look towards home. I can see Uncle Joe pull in with Mama. I hate to let go but must. "I need to talk to Mama now, Sam. I'll be back!" He nods okay. Ruby and I run home. We don't even do our usual, "See ya later, alligator!"

Mama sits down on the couch like she is exhausted.

I feel extra bad now, that I fought with Bella. "You okay, Mama? Is Loren okay?"

She cannot talk. She is crying. I am scared. I get her tissues and sit down beside her. "He is gone, Patsy. Mrs. Stewart was holding him in the car on the way to the hospital when he took his last breath. It was on Route 85 he died. Route 85, the most beautiful drive in Armstrong County this time of year. The most beautiful, now the ugliest." Mama cries harder. I put my arms around her and cry with her. How can this be? A four-year-old child?

I lay my head on her shoulder. "How can God be so mean, Mama. He is a mean God!"

Mama straightens up and wipes her tears. She puts her hands on my shoulders and shakes me. "Don't you ever question God, Patsy! This is his will! He needed an angel today. He took Loren. We have to accept God's will. You will understand someday."

We sit together on the couch for the longest time. We are both numb. Bella, Ruby and Ina are in the kitchen crying. It is getting late. I am worried about Mama. "Let's go to bed, Mama. Maybe we will all feel better in the morning."

We all go to bed, but no one sleeps. Ruby comes into my room at two o'clock. I feel her crawl in beside me. "Can't sleep, Patsy."

"I know, Ruby. I can't sleep either. Let's go downstairs for some warm milk."

We walk down the stairs. Mama is sitting at the kitchen table. Sleep never came to her either. She looks exhausted. "You okay, Mama?"

Mama looks like she has been crying. "I'm okay girls, just sitting here thinking."

"Thinking about what, Mama?"

She is staring at the table, yet nothing is on the table. She is holding a napkin, twisting it. She stares into it. "Thinking about a mother holding her child as he takes his last breath." Mama is silent. Finally, she sighs. "I remember it well. I was holding Thomas when he died. I kissed him goodbye and held him until he was cold. So cold. Mothers don't get over these things."

I want to start crying, but I feel like I need to be strong for Mama. "Mama, you know Loren and Thomas are in heaven. You said it yourself, that God needed an angel today. There is nothing that could have prevented it. When God wants an angel, he takes an angel. You know that, Mama. You know that, right?"

Ruby thinks food fixes everything just like Mama does. She pulls two cookies out of the cookie jar.

Mama takes the cookies Ruby hands her. She smiles at Ruby. "Thank you, honey." She is quiet. We all are. Mama inhales loudly. "It is not for us to question. Loren will be okay girls; he is in God's kingdom now."

"I know he's in heaven, mama, but when will this elephant get off my chest?" I need to know.

"When we accept God's will, Patsy. When we accept God's will. The Stewarts are a strong family. The cross of sadness that consumes them will be the garment they dress in every morning for their rest of their lives. We will think of them every day when we wake up, and every day we will say a prayer for them. They have good family and friends who surround them. Their faith is strong. They will be okay."

I know this to be true. They are more than I could ever be. I feel unworthy to be their friend.

twenty-four
Life Goes on

I try to pick up my spirits with the morning light. Everyone always says things look better with the morning light. Well, the morning light is shining and my heart still hurts. I walk over to Sam's. Sam is talking about quitting baseball. "I'm getting old." He tells me. He is only 28.

I am confused. "Old? You are young, Sam!"

"Maybe young for working and planting gardens, but old for baseball, Patsy."

This doesn't make sense to me. He loves the game. He is physically fit, and he is such a good player. I feel sad he is giving up. "Is something wrong, Sam?"

Sam just laughs. "Just don't want to play anymore, I guess. Dave and Kenny are the newest players and youngest. They are only sixteen, Patsy. The other players are between that and just maybe twenty-three. It is time for me to give it up."

"But you are in great shape and good at the game! Why not keep going? Professional players stay until their late thirties!"

He laughs again. "And they make thousands of dollars to do it! I think I got paid with a candy bar once or twice. There is a time for everything. My time for baseball is over. I had a good time, that's all that counts. I just really like being home more, anyways."

I am hoping it is me that makes him like being home more. I look at his blue eyes and think how young and vibrant he is. He is stronger than anyone I know. Well, one good thing, I'll get more time on his porch with him.

"Or are you just wanting to be here when your package with the red ribbon arrives?" I jest.

His face turns sad. "It's hard to talk about that anymore, since it hasn't come. Seems I'm making a fool of myself expecting it to. Let's talk about something else."

I find this all so odd. Making a fool of yourself? What does that mean? I have known him seven years now. You would think by now he'd tell me what it is. I'm not asking. It is the one thing that bothers me. I want to help him forget about it. Can't do that if I don't know what it is. "How about you forget about red ribbons and think purple. Purple grapes, homemade wine. You'll have time to make it, Sam!"

He smiles at me with those beautiful blue eyes. "Maybe. But you aren't getting any until you are twenty-one!"

Until now, I did not know he was paying attention to my age. At eighteen, I am not innocent when it comes to nipping wine. "You don't need to worry about it. Slick and Utz get me and Ethel wine when we want it."

"Patsy, tell me you are fibbing. You aren't drinking, are you?" He seems worried.

"Really, Sam? You never had a nip when you were eighteen?"

"You have a point." He has to admit. "Not going to lie. But I worry about you. Promise me you'll never overdo, okay?"

I love that he worries about me. "Sure thing. I'm no lush, honeybun!" I pretend to knock ashes off a cigarette in my hand, like the ladies at Valley Hotel. Sam laughs.

Homemade wine and moonshine are plentiful in our Valley. The taste of sweet grapes trickling down the throat is a delight. Each wine maker brags that his wine is the best. Many of them enter wine making contests to bring home the blue ribbon. The young boys in town are often in the fruit cellars with the men making the wine. They always come out of the fruit cellar drunk. That is the point of them helping.

Besides making homemade wine and moonshine, there is a lot of butchering goes on in these towns. Early fall is butchering time. Slick and Husker's dads go around to help farmers kill the pigs. They then scald them and hang them. Thanksgiving Day is always butchering day. After butchering, the two men take the horse drawn meat wagon around town selling the meat. I used to like to hang around when the farmers were butchering. I got older though and found it rather disgusting. Now, though, Ruby wants to be there when they butcher. I take her, as much as I hate butchering time.

Ethel's family and mine get a gallon of milk twice a week straight from the cow on Mr. Kroh's farm. Bella and Gibs always go with Ethel and me to get the milk. Today is Wednesday, milk day. We walk arm in arm to the Kroh Farm. Mr. Kroh is always happy to see us. "The four musketeers!" He always hollers to us. Once we get our milk, we head the long way home, past the company store. There we can flirt with the boys leaning on the log outside. Blitz, Slick and Utz are at the log today. Blitz takes the piece of straw out of his mouth to talk. "Hey, Patsy, what you girls doin'?"

"Got milk for home. That's all!" I would never let them know we came this way to flirt.

Blitz is no dummy. "Hmmm, now why would Patsy walk this way home from the Kroh Farm when it would be much closer to go over to First Street?"

I am embarrassed. "Just wanted to see who was hanging out here. That's all."

Blitz just smiles. "If you're satisfied with what you see, then take that milk home and meet us at the school."

"Maybe." Don't want them to know I am interested. "We'll see!" We walk past them and up the hill very slow and casual. We, for sure, don't want to look anxious. As soon as we are out of their sight, we run like the wind to take the milk home and get to the school.

We go to the school playground often with boys we have flirted with at the log. Not always the same boys, but always familiar faces. There is never anyone that I want for a boyfriend. I just have fun flirting and hanging out with them. Blitz still likes to flirt with me, but he and Jenny are together now. She can have him. We four girls swing as the boys lean on the poles of the swing flirting with us. Sam's car is coming up the hill. He slows down when he sees us and seems to come almost to a stop. Finally, he moves along. Surely, he isn't spying on me! Why would he do that? After all, he isn't my boyfriend or anything, not at all. He is just a friend. A good friend. I will have to ask him why he did that. Strange!

twenty-five
Fear For Tubby

After breakfast, I want to just hang out with friends. I don't really have to ask anymore. Not as long as my chores are done.

Ruby is fussing to go and Mama scolds her. "No, Ruby! Patsy doesn't have to always have you tagging along. You go ahead, Patsy!"

Ike, Tubby, and Ethel are waiting at the school. Tubby has gotten so tall. He has thinned out some. He is glad to see me. "Hi, Patsy! Hey, Husker is still at the Lauster Flour Mill working. Let's go by there when he's done and do something fun!"

The Lauster Flour Mill supplies all the farmers around. The sign on it says, "HAY OATS FEED FLOUR ETC." If we turn down by Avi's Bar, it is right down the street on the left. Since Husker's brothers and sisters are older now, he isn't so tied down to taking care of them when he isn't working. As he has gotten older, he is much more friendly and outgoing.

I've got a great idea. "After we get Husker, we should go steal fruit, 'cause right past the flour mill is the McCartin farm. We can steal grapes and apples!"

Ike likes my idea. "Sounds good to me!"

We all walk the back alley to the Flour Mill where Husker is just winding up his shift. I see him taking off his apron. "Come on, Husker! We're going to the McCartin farm to steal fruit!"

Husker throws his apron in a bin and jumps into the path with us. We soon arrive at the farm. We come onto the orchards first. The old farm house is to the right through the trees. No one can see us.

The applies are green but just the way we like them. We all eat apples like crazy and stick one in each pocket. When we get our bellies full of apples, we go over to the grape arbor to pick grapes to eat. Though we are all getting older, we are still silly sometimes. "Husker, you look like you need some vegetables!" Tubby laughs as he gnaws on another green apple. "We can go to Lloyd Smith's garden for tomatoes. Lloyd is always at the Grange on Thursdays!"

We all run until we reach Lloyd's garden. The tomatoes are thick and ripe. We pick and eat until we cannot eat anymore. Tubby is starting to look a little funny. His face is white. Sweat is pouring from his forehead. "Tubby, what's wrong?" I ask.

"I'm feeling sick, real sick!" He whimpers and doubles over in pain.

I shoot orders to Ike and Husker. "You boys get on either side of him. Let's get him home!"

It is a struggle getting him down across the black road to the flats. He is so sick. He is having trouble walking. "Leave me here, I can't walk!"

"Keep going, Tubby. You can do it!" I beg him. Ike and Husker face each other and lock their hands together, making a chair-like effect for Tubby. Now they can carry him.

We finally get to Tubby's house. His daddy meets us at the door with a beer in his hand. "What the hell's wrong with you, boy!"

I am rambling. "We were just eating apples and grapes and tomatoes and Tubby got sick. He's real sick."

His daddy is mad. "It's those damn green apples, I told him not to eat those! Get him in there on his bed! He can lay there until he pukes! He'll be fine!"

Husker and Ike struggle to get him into his bed. His mama follows them in. She is worried. "Where does it hurt, Tubby?" Tubby pointed to his lower side, and cries in pain. Tubby doesn't cry that easily. This is bad.

His mama runs to the kitchen and begs his daddy. "Jib, we gotta take him to the hospital. He's real sick, Jib!"

His drunken daddy refuses. "Let him suffer it out. I told him not to eat those green apples!"

I am so scared for Tubby. Ike and Husker are scared too.

Jib is mean. "You kids git outta here now. We'll take care of him!"

Tubby's mama is crying. We run out the door. I go as fast as I can to home, to Mama. She hears me burst in the door. "Mama! Tubby is sick! REAL sick! His daddy won't let his mama take him to the hospital. Mama, I'm afraid he dies!"

Mama grabs her purse and marches out the door and across the street to Uncle Joe. I follow. The three of us go to Tubby's in Uncle Joe's Chevy. Tubby's daddy is by the barn now. Tubby's mama answers the door. Mama is firm as she speaks. "We are here to take Tubby to the hospital.

Tubby's mama is crying. "Thank God for you, Isla. Thank God!"

Just then Tubby's daddy came up to the porch. He gets in front of Mama. 'You ain't takin' my boy nowhere. He ate green apples. He can suffer it out. THAT'S IT!"

Uncle Joe starts toward him as if to punch him. Mama gets in front of Uncle Joe. Mama is angrier than I have ever seen her. "Git out of my way, Jib. Take that damn beer bottle with you and git out of my way!"

I never heard mama swear before. Jib doesn't know what to say. He mumbles something in his slurred drunken speech and backs down the porch stairs, sitting on the bottom step. He keeps his head down as we all help Tubby to the car. We almost have to carry him.

Tubby's mama sits in the back seat with him. Tubby's head is on her lap. Uncle Joe and Mama are in the front, so there is no room for me. "It will be okay Tubby, hang in there!" I holler as I head towards home.

Passing Sam's house, I see him on the swing. I sit beside him. "Tubby is really sick, Sam. REAL sick!" Mama and Uncle Joe took him to the hospital!"

"What happened, Patsy?" He is so concerned.

I explain our adventure to him and that Tubby's daddy thinks it was just the green apples.

"Not likely." Sam surmises. "You don't get that sick off green apples. Good thing Tubby has you, Patsy!"

I feel good about that. "I suppose so. I am just glad I was there for him."

I stay at Sam's a couple hours or so when I see Uncle Joe's car pull in. "Bye, Sam!" I jump down the stairs and start to run.

Sam is hollering to me as I run. "Let me know if there's anything I can do!"

Mama looks tired. "Tubby was rushed into surgery; his appendix had burst. The doctors said another half hour and he would have been dead! His mama stayed with him. We will go get her in the morning."

I feel sick. Poor Tubby! Thank God we got him to the hospital!

I went with Uncle Joe the next morning to pick up Tubby's mama at the hospital. She will rest awhile, then Uncle Joe will take her back to the hospital again this afternoon. When we pull into Tubby's house, we walk in with her. Jib is sitting at the kitchen table drinking a beer. Tubby's mama grabs his beer bottle and throws it at the wall. Beer flies everywhere and the glass shatters. Jib looks at us. He turns and slithers out the door. He will probably sleep it off in the barn. If she did more of that, maybe her life would change. I think to myself how tall Tubby is now. He could flatten his daddy if he wanted to do that. I hope he wants to someday!

twenty-six
Into Adult Life

May came in like a lion. We had the strangest rain storm last night. The clouds came over the valley dark and thick. Lightening illuminated the sky. Then instead of rain falling, hail fell, and hard. The hail dented Uncle Joe's car. Now that is a hard hail storm!

After breakfast I run to Sam's to see if he has any damage.

"None that I know of. That was one heck of a storm!"

"Sure was, Sam. By the way, I've been meaning to ask you something. Were you spying on me the other day when I was at the playground with the boys?"

He looks surprised. "Me? Spying? No, not at all! I saw you there, but I was looking at that one swing you kids were swinging on. It looked like the chain wasn't hooked right at the top. Just stopped to see if it was okay. It was, so I kept going."

"Ok, just was wondering." Though I really think he was spying on me. I don't really mind if he was. "Next question, Mr. Kaminsky. You want to come to my graduation in two weeks?"

Sam grins. "Thought you'd never ask. Of course, absolutely, without a doubt sweetheart!" He pretends he is flicking the ashes off a cigarette, as he talks like a gangster. He is so adorable when he does that. "Where do you want me and when, lady?"

I laugh at him, "It's in the field beside the school, 7:00. You will sit with Mama and my brothers and sisters."

He gets serious, as he asks, "What shall I wear, my Sunday best I presume?"

"You wear what you want, Sam. It doesn't matter to me!! Casual is good!" I'm so happy right now. I just want him there. He can wear a feed sack for all I care!

Graduation night is a beautiful evening. On the field is a stage, decorated with ribbons. There are orange carnations in vases on both sides. There are seventy of us graduating. Mama bought me a white dress from the Sears-Roebuck catalog. My hair has changed as I've aged. It is not so outrageously curly. It has more of a wave, than obnoxious curls, and it has gotten darker. I let it grow long. I think Sam likes it. I look pretty good in my makeup. I've done a little extra rouge, and some lipstick. I bought a sweet barrette with pearls to sweep one side of my hair up. I put my black graduation gown on to walk across the street to the school with my family. Ruby holds my hand, as usual. My sisters are being nice to me tonight. Sid and Doug are teasing me, as usual. As I approach the field, I see Sam. He walks over to me. "You look pretty dapper, young lady!" His eyes look extra blue tonight. He is wearing a light blue button-down collar shirt with a necktie. He looks very handsome.

Ruby grabs his hand. "Come on, Sam, me and you sit together!" She leads him away.

He turns around and looks back at me. He winks. I am so glad he is here. It means a lot. I care very much what he thinks of me.

The ceremony seems long. Jenny is valedictorian and she talks way too long. She tells us how we should be achievers and doers and blah blah blah. Slick is the class president so he has to do a speech too. He is stumbling a good bit. His head is down reading from his paper. When he looks up, we taunt him, trying to get him to laugh. He will give us all heck later. Finally, they are giving out diplomas. It is my turn to walk across the stage. I never liked school. I spent a lot of time wishing it would go faster, go away. Now I feel myself start to cry as I walk across the stage. I will miss school. I will miss my friends. I will miss being a kid. Another chapter is beginning for me. I don't know what to expect. But I am an adult now and will have to act like one. I am starting to wish I would have appreciated more being a kid and being in school.

The high school chorus sings our alma mater. We all stand up and sing along. I cry a little as I sing. The ceremony ends and we march out to the graduation march being played by our high school band. I cry more. I just can't stop. All the parents and guests follow us out. Everyone is trying to find their graduate to congratulate them. Sam finds me first and puts his arms around me. With his hand he wipes the tear from my cheek. His lips meet my cheek for a soft kiss, as he talks softly. "I told you that you liked school! I'm so proud of you, Patsy, and you look beautiful tonight." A tickle runs down my spine.

Ruby runs into my legs, hugging me around my waist. I bend down for a proper hug. "This will be you someday, sweetheart." She just giggles. Mama, my sisters and brothers all hug me. After all the congratulations, the graduates are all gathering to take off for the evening for their little celebration parties wherever.

Ethel is begging me to come. I hug her so hard. "Ethel, I don't know what I will do without you!" Ethel is going away to nursing school. My heart is breaking.

"No sadness tonight, Patsy! We are celebrating! Let's go! The guys are waiting!"

I look back at Sam. He motions for me to come over to him. "I'll be right back, Ethel."

She looks at me with a look of concern. "I'll wait for you over there. Patsy, hold on to your heart!"

What does she mean by that? I don't know. Sam grabs my hand. "I have something for you." He reaches into his pocket. "Hope you like it." He hands me a flat box wrapped in silver with a silver bow.

"You didn't have to buy me something, Sam!" But I'm excited. I open the silver paper slowly. The box says "Pribicko Jeweler" on it. I lift the lid. It is a gold bracelet. The chain has tiny, delicate links and in the middle is a charm. It is a heart, with little stones around the heart that sparkle. I throw my arms around him. "I love it, Sam! I love it!"

I feel him loving my embrace. He whispers in my ear, "I'm glad you like it!" When I release from the embrace, he unhooks the bracelet and hooks it around my wrist. "I bought a heart because you are a girl with a big heart." He smiles at me and I feel love pouring out his blue eyes. I am sure of it. "Now get going! Have fun with your friends. And, Patsy, NO DRINKING!"

I give him one last hug. "See ya later, Sam!"

"If the good Lord's willin' and the creek don't rise!" He smiles as his eyes follow me.

I rush to catch up to Ethel. One last night with all my friends. Then, this part of my life is over. Tomorrow, or soon, most of them will be going off to college or to jobs. Life, as I know it, will change. I hope I am ready.

When Monday arrives, I walk to Palilla's Market to ask for a job. Lucio always liked me, as he responds, "We'd be happy to have you, Patsy!" I am thrilled.

I run home and stop by Sam's to tell him. "I'm a working girl!"

He is happy for me. "That so? Good! Now I will know who to go to when I need a loan!" We both laugh.

By Tuesday, I am working. Dee shows me the ropes and I will get four days a week work with three days off. I will get minimum wage, forty cents an hour. I'll be able to help Mama and there will be some left over for me.

I'm happy with my new life as a working girl. Plus, I will still have time to do what I want, like visiting Sam.

twenty-seven
Childhood Pains

With working so much the days fly by. Our neighbor's daughter got married in June. The wedding was at the Catholic Church but we went back to their house basement afterwards. I drank wine, lots of it. Bella drank way too much too and was sitting on everyone's lap. It was fun. I hope that is me someday, getting married I mean!

Before we know it, August is here. Time for school. It is the first day of school for Ruby. She is nervous. I help her get dressed in her little black shoes with the strap and her white socks. Mama has made her a pretty dress which is blue and white plaid. A white ribbon will work perfectly in her hair. I hold Ruby's hand as we walk the mile up the road through Rural Valley to the grade school on Main Street. Rural Valley Elementary is in the middle of town. It is two stories with lots of windows, and it is huge! We can smell the oiled floors as we enter.

I assure her that she will have lots of fun in school. An elderly man greets us, with little round glasses and a bald head. "Hello, I'm Principal Holmes."

Ruby squeezes my hand tight, as she replies. "I'm Ruby." I am surprised she answered on her own.

I reach my hand to shake his hand. "I'm her sister, Patsy. Ruby is a little nervous today."

He kneels down to Ruby. "Now, Ruby, nothing to be nervous about. You are going to have a lot of fun in school!" He then stands up to greet the next student.

I bend down to be at her eye level. "I will be here to get you when school lets out, don't worry." She looks scared.

Her teacher, Mrs. Weaver, greets her with a smile. "Good morning, Ruby, would you like to come with me?" Ruby nods yes. "It is a tour of the school, Patsy. Please join us!"

Ruby looks at me with fear. I simply nod my head and follow.

The cafeteria is down the steps, into the basement. We walk under all the heat pipes, water pipes, and vents. We pass an eraser cleaner and someone is cleaning erasers. It is just a belt that goes around and around. Chalk dust is flying everywhere. Ruby sneezes. We continue to weave through the narrow passage, with Mrs. Weaver leading. We end up at a kitchen where little ladies wearing hairnets are making food. This is where Ruby will pick up her lunch. Then Mrs. Weaver leads us back a hallway and up another set of stairs, showing Ruby how she will bring her lunch tray back to the classroom. Next stop is outside Principal Holme's office. Mrs. Weaver talks sternly. "This is where I will send you if you get in trouble, Ruby. You don't want me to send you here, right?"

"No ma'am." Ruby whispers. I can see this scares her.

"Now we will go to the classroom and I will assign you a seat." Mrs. Weaver announces.

She bids me leave and I wave to Ruby. She waves back and her hand is shaking. I smile as I give her a thumbs up.

I am working at Palilla's today but Lucio will let me go in time to pick up Ruby. Three o'clock comes quickly. As I walk up the sidewalk to the school, I see Ruby with two new friends. "This is Ellen and that one is Shelly." She proudly announces.

"Nice to meet you girls. Do you want to walk home with us?"

Neither answers, but both nod yes. We begin the trek down the street. Shelly lives halfway through Rural Valley, in a small house on the left. "Can you come meet my mama?" She asks.

"Of course, we can."

As we walk into the house her mama greets us. "Hi there!" She is sitting in a wheelchair mixing cranberries in a bowl at the kitchen table. "I'm Erma. Now who might you be?"

Ruby surprisingly answers for me, "I'm Ruby, this is Ellen, and the big one is my sister, Patsy."

The big one? Really?

Ruby stares at Erma, as she asks, "Why you in that wheelchair?"

I nudge her to let her know she should not have asked that. But it did not bother Erma at all. She simply smiled, and replied, "I have something called MS, Ruby. I have had it for years. I wasn't always in a wheelchair. But the disease progressed through the years. It progressed to the point my legs don't work, so here I am! It's okay, Ruby. My chair takes me where I need to go."

Ruby looks at the bowl. "Whatcha mixin' there?" Ruby is so nosey.

Erma laughs. "Cranberries, honey. Do you know where I got them?"

"No, where?" Ruby asks.

"At the bog!" Erma laughs and sees Ruby is puzzled. "The bog, honey. That is where cranberries are grown. You learned something today!"

Erma is so easy to talk to. I shake her hand. "I'm so glad we got to meet you, Erma. I will walk Shelly home from school every day. I will be walking Ruby home anyways. It will be my pleasure."

"So kind of you, Patsy." She turns to Shelly. "Shelly, you be sure to thank Miss Patsy every day, too." Shelly just smiles.

I hope to visit Erma again. She is an interesting woman to talk to. I hope Ruby can see that even in the worst situations, a person can be happy, like Erma.

We continue down the street to deliver Ellen home. She lives above one of the bars, on the top floor. She opens a door beside the bar and starts up a dingy staircase. It is dark. I can hear a man yelling upstairs. Every now and then, there is a woman's voice. Both seem angry. Ellen looks at us with fear in her eyes. I am nervous. "You okay, Ellen?"

Ellen nods yes, but her eyes are sad. "Bye, Ruby!"

Ruby seems mad at Ellen for something, so her reply is a simple hand wave. Strange.

We reach home. Ruby grabs a cookie. "I want to go to Sam's house."

I never mind that, so why not. Off we go.

Sam is on his swing. Ruby jumps onto the swivel stool. He just got done mowing his lawn. He smells of grass and sweat, but a good smell.

He is always happy to see us. "How was your first day at school, Ruby?"

"It was awful!" She burst out. A kid named Mitch kissed me on the playground. I was coming down the slide and he waited there at the bottom and planted his ugly lips on me!"

I can feel Sam trying not to laugh. "Well, what did you do about that, Ruby?"

"I told my teacher and she did nothing! She just laughed and said, "don't worry about it." I bet she'd worry about it if he put his ugly lips on HER cheek!"

"Now, Ruby, be nice. All you have to do is stay away from him. Stay away from the slide if you have to."

"NO! I am going on the slide if I want to! He isn't getting the best of me. If he tries it again, I'll just punch him!"

Sam looks at me with a frown. "Oh my."

I better get control of this, though I'm wondering why she didn't tell me on our walk home. "Ruby, you will not punch anyone. Do you remember the Principal's office? You want to be sent there? You just stay away from this Mitch, that is all. It is your job to do that."

"Whatever!" She swivels the whole way around on the stool. "And that ain't all!" The stool stops. She is scratching the wood on the seat of stool between her legs. I can feel she is nervous as she starts to talk. "Ellen told me how babies are made!"

Sam and I look at each other not knowing what to say. He speaks first. "What? What do you mean?"

"Ellen said that a man and a woman get together and do dirty things. I told her that is disgusting. I know she is just trying to scare me. It made me mad!" She keeps scratching the wood of the stool. She won't look up.

I am speechless. These kinds of things I don't talk about with Sam. Why didn't Ruby tell me? I recover quickly. "You ignore that, Ruby. Forget you heard it. That is not something you need to be talking about at your age. You have lots of time for those conversations."

She jumps down off the stool seeing a rabbit come out of the bushes. She always thinks she can catch a rabbit. Down off the porch she goes to chase the rabbit around the house.

I look at Sam, and I see his bewilderment. "Sam, how would Ellen, a first grader, know these things?" Then it hit me. The fear I saw in Ellen's eyes walking up those stairs. The man and woman hollering upstairs. What is going on in that house? How does Ellen know about sex? "Oh my, Sam. I am worried. When I dropped Ellen off, she looked scared. She lives above a bar. I could hear yelling from upstairs. Do you think…..?" I couldn't say it.

"I don't know what I think, Patsy. But we can't ignore this. An eight-year-old should not know this stuff."

"I will tell Mama and Uncle Joe. I don't think we can ignore this either, Sam."

"I think you are right to talk to them first. Let me know if you need me also to do something. I'm willing, you know."

Ruby comes around the house. Without the rabbit, of course. "Let's go, Patsy. I'm getting hungry."

I start down the wooden stairs. Ruby already seems to have forgotten about what she told us. "Hey Sam, did your package with the red ribbon come yet? I'm getting tired of waiting!" Ruby just won't forget about that.

Sam looks at me, then Ruby. "No, Ruby, it didn't." Again, Sam's sadness is evident.

She is stomping on an ant on the sidewalk. "Well, you said before it might take a long time, and it is. You can wait for it!"

He follows her every movement. "I suppose I can. I'm lucky I have you and Patsy to keep me company until it gets here!"

I'm still trying to digest why Ruby didn't talk to me first about what Ellen told her. I'm troubled about Ellen. "I'll bring you some of Mama's homemade bread tomorrow, see you then Sam!"

Sam smiles. "If the good Lord's willin' and the creek don't rise. Ruby, stay off the slide!"

I tell Mama about the conversation Ruby had with Ellen. I tell her about where Ellen lives and the hollering from up the stairs I heard. I tell her about the look in Ellen's eyes when we left her. Mama is concerned too. She calls Uncle Joe over to tell him about it.

"There could be a problem there." He sounds concerned. "I knew her daddy from way back. He is a drunk. He is also rotten mean. He had a fight a couple years back, in the coalmine. He put another fella in the hospital."

That tells me something about Ellen's daddy. "Do you suppose he is doing something to Ellen?"

"I sure hope not, but we can't ignore this. Can we?"

I am troubled, more than troubled, "What can we do?"

He hesitates a moment. "Leave it to me. I will go there tomorrow."

"I'm going with you!" I announce. He does not argue with me.

The next day Uncle Joe and I drive to the apartment where Ellen lives. We walk up the wooden stairs. Knock, knock, knock. A woman opens the door. Uncle Joe does the talking. "I'm looking for Chet, your husband." He states matter-of-factly.

She hesitates a minute. "Well then, go to the Kittanning jail, that's where he is!" She turns her head sideways to be sure Ellen isn't in the room. We can see her black eye. She realizes we have seen it. "Yeah, he beat me up bad last night."

Uncle Joe is troubled seeing the black eye. "Are you alright?"

"I'm fine. Ain't me I'm worried about. It's Ellen."

"What about Ellen?" He is quizzing, but he thinks he already knows.

She wrings her hands into her apron. "When Ellen came home from school yesterday, Chet was drunk and fightin' with me. Ellen tried to break it up, screaming at him that he was a pig, that he was doin' things to her and stuff. I wanted to kill him. I pushed him hard and picked up a knife. If he hadn't punched me in the face and knocked me out, he'd be dead!" She keeps wringing her hands. "Once he knocked me out, he ran out the door. After she knew he was gone, Ellen ran and got a neighbor to call the police. I had come around by then." She looks back towards the bedroom again where Ellen is. Looking back at us, she says in a low voice, "No one needs to worry about him no more. Cops say he ain't comin' back. Cops got hold of him runnin' down by the company store. I can tell you this! If he ever comes anywhere near us, I'll kill him myself for what he did to my girl!"

Uncle Joe looks nervous and concerned. "I'm sorry that happened to you. We were worried about Ellen. That is why we are here. We are glad to hear he is gone."

"Don't worry no more. Ellen will be safe now. She is safe with me. That no good SOB will never set foot here again."

Uncle Joe is still troubled, but he knows, for now, he has to trust what Ellen's mother has told him. "How about I stop back when I go by here just to check on you and Ellen?"

"That would be nice." She manages a faint smile.

I put my hand on hers. "I'll be glad to bring Ellen home from school each day. And if there is anything else I can do, I will. Please call me."

"Appreciate it much. Gonna go be with my girl now." She turns and shuts the door.

I tell Ruby to forget about what Ellen said and try to be her friend. She needs a friend. Somehow, I think Ruby understands.

Ruby scoots through this year of elementary school with minimal work. She is smart, but she likes being the class clown. She is in trouble often. Sometimes she drags her friends into her schemes, getting them in trouble too. First grade is going rather fast. Her summer will be spent helping in the garden, fishing with Sam, doing her chores, and playing with her friends. She goes with me everywhere. She never misses our visits to Sam. She wants to go to Swede Alley often to play with Frankie, Jimmy and their sisters. Her puppy love for Jimmy is growing. She is like me at a young age, I loved my friends. Still do.

twenty-eight
Mischievous Ruby

School ends in May and summer flies by. It's Dayton Fair time, my favorite time of the year. Today is Wednesday. The fair rides are half price on Wednesdays. "Wanna go to the fair with Ruby and me for the afternoon, Sam?"

He seems a little down today. "Nah, Pats! Just not up to it!"

I laugh, "You just want to be here when your package with the red ribbon gets here!" I am starting to joke about that. It seems like a joke to me. It's been years now he's been waiting for it!

Sam doesn't smile today. "It's best I quit talking about it. It was just a dream. That's all."

I am shocked at this. He has given up! What the heck is this package? I feel bad for him now. Shame on me!

"Dreams are worth having, Sam!" I smile at him and put my hand on his shoulder. "So-be it then, Mr. Kaminsky. Stay home and eat a bologna sandwich. I will, meanwhile, have a funnel cake for you at the fair, plus some greasy French fries, okay?" I chuckle, trying to get him to smile.

Sam smiles slightly, but there is a gray cloud above him today. "You go ahead with Ruby and have fun."

I know I'm not visiting him as much now that I am working. Maybe that's the problem. I must try harder.

We get home from the fair in time for dinner. Bella has a bunch of friends in tonight. Gibs is here too, of course. I'm not crazy about Bella's friends. They have foul mouths and they all smoke. Mama makes them stay on the back porch because of all the cigarette smoke. Ruby loves sitting out there with them, though I wish she would not.

A week after the fair is over, second grade starts for Ruby. Ruby still lets me walk her to school. I know she will outgrow that soon. As we enter, Aunt Bertha is standing outside her classroom. Thank goodness Ruby didn't get her for a teacher! Aunt Bertha shakes her finger at Ruby, as she scolds, "You be a good girl! Don't let me hear you were naughty!" Old biddy. She needs to mind her own business.

Ruby's first day is in Mrs. Smith's class. I deliver her to classroom five and Mrs. Smith is here to greet her. Unlike first grade, Ruby is no longer nervous and runs into the classroom. "See you later, Ruby!" She ignores me.

I'm not working today. I am going to help Mama bake chocolate chip cookies. Especially since I want to take some to Sam. Mama and I have lunch and finish our cookies by 1:00. Our phone is ringing. "Hello?" It is Mrs. Smith.

"You won't have to pick up Ruby today, Patsy. I will be walking her home."

I am surprised, but who am I to question. "Okay, that is very nice of you."

Mama looks concerned. "That's not good."

Shortly after three o'clock, a knock came to our door. Mama and I answer it together. It is Mrs. Smith and Ruby. Mama opens the door wide for them to enter.

Mama speaks first. "What's going on? Is something wrong, Mrs. Smith?"

Mrs. Smith pauses just a moment then begins. "Well, seems as though your daughter likes to tell dirty jokes, to the entire class!"

Mama glares at Ruby as Mrs. Smith keeps talking. "I can't allow this kind of behavior in my class. She has had to have heard it at your house!"

Mama grabs Ruby by the arm and shakes her hard. "Where did you hear it, Ruby? Where?"

Ruby is crying. "On the back porch last week. I didn't know it was dirty, mama. I didn't! Bella was telling her friends; they were all laughing. I thought it was just funny, not dirty!"

I feel bad for Ruby. "Mama, I am sure Ruby doesn't know what a dirty joke is. I am sure she wouldn't have said it if she had."

Mama doesn't answer me. She spins on her heels and hollers up the stairs. "BELLA, GET DOWN HERE!" Bella bounces down the stairs, cocky as usual.

As Mama starts to scold her for talking like that on the back porch, Bella fights back. "Oh, for heaven's sake, I can't help it there's an eight-year-old in our house! I'm old enough to talk how I want, Mama! Make the little twit stay in her room where she belongs!"

The family argument that is forming is uncomfortable to Mrs. Smith. She bends down to Ruby, "I'm going to let this one go, Ruby. But you have to learn what is right and wrong. You can't bring these kinds of stories to school!"

"I know." Ruby is sobbing. "I'm sorry."

Mama is so embarrassed. "I apologize for what Ruby did and I especially apologize for my other daughter's rudeness, Mrs. Smith!"

Mrs. Smith speaks with sympathy. "I am raising daughters as well. We all know we can't control everything." Mama feels better. Mrs. Smith seems to understand.

As soon as Mrs. Smith leaves, Mama runs through the house looking for Bella. She wants to swing at Bella, but by now Bella has gone out the back door and up the back of the yard by the shed. "That's fine, Bella!" Mama hollers out the back door. "You are going to get hungry sometime and have to come in! Wait 'til you see what's waitin' for you when you do!"

Punishing Bella isn't easy since she is older now, but Mama figured it out. She makes her feed the chickens for the next two weeks plus run the wringer washer. I would have laughed if she caught her boob in the wringers! Bella pouts around like she is mad at everyone. "You spoil Ruby so badly, Patsy! She is a little prima donna! She was the one with the big mouth! Not me!"

I decide to not fight with Bella about this. It is no use. I never win.

twenty-nine
Catastrophic Loss

I t is August 30th. The sun is bright and the air is warm. My goal today is to sit on the steps of the gymnasium in Rural Valley. The many steps that go up the front are where all the kids gather. The steps are cement, some crumbled. The banisters are made out of pipes and have lost their paint. The auditorium itself is old. It was built of cement block. There are many basketball games played here. On a cold windy day, the wind will come through the cracks in the cement block. The stage of the auditorium is all wood with old wooden steps going up both sides. Many things happen here on this stage. There was the Tom Thumb wedding last year. The young kids in town played the parts of the bride, groom and attendants. A lot of my friends had younger siblings in it. Everyone in town came to see it. It was very cute. I wanted Ruby to take part, but she wouldn't. There are minstrel shows here too, where many of the town's men sing. They paint their faces. They do skits and comedy and belt out songs with their nasal voices. Most are three sheets to the wind before the show even starts!

I am glad Ruby's friends are here. She is thrilled to see Frankie and Jimmy. Ellen and Shelly came also. It is a warm day. The boys have their bikes with them. Ruby sits with the girls on the gymnasium steps. They are talking about hair dye, and how to make your hair red in the summer. Ellen seems to know how, and her hair shows it. "Just pour peroxide in there, Ruby."

Ruby's hair is a soft auburn now. It is very pretty how it is just slightly curly and falls around her face softly. She is intrigued about how to streak her hair with red. I have to stop some of the things Ruby wants to try. "Now, Ruby, you know you are too young to do that. Mama wouldn't like it."

Ruby doesn't like me chiming in. "If you wouldn't say anything, Mama wouldn't even know!"

"I say no, Ruby! No is no!" She pouts and moves up two steps away from me. The girls continue discussing the peroxide deal as Ruby shoots me dirty looks. Frankie and Jimmy are throwing their football back and forth to each other in the grass at the side of the gym.

School will start the day after Labor Day. I'm glad the kids are enjoying one of their final days of summer.

"Hey, Frankie and Jimmy! Do you want go up to the football field and look for coins?" Ruby pleads as she runs down the stairs to join them. She got tired of the girls really quick. She is like me when I was young. She likes being with the boys more than the girls. The boys quickly agree, and I follow them. I just don't totally trust Ruby yet on her own. Especially since she is so in love with Jimmy!

The three of them run up the hill to the football field. I walk. Can't keep up with these young kids! I plant myself on a bleacher near them. Under the bleachers they search. Jimmy comes up with 5 nickels, a dime and a quarter. Frankie has in his hand 3 quarters, 5 dimes and a nickel. Ruby has 2 nickels, and they have a good laugh at that. It isn't her lucky day.

Ruby gives up, "Race you across the field to the goal post! Winner gets all!"

They run like the wind and keep the football goalpost in their sight as they race. Jimmy wins with Frankie not far behind him. Ruby is way last. All three of them fall onto the ground when they reach the goal posts, handing Jimmy their coins and laughing. They turn on their backs and watch the white clouds in the sky. I sit on the bleachers and listen. Ruby loves looking at the clouds. She points to the sky. "That one looks like a turtle."

Jimmy points in the opposite direction. "That one over there looks like a soldier, and he is moving, watch him, he is going to attack that one that looks like a tank!" The three of them lay on the ground facing up for a long time, just talking.

Ruby is looking at her hands. "Digging for coins made my hands dirty!"

They all laugh and Jimmy turns to her stroking her cheek. "Ruby, Ruby, she's so snooty." Ruby slaps his hand away, but I can see she loves it. She is in puppy love with Jimmy, and he with her. Not sure if I should step in. They act like they don't even know I am here. It is just puppy love. I will let them enjoy it.

They swing back onto their backs and the clouds entertain them for a while. Finally, I have to break this up. Need to get home. "Come on you guys, we gotta go!"

Ruby is mad. "Why do we have to go, Patsy?"

"I have chores to do at home. You need to come. We can come back tomorrow!" They weren't happy but meandered down the hill to the gymnasium with me. They swing one last time like monkeys on the steel banisters that lead up the stairs.

It is hard to get them moving. "Stop that you kids! We gotta get home. We've been here too long already!"

Frankie and Jimmy start down the street, pushing their bikes through Rural Valley. Ruby and the girls follow alongside me.

Ruby runs to catch up to Jimmy. I see him smile at her. "Knew you couldn't resist me, Ruby, Ruby." She walks the rest of the way at his side. I can almost see the little flutter going on in her chest.

Ellen and Shelly go into their homes as we pass them. Ruby and I make the right to go to our house up the hill. The boys continue on to Swede Alley. "Bye, Jimmy!" Ruby hollers. She is so smitten with him. It is still only 3:00 in the afternoon. I know they want to play more today. I will try to get my chores done and walk her to Swede Alley later to play a little longer.

Ruby knows my plan and helps me fold the laundry. Her mouth is going a mile a minute. "Jimmy said he likes my hair. I suppose I won't put any red in it then. Not because you told me not to, Patsy. Because I decided. Jimmy said he would come here to ride bikes with me. He has a really nice bike, don't you think so, Patsy? I think he likes me better than any other girl. I'm pretty sure he does? I sure hope so, because I like him. I like him a lot!"

I feel like she isn't stopping to even take a breath. She is in love.

It took me longer than I wanted to get my chores done. Mama had me scrub the kitchen floor and whatever was stuck to the floor was hard to get off. Gosh, it is already suppertime. We might not get down to Swede Alley today. Ruby will just have to understand.

Suddenly, the walls of the house shake simultaneously with a loud KABOOM! An explosion! It was loud, very loud. I run out the door. Ruby is behind me. Everyone is on the street. They are hollering. "Where did that come from?" We see smoke coming from Swede Alley. We hear screaming, lots of screaming. We start to run to Swede Alley.

As we pass Mrs. Benson's house, we can see Frankie is sitting in his front yard being consoled by his parents. The chaos is confusing. What happened? As I run up the street holding onto Ruby's hand, she falls in front of Frankie. He is crying, hard! "Frankie!" Ruby pleads, "What's wrong? What happened?"

He struggles to talk through his tears. "We were playing with a big bullet. I don't know what happened! I can't see Jimmy. I CAN'T SEE HIM! They won't let me go over there!"

Ruby tries to run towards Jimmy's house, but I grab her and fall onto the grass with her. She is screaming. "LET ME GO! LET ME GO!"

Mama has come with Uncle Joe in his car. She sits in the grass with us and puts her warm arms around us, rocking us. Uncle Joe joins the men to see what he can do.

People are everywhere, rushing around us. As Mama and I hold onto Ruby, I look over at the cars parked on the street. It looks like they were all shot up with a machine gun. The big maple tree I am sitting by has most of the bark ripped off. I can see the priest going into Jimmy's house. Jimmy's daddy is being held back by two police officers as a stretcher is loaded into an ambulance. Jimmy's older brother is screaming. He starts to run up Tarzan Hill. I see neighbors going after him.

Uncle Joe walks back to us. He gets on his knees and takes Ruby's hand. "Honey, Jimmy is in heaven."

Ruby leaves out a wail. It is a wail of pain, terror and grief. She tries again to get out of my grasp to run to the ambulance, but I grab her. She is hysterical. "JIMMY! JIMMY!" She is devastated. She loved Jimmy. It is just too much for her. She collapses. Uncle Joe picks her up and puts her in his car. I get in beside her. I put her head on my lap and stroke her hair. There is nothing anyone can say, nothing anyone can do.

Frankie's mama takes Frankie inside the house. His daddy is talking to Uncle Joe outside the car. With my window open I can hear him. "It was awful, Joe. I called Frankie in for supper twice. He was taking his good old time, but was finally at our front door when I heard Jimmy yelling to him, WATCH THIS! I was annoyed at Frankie for not coming the first time I called him, so I hollered to him "Get in here!" I looked out and saw that thing going through the air. Next thing I remember is thinking we were being bombed. It was awful. When it hit the hard road, the explosion happened. Frankie stepped into our house just in time to save his life. But, Jimmy was caught in the blast." He begins weeping. Uncle Joe pats him on the shoulder. "Nothing you could have done, nothing at all. Be thankful you have your boy." Frankie's daddy gives a faint nod and retreats into his house.

Uncle Joe and Mama take us home.

Men from WWII brought home many keepsakes, including WWII shells. This anti-tank shell was 18" long. It had the powder removed, but the warhead was still in place. It was a live warhead with a timing device, which no one knew. The live warhead had exploded, causing this devastating tragedy. The next day, they found Jimmy's belt buckle in the trunk of a neighbor's car and the casing of the shell was found 250 ft. away.

Frankie and Jimmy had played with this warhead several times before. Someone had left it in a basement with a bunch of other junk. They always just threw it into the grass, retrieve it, throw it again. The grass kept it from exploding. The hard red dog on the street did not.

I put Ruby to bed, the same way mama put me to bed when Arnie died at the ballfield. I feel her pain. She won't stop crying. She is cold. I cover her. Then I curl my body into hers on the bed and just hold onto her. I wish I could take her pain away, but I can't.

The newspaper read the next day: "Blast Kills Yatesboro Boy!" Soon after that the newspaper advertises for anyone who owns these shells to turn them in. It was too late for Jimmy.

Ruby spent two days in bed. I try to get her to drink and eat, but she will not. On the third day I scold her, "Ruby, get up and out of bed! Get dressed! We are going to Sam's house!

"Don't wanna!"

"I said GET UP! It was not a question. GET UP!" Ruby slowly sits up. I don't want to be mean, but I have to snap her out of this. I help her get dressed. As I comb her hair, I try to comfort her, "Ruby, Jimmy wouldn't want you to be like this. You know that don't you?"

"Well Jimmy doesn't get what he wants! He ain't here, is he?" She cries more.

"I'm here. Sam's here. You have us. It's going to be okay; you will see." I take her by her hand, as we walk down the steps. I make her eat toast and milk before we walk out the door to Sam's house.

Sam is waiting, knowing of Ruby's devastation. "There's my girl!" he exclaims, smiling at her. Ruby doesn't speak or smile. She goes to her stool to sit by Sam and looks down at the wooden porch floor. "I got a candy bar here for you, Ruby!" Sam says.

"Don't want it!"

Sam is quiet for a minute. Then, he kneels in front of her. "Jimmy will always be right there in your heart." He points to her chest.

She is angry. "Then hows come my heart hurts?"

He takes both her hands in his. "Dying is not the end of everything. We think it is. But what happens on earth is only the beginning, Ruby. Jimmy is in heaven. Heck, he is in a better place than we are! And you will see him again! I promise!"

Ruby doesn't look up. She won't talk. Her tears just continue to drip onto the old beaten wooden boards of Sam's porch floor. Sam puts his arms around her. She buries her head in his shoulder and cries. My heart breaks for Ruby. I hope Sam's warmth gives her heart comfort. I know that it will.

I watch them in their embrace and know how lucky Ruby is to have Sam right now. Since he is on his knees, I see his hair is thinning right in the middle on the top back of his head. I wonder if he knows that? Doesn't matter, it is endearing. It just makes him more handsome.

I don't talk to God often. Maybe I should. But, as I try to fall asleep, I look towards heaven. "God, thank you for that kitchen floor I had to scrub. It kept me from taking Ruby to Swede Alley. We could have been there when it happened. I hope Ruby and I can do you proud of whatever it was you saved us for. And, God, please forgive me for not taking Jimmy fishing that day."

thirty
I See the Sun Again

t is a long time until Ruby smiles again. In June, Uncle Joe, seeing Ruby's sorrow, proposes taking our family to Geneva-on-the-Lake for a one-week vacation. This is unheard of for our family. A vacation! We are all so excited, especially Ruby. It has been two years since the cancer took Aunt Alice. This will be good for Uncle Joe too.

Only Mama and Bella can go with us. The older kids have jobs they cannot leave. My boss, Lucio, told me to go. "You don't get many chances like that, Patsy!" I bought myself a new swimsuit with the money I earned from the grocery store. I got Ruby one too. The day finally comes to leave and we pack Uncle Joe's car up with our bags of clothes and off we go.

The drive seems long, but it is only a couple hours. Upon arrival we walk into a little cottage Uncle Joe has rented. It looks over the lake! The cottage is painted white. The big front porch has a seat for everyone. Inside there is a kitchen where we enter. A little sitting room is next with a pot belly stove. Beyond that are three bedrooms. One for Uncle Joe, one for Mama and Bella, one for Ruby and me. The excitement of this trip is just more than this family can imagine. Ruby begins to smile again. We walk the strip where everything is happening. Uncle Joe buys us a foot-long hot dog. "Can't come to Geneva-on-the-Lake and not eat a footlong hotdog!" He laughs.

There is miniature golf, an arcade, and music is playing everywhere in the warm night. Uncle Joe buys us each a shirt. On the front it says, "I was at Geneva-on-the-Lake."

We meander back to the cottage and sit in the Adirondack chairs that are on the lawn. Staring up at the starlit sky, the sound of the waves hitting the rocks on the shore is soothing. Every now and then a light faint spray of water touches our faces. Uncle Joe points to the sky. "You see that big star up there to the right, Ruby?"

"Yep!" Her one-word answers are common since Jimmy died.

Uncle Joe looks at her with love. "That is your Aunt Alice. She watches over us from heaven you know."

Ruby seems moonstruck. "Yep!"

Uncle Joe then points to a star over to the left, bigger than the one before, "You see that one over there, Ruby? That great big one?"

"Yep!"

"That's Jimmy in heaven looking over you, and he is smiling."

Ruby smiles and stares at the sky; she has no words. Her eyes fill with tears but her lips are smiling.

After a week of sand, water and fun, we return home. Ruby seems a little better after this vacation. She starts to play outside again and skip to Sam's house to hop up onto the wooden stool beside him as she used to do, cheerfully.

Summer slithers on out as fall approaches. Ruby starts to prepare for third grade. She is now able to remember Jimmy as he was, always laughing, running, smiling. She is almost ten now and growing so tall.

Sam and I love watching her grow, yet we want her to stay a little girl too. I guess we can't have both. He has her help him in the kitchen now, cooking. Watching them together is heartwarming. I love the bond they have formed. I don't even mind sharing him with her.

thirty-one
We Almost Lost You

I go to Sgro's Sunset Grove more often now. Friday nights are teen dances. So many of the boys want to dance with me. I suppose, though, they aren't truly boys anymore, like I am not a girl anymore. I like that they want to dance with me, but they are just friends. Hope they know that. They all tell me how pretty I am. I suspect I'm pretty good-looking. I like to wear dresses to the dances. Tonight, my dress is sleeveless, and fits snug to the waist. Then after the tiny gold belt around my waist, the skirt flairs out. The skirt swirling is a special extra effect when dancing. Sam sometimes seems a little down when I go to Sgro's. He says he just worries about me. I don't know why he does. None of boys interest me. I am still looking for one that is kind and mature like Sam is. I told Mama just last night that I haven't found him yet.

Mama was laughing at me. "Didn't you? You sure?" She laughed again. I don't know what she meant.

Sam has planted a pretty big garden this year. On Saturday, Ruby helps him pick the tomatoes. They will all be coming ripe now, so Ruby goes to his house daily to eat a tomato on his porch with him. Sam is pretty proud of his garden. "We'll make a strawberry patch for next year, Ruby. Then in the spring, we'll be eating strawberries!"

Ruby loves strawberries, so she is excited about Sam's plan. "What do you suppose would happen, Sam, if we planted a chicken bone? Would a chicken grow?"

Sam chuckles. "Well, wouldn't hurt to try, Ruby, Ruby!" You gotta laugh at Ruby.

It is early fall. His grapes are plentiful. "We gonna have grape wine soon?" I ask him.

"Not if you are going to drink it!"

"I turn twenty-one on October first, Sam. You gonna stop me?"

Sam looks at me, shocked. "You are going to be twenty-one already? That can't be!" He seems sad. "That means since I met you ten years have gone by. Ten years, how can that be? Ten years is a long time!"

Just then Mama bellows for us to come for supper. Ruby hops down his wooden steps two at a time. "See you tomorrow, Sam!"

Sam seems deep in thought, but he replies. "If the good Lord's willin' and the creek don't rise!"

Sunday, we wake up to a rain storm. After church the day goes fast. Uncle Joe comes for dinner. Mama invites him often, since he is alone. He is good to our family. He has news today. "Did you hear Sal Matteo died?"

Mama is dishing out mashed potatoes. She stops. Really? "What happened?"

"They think it was a heart attack. She found him dead in the barn!" He reaches for the carrots. "You know that guy never lived a good life. He drank and gambled all the time. Everyone knows he was a Blackhand. He wasn't good to her either. Never minded his kids, none of them!"

Mama is unusually quiet. She hands me the potatoes to pass. "Well, that's too bad. I wonder how she'll manage with all those kids? At least most of them are grown up by now. She should have only maybe four left in school yet." Mama gets up from the table and stands by the sink just looking out the window, in deep thought.

"What's wrong, Mama?"

"Nothin', just nothin'. Just thinking about Mrs. Matteo, that's all."

Surely, she is not worrying that Mrs. Matteo will want Ruby back. Surely not!

By the end of the week Mama, takes Mrs. Matteo a pot of chicken soup and a loaf of her homemade bread.

I quiz her upon her return. "So how was it, mama? What was Mrs. Matteo like?"

"Like a woman who is left alone to raise a bunch of kids. Doubt she'll miss him. I'm sorry to say. But she will struggle. That's for sure. She is strong, though. She'll be okay." She puts her hat on the hook.

"What did she say about Ruby, Mama?"

Mama looks annoyed. "Shush, Patsy! We never discussed Ruby, never! I told you there would never be a problem. Let it go, Patsy!"

She seems angry at me. This seems to be a sensitive subject for Mama. I know I have to let it go. "I won't mention it again, Mama. But I cannot stand to think she'd come back for Ruby. She'll never get her, not over my dead body!"

Two weeks pass before I decide to forget about Mrs. Matteo coming for Ruby. I simply must stop worrying about it. I am off work today. I will take Ruby for a hike up the Roundtop. We pack ourselves a lunch and off we go. We pass the Kroh's farm and stop to pet the goats that are near the fence. Mr. Kroh is here moving hay around. "Hey there girls! What you up to?"

"Going to the Roundtop for our own little picnic." Ruby beams.

He throws more hay onto the wagon with his pitch fork. "That's nice. It's a great day for that. Have a good time!"

We continue up the hill until we reach the top. We can look down over all of Yatesboro from here. I spread out the blanket I have brought and open the basket of little sandwiches Mama made. She packed us some fruit, and a nice big cookie for each of us.

Ruby and I sit for an hour watching down over Yatesboro. We can see our house. I can tell which one by the big garden in the back. We watch Mama as she is in the garden. We can see her pick clothes off the clothesline. She is tiny like an ant, but we know that is Mama. We can see Uncle Joe get in his car and go. The Hockenberry kids are swinging in their yard on the tire hung on the big maple tree. Looking to the left and down across the black road, we can see the smoke from the boney dump burning. A little to the right is the steeple of the Catholic church. Walking by the church now coming up the hill is someone. A woman it seems. We can tell by the way she walks. Not possible to tell who. She is walking slowly, up the hill.

"Wonder who that is?" I think out loud.

The woman stops twice. Must need to catch her breath. She keeps walking up the hill and turns to the right onto our street. She is alone. Who is she? She stops in front of Sam's house. She seems to just stand there awhile. After what seems like a long pause, she turns to walk up his walk. Never knew of Sam to get company other than the two of us. Who is visiting Sam?

Ruby is curious too. "Who is that, Patsy? Who is that visiting Sam?"

"I don't know, Ruby. We'll go over later. Sam will tell us." I am just a little bit jealous. Ruby and I have Sam all to ourselves. Who is it wiggling their way into our territory?

Ruby lights up. "Maybe she brought the package with the red ribbon, Patsy!"

That is an interesting thought. I never thought the package with the red ribbon was real, though. I've just played along all this time for Sam's sake.

I am anxious to get to Sam's house, but I had promised Ruby this day on the Roundtop. We will do some more exploring before we head to Sam's.

We finish our picnic and go hiking through the trails. We spend three hours on the round top after our lunch, hiking and digging up old bottles. That is a hobby I've had forever, digging up old bottles. Only found two today. We check the hole in the base of a tree where a squirrel lives. It is empty today. Before our outing ends, we climb the water tank to see if anything new is floating on top of the water. There are lots of leaves and a dead bird. It is very late afternoon now. "Gosh, Ruby, we better get home! Mama will wonder what happened to us!"

She did not forget about Sam's visitor. "We gotta get to Sam's first to see who that was!"

We start down the Roundtop. When we reach the Kroh farm, Mr. Kroh is climbing into his old beaten truck. He seems to be in a hurry. When he sees us, he stops, "There's a problem at the dam, wanna go?"

I am surprised he asked us. "What kind of problem, Mr. Kroh?"

He puts his face down for a moment, not sure if he should say, but then looks up and says, "Seems as though a guy tried to kill himself."

Me and Ruby jump into the front seat with Mr. Kroh,

I am nervous. "Do you know who?"

"No, I don't. My neighbor is a fireman. He got called and hollered out his car window to me just two minutes ago."

When we get there, we have to park a good way back. There are cars everywhere. I fling open the passenger side door, and with Ruby behind me, we run to the cement wall of the dam. We squeeze our way through all the people standing. When we get through the last person, we can see a man lying on the cement. It…. It…. IT'S SAM!

"SAM, SAM!" Ruby screams.

I fall onto my knees beside him, "SAM, TALK TO ME SAM!" He is moaning. He is alive!

Mr. Johnson is here; everyone knows how close Ruby and I are to Sam. Mr. Johnson is all wet, trying to explain to me. "I vas eatin' lunch and seen him go past my place, Patsy. I just had a feelin' sometin' vas vrong. Could jist feel it, you know? I lift him go and took anoder bite of my lunch, but sometin' was tellin' me, 'go, go to da dam! So, I gut up and I run to da dam. It vusn't five meenutes afta he hud past me, dat I gut here. I come straight to dis cement vall and saw his shoes here on da cement. I knew den dat he jumped in, so I jumped in and fund him quick. He vas near za vall here, maybe ten feet down."

As I try to listen to Mr. Johnson, Ruby is yelling, "SAM! WAKE UP, SAM! WHY? WHY? WHY DID YOU DO THIS? SAM, WAKE UP!!"

I feel like I've been hit with a truck. My head is floating somewhere. I don't think my heart is beating. I look close at his face and scream to anyone who is listening. "Help him! SOMEONE HELP HIM!"

Mr. Catardy grabs me, "Patsy, he is okay. He is breathing and the ambulance is on its way."

By now Sam is starting to awaken, but he is groggy and confused. Mr. Catardy lets go of me and I kneel again, "SAM, WHY? TELL ME WHY?" I shake him. His eyes are fluttering. I need him to answer me. Sam can't answer. He just moans. As the ambulance arrives, Ruby and I are still pleading, "WHY, SAM? WHY?"

Three men put him onto a stretcher and load him into the ambulance. I try to stay with him, but they are pushing me away. They shut the ambulance doors. Ruby and I bang on the back door of the ambulance. "SAM, TELL US WHY! WE LOVE YOU! SAM, YOU HEAR US? WE LOVE YOU!"

The ambulance pulls out with sirens blaring. Ruby and I are numb. This beautiful day has turned into horror. We have had so many special moments with Sam. We thought we made him happy. How could he have done this to us? I am so confused and troubled. He has no one, just me and Ruby. Aren't we enough? Oh, how I wish that damn dam would dry up!

thirty-two
She Is Gone

Three days pass before I can see Sam. He is not allowed visitors the first three days. On the fourth day, Uncle Joe is happy to take me to the hospital. Ruby can't go. The hospital does not allow visitors under fourteen. Mama comes along for moral support. The hospital smells of medicine as we enter. Approaching the desk, we meet a middle-aged lady with her hair on top of her head in a bun and her glasses halfway down her nose.

I can't find my voice. Mama speaks for me. "Patsy is here to see Sam Kaminsky."

The woman with the bun makes a phone call and hands us all a tag to wear around our necks. "Elevator over there. Go to second floor. Then a left to room 206."

Mama puts her hands on my shoulders. "Uncle Joe and I will stay here in the waiting room. Sam will need to talk to you alone, Patsy. Take it slow. Give him the time he needs. You go. Give him a hug for us. I'm here if you need me."

The elevator goes up very slowly. I am so nervous. I feel tears welling up in my eyes. I must stop this. I have to be strong. The little window above the elevator door reads FLOOR 1, then FLOOR 2. Then, ding! The doors open.

The sign on the wall as I step into the hallway says, Rooms 200-210 left. I turn left and pass several people. They seem

THE CREEK DON'T RISE

like statues. I feel like I'm walking through a picture. A dream maybe. I think to myself as I walk. "Just keep in mind, he is sick. He could not have known what he did. I have to help him get better."

I pass Room 200, then 202, then 204. I am here. Room 206. The door is open only a little. I push it softly. The room is dark. It smells of medicine. There is a white curtain pulled around a bed. I pull the curtain back. Sam is sleeping. He has a few scratches on his cheek and he seems frail somehow. I lay my hand on his hand.

His eyes flutter. They open slightly. He mumbles. "Patsy."

I don't know what to say. "I am here, Sam. How do you feel?"

"Just so tired. Can you make my bed sit up and get me a drink of water, Patsy?"

He wiggles his head like his neck is sore. I can see he has a bruise on one side of his face. His eyes seem dark. Not even blue like they were. I am trying to be patient. It is hard. I need answers. I quickly wind the crank to sit him up. I get him a glass of water. He takes a drink. He sits with his head down. "Are you and Ruby okay?"

My voice came back. "NO! We are not okay, Sam! Why'd you do that to us? Why?" Oh gosh, I sound mean. My heart is pounding. I feel a flush moving up my face. I am sorry. Yet, I am not sorry. "Forgive me, Sam. I was just so scared. Just so scared!" My tears start to flow.

He grabs my hand. "I'm so sorry, Patsy. So sorry for what I put you through." Sam takes a deep breath. He picks up his head. "I owe you an explanation. Give me a minute."

I am angry. I don't want to be angry. But I am. "I am all ears, Sam."

He takes a drink of water. He holds the glass in his lap, looking at it. He won't look at me. He begins, "Sit here beside me." He pats the bed beside him. I sit down, facing him. "First, I want to tell you about Betsy."

"Betsy?" I ask. "Betsy who?"

Sam looks up at me, puts his head down and takes a deep breath and lets it out. Seems like he is having trouble talking. After a pause he talks. "Betsy Kaminsky, my wife."

I feel like I want to throw up. "Your wife? You have a wife?"

He looks like he is in despair, "Patsy, please just listen. You will understand."

I recall what Mama said. Take it slow. Give him time. I take a moment to inhale.

He looks into my eyes. He is just silent. I see pain in his eyes.

His head is down again. "Yes, I had a wife. She was the love of my life. We were together since high school. She was beautiful, with auburn hair that curled around her face, sparkling eyes that danced, a wee little nose, and she had dimples on both cheeks." He grins sheepishly as he describes her. "I loved her more than life itself, Patsy."

I am in shock. It always seemed like he had no one in his life, ever! I'm jealous! He is not mine, but yet he is. I've been here for him, for years! I never asked him to be my boyfriend, but doesn't he know how I feel about him? He has a wife? He is in love with someone that passionately? How could I not have seen it? "How could you keep that from me, Sam?"

Sam's face is sullen, as he explains. "I promised myself to not speak of her, to anyone. And, I would allow no one to mention her name." He puts his glass on the table beside his bed.

"Why?" I don't know what my emotions are at this point: disappointment, betrayal, anger? Which? Or all? He can see the confusion in my eyes.

"Just please listen, Patsy. This isn't easy." He pleads. "I was one year older than her. She came here as a freshman. She had just moved here from Johnstown with her mom, after her dad died. They moved in with her grandma on the Hill. His shoulders slumped. "I had eyes for her right away, but for a long time she dated Bruno Matteo from the Hill."

"I know that name, Sam."

"Yep, Sal Matteo's brother. Betsy and him dated a long time. When she started her junior year, they broke up. That was when I stepped in. So, we were together in my senior year. I fell madly in love with her. When I graduated, I went to work at the car garage, so we could get married. That next year she graduated on a Friday and the next day we got married, just privately at the church. Her mama was sick with cancer at the time. Within the next few months, she lost her mom and her grandma within weeks. You would have liked her, Patsy."

I can't stop staring at him. "I am sure I would have. But, Sam. You were married?"

"Yes, married. She was sweet and funny. She always wore a red ribbon in her hair. She was so silly about that red ribbon. She told me red means love. She'd laugh this silly school girl laugh about it. She promised to always wear the red ribbon in her hair. She said because she loved me so much. That is what she said, anyways. I know it was silly, but I liked it."

I am starting to soften. "I'm sure she did, Sam. Who wouldn't love you!" It takes me a moment to gather my thoughts. Then it hits me. "Sam, she is the package with the red ribbon!"

Sam is quietly crying. I see tears dampening his cheeks. "Yes, Patsy. She was the package." He adjusts himself on the bed and clears his throat to halt his tears. "I pictured her walking through my door with that silly red ribbon in her hair. Pictured it for ten years now. We were happy together. Just so happy. Just sitting on the porch swing with her was heaven. We talked so much. She never got tired of me talking."

"I don't get tired of you talking, Sam!" I'm full of emotion.

"I know you don't, Patsy. I'm just trying to describe her. I loved coming home from work. She was always on the porch waiting for me. She stopped everything to just sit with me. She loved being with me, I thought. I know that I loved being with her. She always knew what I was thinking. I thought I always knew what she was thinking too." His tears return. "But I guess I didn't."

I sit on the bed facing him. I take his hand. "Tell me, Sam. I'm listening."

He talks softly back to me. "We lived in the house I am in now. My mama lived there too. She was still alive."

I am still struggling to stay calm. "Why didn't you tell me about her, Sam? Why?"

"Because I was afraid it was bad luck if I mentioned her name, and then I'd never see her again." He exclaims in just a whisper.

"Never see her again?" I am confused, "What happened to her? Where is she?"

Sam put his head down. He doesn't seem willing to answer that. He just wants to talk about Betsy. "She was warm as the sun on your cheeks, I couldn't wait to get home to her every day. She was happy. Always happy. Like you are, Patsy, always happy."

I listen intently. I am so confused. "I don't understand, Sam. What happened?"

He pauses a moment. "The Blackhands happened. That's what happened!" His face grows dark.

I feel like I can't breathe. "How? What? Tell me!"

Sam looks at me and his eyes seem angry. "Betsy used to go in the woods to pick huckleberries for Mama's pies. All those Blackhands hung out down there in that red brick building by No. 4 dam."

I have to admit to him. "I know, Sam. I saw that place."

He seems so troubled. His voice is low, "It was in those woods near the red brick building that Bruno Matteo got a hold of her. He was a Blackhand. He had money. He rekindled their flame with his money. He swooned her with jewelry and promises of a wonderful life. She started meeting him there." He draws a breath, "I felt the spark fade from her. I'd come home from work and she'd just ignore me. I knew something was wrong, but I didn't know what."

"How did you find out?"

"Mr. Johnson saw me one day at the company store. He told me he didn't want to be in my business, but he thought I should know that he had seen Bruno Matteo talking to her down by the dam. More than once, he said."

My stomach is starting to churn. "Oh Sam, I'm so sorry."

Sam looks down. "I couldn't believe it. I WOULDN'T believe it. I went home that day and asked Betsy about it. When she answered, it was like it was someone else talking. Not Betsy."

"What do you mean?"

"Betsy told me it was true. That Bruno is going to give her the good life! Why would she say that, Patsy? She had a good life with me! Does just expensive jewelry mean so much?

"Expensive jewelry, Sam?

His face is drawn, "She picked up her wrist and showed me the bracelet he bought her at McClanahan's. It was gold. Money! Money is more important than love! She liked his money. She had drifted from me. How did I miss that, Patsy? How could I have been so dumb?"

"It's easy to miss things, Sam. Especially when you are so in love." I'm trying to be calm, though I am angry. I am angry at Betsy now, more than him. "What did you say to her, Sam?"

He pauses before he speaks. "My heart was breaking in two. I didn't know if I wanted to throw up or put a hole in the wall. I just broke down and cried."

Sam scratches his chest. "After I cried, she softened. I guess she felt bad. The old Betsy came back into her body. She told me she loved me. She said she would never leave me. She just made a mistake, and could I forgive her? She threw the bracelet on the floor. She took her red ribbon off and put it over my head to pull me to her. She begged me to forgive her."

"Did you forgive her, Sam?"

"It was hard, but yes. I told her I could forgive her. I could not live without her. I loved her so very much. So much it hurt!" He is twisting the bed sheet in his hand. "She even said to me that day that she will never take the red ribbon out of her hair. She said her love was for me only, and for always. That stupid silly red ribbon."

He released my hand. "You didn't deserve this, Patsy."

"I'm okay, Sam. I am here for you."

"Anyway, we just put it behind us and moved on. I tried to be more attentive to her. I brought flowers home. I took off work so I could be with her. I took her on picnics and walks. I just loved her the best I knew how. I did everything I could. She loved me back too. At least I thought so. I thought everything was okay."

I am puzzled. "Then what, Sam? What happened?"

"She was just gone, just gone." His face was drawn with grief. "I came home from work one day and she wasn't there. Mama had sent her to the company store for bread and she never came home. I knew Bruno Matteo had her."

He seems devastated. I wrap my arms around him. He lays his head on my shoulder and sobs. "Oh, Sam, I am so sorry. So, so sorry." I feel the warmth of his body. I feel his grief. I pull back to look into his eyes. "What happened next? Did you look for her?"

He is trying to get a hold of himself. He pauses and draws in a deep breath. "I looked for her. I looked and looked. I ran through the woods, down to the brick building. There were men in there. I had my baseball bat in my hand. I screamed to let Betsy go, LET HER GO!" He seems exhausted telling it.

I have his hand in mine now. "Then what happened, Sam?"

"Two big men came out of that building. They started screaming at me to get out. They said she wasn't there, and that

I'd never see Betsy again. One guy was hollering at me that she chose Bruno, and that she left town with him! Another guy came at me yelling, "Don't ever come back, or we'll kill you AND your Mama!" Then one grabbed me by the neck. I remember a fist coming towards me. I don't remember anything after that."

"Oh my God!" I am starting to feel sick. "You are lucky to be alive!" I am sobbing. My heart is broken for him.

"Don't cry, Patsy. I'll be okay. Just talking to you about it feels good."

It seems as though he has bottled this all up for so long. It is flowing out like a river. "I woke up on Mr. Johnson's couch. He had heard the scuffle and came to get me. They let him take me away, luckily. I suppose they would have killed me. That's where I got this scar on my face. Not from baseball like I told you, Patsy. From Blackhands! I had a couple broken ribs too, but they healed. They probably kicked me after they knocked me out. Anyways, after I could walk without pain, I walked everywhere looking for her. I called the cops and they hesitated to help. They too just felt she chose another man. But they made a lame effort to investigate anyways. Bruno disappeared from town. His brother Sal claimed he did not know where he went. Sal told the cops she went of her own free will. The cops said they couldn't do anything since that was the case. I told them, "NO, she didn't! He took her! No one would listen to me."

It's okay, Sam." I rub his arm trying to calm him. "Take a deep breath."

Sam looks at me with angry eyes, not meant for me. He is reliving the moment. "The Chief of Police came to my house. He acted like I was bothering him. He told me, "This happens, buddy. She found herself another fella. You need to let her go!"

Sam looks beaten. "It cut me like a knife, Patsy. Anyways, I just kept trying to find her on my own. I couldn't get much help from the cops. I asked questions everywhere. I tried to not go back down to the red brick building for my Mama's sake. I knew they would kill my Mama. I tried to get the FBI involved but they said no, it was out of their jurisdiction."

My head is swimming. "My God, Sam! How awful!"

It is all spilling out of him. "I went to Matteo's house when I knew her evil husband was at work. Mrs. Matteo told me she was with Bruno, and she wanted to go. I argued with her that she was kidnapped. She told me "No, Sam. She wasn't. She wanted to go. Please stop looking for her, Sam. Please stop looking!"

"Did Mrs. Matteo know where Betsy was with him, Sam?"

He picks up his head. "She told me she didn't. She kept saying she knew Betsy was okay and she had talked to her. She said Betsy called her and told her to tell me to stop looking for her because she was happy with Bruno. She had chosen a life with him. She said Betsy refused to leave a number or tell her where they were, that Betsy wanted this new life free of the past."

"Did you stop looking, Sam?"

"Not for a long time. The cops quit helping. I knew they were convinced she just chose another man. They kept telling me to accept it. Between that, and Mrs. Matteo pleading with me so sincerely to stop looking, I had to believe Betsy wanted to go with him. I remembered how close they were in high school. She must have decided that was what she wanted." He wipes his eyes with his hospital gown. "But even if it was so, I always felt she was going to change her mind and come home. I thought someday I would hear footsteps and she would be walking up my porch stairs, wearing that silly red ribbon in her hair."

I put my arms around him and he lays his head on my shoulder. I caress his hair. "It's going to be okay, Sam. I'm here for you."

He stops and draws in a deep breath pulling away from our embrace.

"I went back to Mrs. Matteo again one day. I begged her again for more information. She claimed she had none. She said that she never heard from Betsy again. Then, when I was driving out her lane, Sal Matteo was pulling in, so he saw me. He showed up at my door the next day. He pushed himself into the house. My Mama was there too. He was screaming at me. "Stop looking for her if you know what's good for you! She is with my brother because she wants to be! How stupid are you!"

"Oh my!" I was at a loss for words. "That's horrible!"

Sam's body tightens. "It doesn't end there. He grabbed me by my collar and put a knife to my throat!"

I let out a squeal. My hands go to my open mouth to cover it. "Did he cut you, Sam?"

Sam was warmed by my concern. "No, but he told me that after he was done killing me, he would kill my mama if I didn't stop looking for her. That evil man said to me, "You are a fool! Your wife left you for another man and you just don't get it! Quit making a fool of yourself!"

At that point Sam just grew quiet, like spilling all this has drained all the blood out of his body. His voice is low. "I had to quit looking, and just wait and hope instead. As the years passed, I had to accept that she may have wanted to go. I had to accept it. Yet, I still felt in my heart she would come back. She would come to her senses. I was sure of it. Our love was just too strong for her not to come back."

I am trying to collect my thoughts. He looks destroyed. I rub his arm. "It could still happen, Sam." You said it yourself. It could take a while."

Sam's face grew drawn and the tears fall down his cheeks. "Mrs. Matteo visited me on Sunday."

Then I knew that was who we saw going to his house. "Sunday? Ruby and I could see a woman coming to your house. We were on the Roundtop. Was that her? What did she want?"

He took a breath and puts both his hands on his chest as if his heart is going to fall out. "She came to tell me Betsy is dead!" He clutches his chest and sobs. I throw my arms around him.

He is shivering. His body is warm. Yet cold. His skin is soft. Yet hard. He cries into my shoulder. I weep with him. Finally, he stops and withdraws. "Oh, Patsy. I am so sorry I'm such a crybaby today. There is so much I haven't talked about for so long. I guess it is all just too much for me."

"Stop it, Sam. You have every reason to cry and no reason to apologize. You loved her!"

"That I did." He sat up straight. It takes him a minute, but he is calmer. He wants me to know everything." She died ten years ago, Patsy. Mrs. Matteo knew it all this time. She couldn't tell me. Her husband threatened he would kill her if she told me. So, all that time I'm sitting waiting, talking about the package with the red ribbon coming, she was gone. What a fool I've made of myself!"

"Oh, Sam. You are no fool! You are a kind, generous man who loves deeply. I am so sorry! I don't know what to say!" My heart breaks for him. Suddenly it occurred to me. "So, now that her husband isn't here to threaten her, Mrs. Matteo came clean!"

"Seems so. But, Patsy, my Betsy has been gone ten years! Ten years I've been waiting for her to walk through my door, TEN YEARS! She has been gone all that time! The thought of her walking through my door was what made me get up every morning!"

I sit on the bed and embrace him. "SHAME ON MRS. MATTEO! SHAME ON HER!"

He whispered, "I'm not blaming anybody. I felt her fear. Poor lady lived her whole life in fear."

"Did she tell you how she died, Sam?"

"She said her heart just stopped. There was nothing anyone could do."

I am quiet for a moment. I feel his body tremble. "Is that why you jumped in the dam?"

It took him a minute to answer. "I guess. I remember feeling hopeless. All those years of hope wiped out in an instant. I remember Mrs. Matteo at my house, but I don't even remember her leaving. It was like I was watching the figure of a woman in a dream. I felt like my body was sinking into a deep dark hole. I don't know how I got to the dam. I don't remember walking there. I don't even remember it."

"Sam, it wasn't you that jumped in the dam. It was the grief that took over your body. Grief became a human form. You aren't responsible. We can work through this, Sam. Will you let me and Ruby help you?"

Sam looks at me. His eyes are still sad, but the blue has come back into them. I feel like I am looking into an ocean. There is something in the way he is looking at me. Something. "Of course, Patsy. You know that you and Ruby make me so happy. I can't explain why I did that. I lost my sense of what was real."

Thinking of how we almost lost him, I start to sob. "I can't think of life without you, Sam. I was so scared!"

He grabs me and pulls me in. "I'm sorry, Patsy. I am so sorry I hurt you and Ruby that way. It will be okay. I will be home soon and everything will be okay." He releases his grasp. "We've got to make that wine you know!"

He makes me smile. "Promise to never leave me, Sam. Promise!"

"Never!" He puts both hands on my cheeks and pulls me close to his face. I feel his breath. I smell his skin. He looks at me like he is reaching into my soul. "I'll never leave you, Patsy. I promise. And, don't you ever leave me!"

"Visiting hours are over!" Nurse Crabby Pants is at the door to chase me out. My moment is gone.

I throw my arms around Sam. "We'll be on your porch waiting for you, Sam."

He embraces me back. He squeezes me hard. "I will be looking forward to that."

As I enter the waiting room where Mama and Uncle Joe are waiting, my head is floating and my thoughts are scattered. I feel like a bomb just went off in my head. Mama stands when she sees me. I feel like I am glaring at her. "Mama, you knew. You knew about Betsy."

"Betsy?" She seems surprised. "What about her?

"What about her, Mama? She was his wife! How could you not tell me about her?"

"I am sorry, Patsy. Sam asked us to never mention her. Marriages fail you know. It happens all the time. It was in his past. Daddy tried to talk with him about her and Sam asked us to never mention her name. We wanted to honor his wishes, even though we knew he was hurting. If he asked us never to mention it, then it was no business of ours."

"Did you not wonder where she was, Mama?"

"Not really. Rumor had it she had left with another guy. The whole town kind of forgot about her."

"Did you forget about her, Mama?"

"I tried not to, Patsy. But Daddy said Sam seemed so angry when he asked that we not mention her. Because of that, I tried to forget about her. She had left town."

"Angry? Angry? Oh Mama, he wasn't angry, he was scared to death. Scared for his life and he was keeping you safe too. And Betsy didn't fall for another guy, she was kidnapped!"

"What? What are you talking about?" The color has drained from Mama's face.

"It is too much to tell you now, Mama. Let's go home and I will tell you all about her."

I get most of it out on the car ride home. Both Mama and Uncle Joe are shocked. Mama is sad. "If we only had known. Poor Sam, poor poor Sam."

Two days later Sam is discharged from the hospital. Uncle Joe brought him home. He seems frail and weak, but we will get him strong again. Ruby and I are on his front porch. We both hug him and he hugs back. Ruby made a sign, "Welcome Home, Sam!" Sam smiles at the sign and thanks us, but he doesn't want to go inside. He just wants to sit on his swing on the front porch, as he always does. Ruby sits on her little stool and I lean against the wooden banister.

"Mama has made a meal for us. You hungry, Sam?"

His soft smile is back, "Guess so."

"I'm going to go inside and warm up our meal. You okay out here?"

"How could I not be!" He grabs Ruby's hand. "I've got Ruby, Ruby!"

I had explained this all to Ruby, with mama's help. She is old enough now. She seemed to understand it all. She is incredibly sad for Sam also.

Ruby finds her voice. "Sam, you really scared me. How'd you think I was supposed to live without you?"

"I wasn't thinking, Ruby. My mind wasn't working at all. It's working now. I'm here now. I'm sorry I did that to you."

"It's, okay Sam. Let's just be happy now. You have Patsy and me. We ain't goin' nowhere."

In the kitchen, my emotions are all over the map. I am angry he did that, yet I am so thankful he is here. I am happy he told me he will never leave me. Yet, I am jealous of Betsy. My heart aches for him. Next minute I'm mad again. I'm mad at Betsy. To have been loved like that! He said, "I loved her more than life itself." She was a lucky woman. If she went with Bruno Matteo on her own, she was stupid. STUPID! Will I ever find someone to love me like that? I am perturbed he didn't tell us about Betsy. Yet I understand. Most of all, I am angry. Angry at Mrs. Matteo. She has some answering to do!

thirty-three
Unloaded Burden

I spend day after day with Sam since he found out Betsy died. If I am not working, I am at Sam's house. I ask him many questions about Betsy. "What kind of things did she like to do? Did she like listening to music? Did she like good movies?" I keep asking him things because the more he talks about her, the better he is. I want him to remember all the good things about Betsy. I want him to hold on to his memories of her.

"She loved catching fireflies." He smiles. "And when she saw a spider, she'd squeal like a child. She hated spiders, that girl!"

"She sounds wonderful, Sam." I am jealous though. "You sure loved her."

He looks at me. "She was easy to love, Patsy. Kind of like you."

I don't know what that means, but I like it. I put my head down like a school girl. He laughs. "Want to have a beer with me?"

"Me?" I am amused. "You talking to me? The girl you told not to drink?"

"There's no girl here anymore. Seems to be a woman sitting here now."

He is right. I am 22 going on 23. I look down at my body and pretend I am shocked. "My gosh, I am a full- blown woman!"

Sam laughs as he gets up to get our beers. "I noticed. You are the one that didn't!"

He noticed. I like that.

We sit down together on his swing on the back porch to drink our beers. He seems calm and at peace. "I can't say enough times how sorry I am what I did to you and Ruby, Patsy."

I look at his face and see the sincerity in his blue eyes. He grins at me. Little wrinkles appear at the sides of his eyes. I think they are cute. I tap my beer bottle to his. "This is a toast to today. The first day of the rest our lives. The past is gone. We won't revisit it."

His smile becomes bigger and he puts his arms around my shoulders. He pulls me in for a warm and fuzzy hug. It feels so good. The smell of musk embraces me. The warmth of his body sends electric through mine. I would love to stay in this hug, but I hear Ruby coming through the house. We quickly part. "You came to Sam's without me!" She scolds.

"You were helping Mama, Ruby! And anyways, you know the way yourself!" I scold her back. She plops herself down on the top step of the back porch. My moment with Sam is over.

Sam always laughs at Ruby, even when she is being nasty. "You want a beer, Ruby?"

"You know I'm not old enough, Sam! What's wrong with you?"

"Same thing that's wrong with you. Too much stress lately. How about you tell Patsy that you love her?"

"That's corny!" First, she scowls then she grins. "Okay! Patsy, I love you. There!"

"See, love fixes all!" Sam laughs out loud the first time since all this happened. "Now let's go back to life the way it was. Okay?"

"Whatever!" Ruby chimes, laughing and running towards another rabbit.

I still have a thirst for information. How exactly does a 20-year-old die? Did Bruno take her or did she go willingly? Why did Mrs. Matteo keep this secret for ten years? I am going to get some answers.

We stay until Mama hollers that supper is ready. "You want to come eat with us, Sam?"

"Not today." He gathers our beer bottles up. "Still don't have my appetite back. I have your mama's leftovers in my refrigerator to use up yet, too."

His eyes are smiling at me. My eyes smile back. "We'll be back tomorrow, Sam."

"I know," he meekly admits. "It's what keeps me going!"

"Bye, Sam!" Ruby hollers as she runs away, "See you tomorrow!" She is already across two yards.

Sam's eyes follow her as he hollers. "If the good Lord's willin' and the creek don't rise you will!" He looks at me and laughs. "Boy, that girl can run fast!"

At supper, I ask Mama to go with me to see Mrs. Matteo. Mama hesitates, "Do you really need me?"

"Well, you know her, Mama. I don't really know her. Won't you go?"

Mama face is troubled. "I will go, but we will talk about Sam and Betsy. Nothing else."

"Well, of course, Mama. That is why I'm going. What else is there? You mean Ruby?"

"Don't ask me, Patsy. I said I would go. I will. Don't ask for more!"

I have to be happy with that, though I don't know why it bothers her so bad. The morning sun awakens me early. Mama is downstairs early too. I ask her why she is up so early.

"Couldn't sleep." She writes a note for Ruby that we'll be back. I don't know what's wrong. She seems unhappy. I guess everyone has a bad day now and then.

Mama and I walk down the hill. We cross the black road, then onto the flats and up the hill to the Matteo house. The house is beaten. The sidewalk leading up to it is overgrown with grass and crumbled in most places. There are old rusty bikes sitting outside among the weeds. Chickens are running around the yard. Knock, Knock, Knock. A young teenage boy opens the door.

I study him for a moment. Maybe fourteen. Nice looking boy. "I'm here to see your mother, is she home?"

He points to the right. "In there." He opens the door for us to enter.

Mrs. Matteo is sitting in a rocking chair, knitting. The minute she sees us, she lays down her knitting needles and stands up. "Isla, good to see you. How are you?"

"I am well, and I hope you are well also, Mrs. Matteo. We were so sorry to hear about your husband passing."

Mrs. Matteo frowns. "He was no damn good. Everyone knew it too!"

"Just the same, please accept our sympathies."

"Thank you! Would you like to sit down?" Mrs. Matteo looks worried, she should be!

I am not as gracious as Mama. "Yes, we will have a seat. I think we have a lot to talk about!"

She looks troubled. "I understand, Patsy."

Mama and I sit on the couch. Mrs. Matteo sits back down in her rocking chair. I am curt as I begin. "We are here to talk to you about Betsy. I'm sure you heard about Sam jumping into the dam!"

She looks down at her hands. "I heard it. It doesn't make sense to me why he would do that."

I am angry. "He loved her, that's why! He was waiting for her to come back! He never lost hope. Don't you know that? And you knew for ten years she wasn't coming back. Why did you do that? Why didn't you tell him? Tell me, please. WHY?"

Mama pats my arm which means calm down.

Mrs. Matteo looks gray. "You know nothing about fear, Patsy. I lived my life in fear. My husband threatened me and my children that if I told Sam that she was dead, we would pay."

I am scowling at her. "So, your husband is gone now and you decided to come clean?"

"Thought it was the right thing to do. I know Sam has been thinking she is going to walk through his door. She isn't. It was time he knew." She squirms in her chair.

I am furious. "The right thing to do? Did it ever occur to you how that would affect him? Did you not have the presence of mind to ask someone to go along when you told him? To be there for him? Someone that cares about him, like ME? That would have been the RIGHT thing to do! We almost lost him. FOR GOD'S SAKE! WE ALMOST LOST HIM!"

She begins to cry. "I'm so sorry, Patsy, I am. But again, I don't think you can know what living in fear is like. You never had to do it!"

Mama steps in. "You will have to forgive Patsy. She is pretty upset about all that has happened. I understand your fear. I am so sorry you had to live like that."

I try to calm down. "I am trying to understand, Mrs. Matteo. I am. But we need answers. "How did she die? She was only twenty. What did she die of?"

"Her heart stopped, Patsy. The doctor was there. Said her heart just gave out. There was nothing he could do."

"Was she sick in any way before that happened?"

"I don't know. I only saw her the day she died, not before. Bruno had called me to come."

My heart aches for Sam. "I need to know. Did she go with Bruno Matteo on her own or did he take her?"

She hesitated, and turned her head away from me. "I'm not sure."

She seems angry too. "I don't know what you want me to tell you, Patsy."

"I want you to tell me the truth! I don't know that I am getting it! I know something isn't right about this. You apparently were in touch with Bruno. You were there when she died. How'd all that come about?"

"He called me. That's all. Then he disappeared."

"So, Bruno was there when she died?"

"Yes, Patsy. A week later he left town. None of us have seen him since."

I feel my blood rising up my face. "If you weren't absolutely sure she went on her own, ABSOLUTELY SURE, how can you live with yourself? Yet shortly after she disappeared Sam came to you. You told him you were sure Betsy went on her own. Why did you tell Sam she did when you didn't really know? He quit looking for her because you told him that."

"I told him that to save his life, Patsy. It is that simple. If he would have kept looking, he'd be dead now."

That sent a shiver up my spine. To think of what could have happened to Sam. I stare at her floor with the threadbare rug. "Poor Sam. Poor Sam." My head comes up and my eyes meet hers. "I hate what this has done to him. What YOU did to him!"

Mrs. Matteo's face seems to fall in vertical wrinkles. She is weeping. "I couldn't help. I wish I could have!"

Mama is so quiet. I look at her and see only sadness. "I don't feel well, Patsy."

Mrs. Matteo gets up to get Mama a glass of water. "Drink this, Isla, see if it helps." She is staring at Mama. "It will be okay, Isla. Remember, this is about Betsy."

Well of course it is about Betsy! Who else would it be about?

She turns to me and speaks softly. "Once Betsy died, Sal and Bruno both threatened me that I could never say I knew anything about her. I wept every time I ran into Sam at the company store. I'd have to run out of there when I saw him. I wept for his pain. I could do nothing. I had to protect my kids, Patsy. Don't you see that?"

I still don't feel like being nice. "So now you are free to talk. Do you know what Sam has been going through for ten years?"

Now Mrs. Matteo's head is down. She is playing with her fingers. "I ain't proud of it. Ain't proud of it at all. But you don't know how hard life was here with him."

Mama nudges me to stop talking. I have no good answers for Sam. I am not sharing any of this with him. He had not asked Mrs. Matteo these questions, so best left alone.

Mama stands up. "Let's go, Patsy. We have taken enough of Mrs. Matteo's time."

"Not quite yet, Mama. Mrs. Matteo, was Betsy at least buried properly?"

"I told Sam she was, Patsy."

I stand up and stare at Mrs. Matteo. "I don't know that I will ever understand."

Mama tugs on my arm. "Let's go, Patsy."

I leave frustrated. I didn't get the answer I want. I have to let this go. I have to focus on Sam. I need to help him move on now. He needs to put this behind him. But there is more to this. I just now there is!

thirty-four
Class Clown

Sam is excited about Ruby going into junior high school.

Ruby, at thirteen, is becoming very pretty. Her hair is thick and long. Soft curls fall around her cheeks. With her blue eyes, her skin is like satin. She is in Shannock Valley High School in grade seven. The school was just built last summer. She is so nervous about going to junior high school. But once there, she adjusts quickly. She has a confident personality. Lord knows she has the gift of gab. I always hope that her mischievousness remains at a minimum, but not sure that is possible.

Ruby still loves to be the class clown. Since she never shuts up, she gets in trouble easily. She started school just two days ago. As we visit Sam on his porch, she is telling us stories about her teachers. "Mrs. Snoden teaches English. She makes us finish every word and sentence for her. It is ridiculous!"

Oh boy! Here we go! "How do you mean, Ruby?"

Ruby always twirls her hair as she talks. "Well, if she is saying the word encyclopedia, she only says encyclo and we all have to say pedia! Isn't that corny?"

I know Ruby is rebellious. "Every teacher has their own way of teaching, Ruby."

She is on a roll. "Then there's old Mr. Creag. He teaches history. He always wears a plaid jacket and a bow tie. He's bald, but not quite. One side he grows long then combs it up over the top with a lot of goop on it. That right there is an ugly bald! He wears little round glasses. He is a geek. He stands at the front of the class twisting his top button around and around while he talks."

It worries me she finds this all so funny. "So, what's wrong with that?"

"He's weird, Patsy! When he went to his closet for a book, Ellen pushed him inside and shut the door!"

"Ruby! That is not funny!"

She laughs hysterically. "He was in there hollering and stuff; but don't worry, me and Frankie let him out of there!"

I think I need to worry about Ruby. Seems like she is a little bully.

She won't stop. "Mrs. Shnider is our home ec. teacher. We call her cat woman because she has 21 cats at her house! Her breath smells like cats. I'm not kidding, Patsy!"

"Ruby, you have to realize some people can't help bad breath. It is a medical condition."

"Medical, Shmedical, Patsy! It's cats and maybe vodka combined! Margie said she saw her drink vodka out of her desk drawer!"

"Ruby, you must respect your teachers!"

I look at Sam. He is already looking at me. He raises his eyebrows to me. His blue eyes sparkle but they are filled with concern. He turns to Ruby. "Are there any teachers you actually like, Ruby?"

"Mrs. Cassidy, gym teacher. She is my favorite. I like gym class except for starching my white uniform and polishing my stupid tennis shoes white. It's painful, Sam. Just painful!"

"Well at least there is a class you like, Ruby!"

Ruby is in a hurry to meet her girlfriends. "See you guys later! Gotta get to the football field!"

Sam is laughing. He looks at me, "Yep, she's a teenager I'm afraid!"

I am not laughing. "She is embarrassing. I am embarrassed FOR her!"

Many girls in junior high school go onto the football field after school and sit at the edge on a grassy embankment looking over the track field. The track team runs just below there. Ruby has noticed a boy named Michael. He is from Sagamore. Ruby thinks Sagamore men are "manly." She tells me, "Sagamore boys aren't spoiled like Rural Valley and Yatesboro boys. Their life is harder. That makes them manly!" Her theories on things are amusing. "His Adam's apple sticks out a mile. He has dimples, and he runs like the wind. He plays football too! He is so cute!"

She never misses a track meet. By the end of the week, he starts to notice her. She is smitten with him. Today there is no track meet so she comes straight home after school. Grabbing a cookie from the jar, I walk with her to Sam's.

Sam is fixing a wheel on his mower. He sees her coming across the yards. "Hey, Ruby, Ruby! "What's up? How's school?"

"Okay, I guess. Sam, do you think I'm old enough to have a boyfriend?"

I am going to stay out of this and let Sam handle it.

He stops what he is doing. "NO! You are way too young. What's going on?"

"Nothing in particular. Just asking." She kicks a rock from his sidewalk into the grass.

"You don't need a boyfriend, Ruby. Just have fun in school. Hang around with your girlfriends. A boyfriend will keep you from having fun, Ruby."

Ruby doesn't like hearing that. "Well, you had Betsy in high school!"

"Yes. That is right. High school, not JUNIOR HIGH SCHOOL!"

Ruby turns on her heel. "Well, we'll see, Sam. We'll see!"

She seems unwilling to come onto the porch. She doesn't want to hear Sam's advice. She takes off across the yards. "See ya, Kaminsky!"

Sam laughs, "You'll see me only if the good Lord's willin' and the creek don't rise! Stay away from those boys, Ruby!"

Sam comes onto the swing on his porch, where I am waiting for him. "I think she is too young for boys. Don't you, Patsy?"

"Yeah, I do." I admit, "She has her eye on a boy from Sagamore. I'm sure it's just puppy love. She was like that with Jimmy four years ago. Maybe nothing to worry about."

"I don't agree, Patsy. When she loved Jimmy, she was a child. It was true puppy love. This is different. She is thirteen now. This love is different. Don't you think she is too young?"

"You might be right about the kind of love it is, but I don't know how to stop it. She's getting that nasty teenage attitude. You know?"

"I've noticed. Not sure nasty is a good enough word. Still, let's keep an eye on this boyfriend thing!"

Ruby finished out the month going to the track field every day after school. Sam is awfully worried. I am worried too. Ruby is just too young to have a boyfriend. When she visits Sam after school, he is more intent on talking to her about it. "Still liking that boy, Ruby?"

"Yep, do!"

"What's his name?"

"Michael. His name is Michael." She says as she brushes a maple leaf off his banister. "He's handsome and he's nice. I think he likes me. He tells me I'm hot."

"I'm not sure what that word means, Ruby. But why don't you just take it slow and let him be your friend. Not boyfriend. I so much want you to enjoy your junior high years!"

Ruby bent down to tie her tennis shoe that had become untied, so she wouldn't have to look at Sam. "We'll see! Patsy should be showing up here soon. She's off work at five."

"Yep, any time now."

My job at the grocery store just changed last week. Lucio made me a butcher. I was just thinking about taking a job at Dixon's Market as cashier, but the butcher job at Palilla's Market pays a little more. Another plus with the butcher job is that I am able to bring home any mistakes on meat that I make, which will help Mama tremendously. Today I am bringing home a ham. I had cut into it the wrong way, so Lucio told me to take it. He couldn't sell it cut that way.

Mama has invited Sam for dinner tomorrow night. This ham will be perfect. I stop at Sam's on my way home from work, "You are coming to dinner tomorrow, right?"

"Oh, I don't know, Patsy." Sam is always afraid he is intruding.

"What you mean you don't know? Mama is counting on you! Me and Ruby are counting on you too!"

Sam, at thirty- four, is getting a few gray hairs above his ears. I think he looks distinguished. I can't believe how fast the years have gone! "You can take a night off from your garden, Sam. Relax, the work will be here when you get back."

"Ah, okay, I can see I can't get out of it!" He chuckles.

Ruby breaks in the door. "Michael asked me to the junior high dance!"

Sam is surprised. "At thirteen you can go to a dance, Ruby? Seems to me that's pretty young to be going to a dance."

Ruby is excited and grabs an apple from the middle of Sam's kitchen table. "Well, I'm old enough. Grades 7, 8 and 9 go, so there!" Out the door she runs.

Sam is standing at the sink not knowing what to say next. I go very close to him and whisper. "Don't worry, Sam. I'll talk to her."

He smiles at me and puts his hands just below both my shoulders. He holds tight. His smile is warm. "I know you will."

I love the feel of his warm hands. He is staring at me. I love the blue of his eyes. I can't answer back. I just want to stand here with his hands on my shoulders. He starts to rub his hands up and down my arms. He seems to be soaking me in. I like it. "Thanks, Patsy." He turns to do his dishes.

Darn, what was that?

thirty-five

Let Us Be There

Sam arrives on time for mama's dinner. Mama has used her best tablecloth and prettiest dishes. Only five of us are at dinner. Besides Sam and me, there is just Bella, Ruby and Mama. Bella is in ripe form. "Well, what do you know! Sam Kaminsky can leave his house!"

I scold her. "Shut up Bella, can't you just sit there and be nice!" Mama glares at Bella, but as usual, it does no good.

Mama starts conversation to filter Bella out. "I remember your parents, Sam. They were good people. Your Dad died rather young though, didn't he?

"He was only 37. Too much coal dust in his lungs. It was a couple years that he struggled to breath. It wasn't an easy couple of years."

"That would be hard on you, Sam. I'm so sorry.

"He came here without us in 1919. Mama was pregnant with me when he left Poland. He lived in the Valley Hotel until he sent for us in 1921, when our house on the hill was ready. By the time we got here, I was almost two. When he died, that is when Mama and I moved over to this street. I was sixteen."

"That is a lot for a young boy." Mama says sadly.

"We were okay. Mama and me I mean. But then Mama died the year after Betsy disappeared." He put his head down. "I don't think she ever got over the fact that she sent Betsy for that loaf of bread."

We are all silent. We don't know what to say. Sam quickly raises his head. "Enough of that. Let's eat!"

Mama has cooked the ham with pineapple and garlic and it melts in our mouths. She has made creamy mashed potatoes with tons of butter mixed in, homemade bread with apple butter, and corn on the cob. Meals like this Sam does not get often.

Mama brings out the peach pie she had made and the ice cream for on top. She cuts everyone a piece, and her own piece is as big, if not bigger, then everyone else's. Her ice cream is piled higher too.

"Mama!" I plead. "Should you be eating all that, with your diabetes and all?"

"Shush child! If I can't live how I want, ain't worth livin'!"

I don't like that answer, but know not to argue. Mama does this every day, eats what she wants, especially sweets. No one can change that.

Ruby hasn't said much. The junior high dance is just around the corner. I worry about Ruby. "You think you are mature enough to go to a dance with a boy?" I asked her.

"Can't you just be happy for me, Pasty? She answers me curtly. "Mama, can I buy a new dress?"

Mama talks as she fills her plate with mashed potatoes. "I can't say I am comfortable that you are going to a dance at your age. But, if that is how it goes nowadays, I have to trust you. Tonight, you and Patsy can check out the Sears-Roebuck Catalog for a dress. We will order it."

Dinner ends and I walk Sam home to sit on his back-porch swing awhile. He is still worried about Ruby and this new boy she likes. "Don't let her get a dress that is too old for her, Patsy. You know what I mean!"

"No worries, Sam. It is going to come up to her chin and down to her ankles!"

He thinks that is funny, "Look for a blue one. It would show off her blue eyes."

I can't stay long. I need to give Ruby the time she needs. She and I sit down with the catalog. Right away she wants a dress meant for a twenty-five-year-old. "Be sensible, Ruby. You don't want to look too old. Sam said you should get a blue dress, to match your eyes. Look at this one!" I point to a darling dressing with blue sparkles in the skirt. It is sleeveless, yet not revealing. The neckline is normal where it should be and the dress fits tight to her waist. Then after the skinny- beaded belt, the skirt flares out. It will be adorable on Ruby.

"I like it. A lot!" She beams.

Mama looks at it and approves. I am so glad this was easy. "Good, then, done! The dress will soon be on its way!"

Ruby retreats to her bedroom to get her pajamas on. Just then the phone rings. It is Mrs. Turnbull, the class sponsor. "Would you like to be a chaperone at the junior high dance, Patsy?" I am surprised to have been asked. I, of course, would love to be there, to keep an eye on Ruby.

"I would be glad to. May I bring someone to help chaperone?"

"Of course! We would be glad for the extra help. See you at the dance, Patsy!"

As I turn to tell Mama, she is smiling. Then it hits me. "You orchestrated that arrangement, didn't you?"

She giggles quietly. "Keep it quiet. It is our secret. I am just not sure about this whole thing, so at least you will be watching her."

"It will be our secret, Mama."

It is getting late, but I'm anxious to tell Sam, so I run across to his house. "Do you want to come to the junior high dance with me in two weeks and chaperone, Sam?"

He looks at me puzzled. "Chaperone, like in keeping an eye on the kids?"

"Yep! We just have to stand around and watch everybody."

"Then heck, yeah! Ruby won't like that at all. But I'll feel better about it! I'll need to get out and buy a suit."

"No, don't. I know one of daddy's suits will fit you. He was about your size and he owned two nice suits, still hanging in our closet. I'll bring them over. Sleep tight!"

He laughs. "You sleep tight!"

When Ruby heard we were both going, she was furious. "You treat me like a baby! I'm not a baby!"

"Well, you're my baby!" I tell her. "And besides, Sam never gets to go anywhere. This will be nice for him!"

Ruby softens somewhat. "Okay, but you two better not embarrass me!"

Her dress came in a week later and it fit perfectly. She loves it. The dance is next Saturday. I better get that suit over to Sam.

I have washed and starched the white shirt. Hopefully the pants and suit coat will fit. I bought a new necktie at Abe N. Cohen's yesterday. Daddy's are old fashioned.

It is a week until the dance. Sam seems pleased with the suit. He takes it upstairs to try on. As he walks down the stairs, he is fussing with the necktie. The pants are the perfect length and the suit coat fits perfectly. He just can't get the necktie right.

He looks dashing in the gray suit. His tan skin against the white shirt with his blue eyes are striking. His hair is messy. I like it messy, but I'll do a little trim to make it neater. He always looks like he needs a shave, which I love. I'll shave him after I cut his hair. I help him tie the necktie. He is staring at me as I tie it. I can't look into his eyes. He keeps staring at me. I am glad when I get it done. "There, you look dapper! Go take the suit off and bring me your razor, shaving cream and scissors." I know he will have to shave again the day of the dance, but I will still shave him now.

He did as I asked. I set a kitchen chair on top of an old sheet in the kitchen. I run the water in the sink until it is warm. I put a towel softly on Sam's shoulders. First, I take the scissors and trim his hair. Sam is being so quiet today. I think he likes the soft touch of my hands. It has been a long time since Sam felt the touch of a woman.

After I finish his hair, I comb it and come around front. I am two inches from his face to get a good look, "Perfect, your hair looks great!" I catch his blue eyes staring into mine again. He looks away quickly, embarrassed. I chuckle, "Now let's take care of that scraggly stuff growing on your face!" I mix up the shave cream with the brush and sweep it softly across his face and chin and on his upper lip. I pull the razor from up to down on this cheeks and chin, then down his neck. I feel the heat of his body. I feel his breath.

When I am all done, I run a washcloth under the warm water and wipe his face for him. With both hands I pat the washcloth slowly on his face, down each check, across his top lip, down his chin and neck. When my hands with the washcloth reach the bottom of his neck, Sam brings both his hands onto mine and holds my hands there at his neck, tight. My heart races. I am not sure what to do. Our faces are so close to each other. The moment stops and hangs in the air. Our eyes are locked. He begins to lean towards me. Our lips begin to faintly touch.

The door swings open and we separate quickly. It's Ruby. "So, did the suit fit?"

"Indeed, it did!" Sam answers nervously and quickly. "And aren't you happy to know I am able to go to keep an eye on you!"

"WHATEVER! If it makes you happy!" Ruby as she runs back out the door.

I love what is happening between me and Sam. It has been here for a long while now. I know it, and he knows it. Our moment is gone, for now. I know we'll get it back.

thirty-six
A Magical Moment

Another week passes quickly. It is Saturday night, the night of the junior high dance. It is a beautiful night for a dance. There is a warm breeze and the sky is illuminated by stars and a full moon. Sam comes to our house in his car to pick us up. He looks dashing. "You clean up pretty nice, Mr. Kaminsky!" I tell him.

"Ain't so bad yourself! In fact, I'd call you beautiful!"

I am wearing a peach evening dress that hugs my slim body and goes to my ankles. It is soft chiffon. I am wearing Mama's pearls. Sam hands me a white rose. I smell it first. "Thank you, Sam." My stomach is doing flip flops.

He then hands one to Ruby. "You look beautiful, Ruby. Your eyes are so blue in that dress!"

"Awe, Sam! That's is so sweet!" She is being so polite.

He is staring at me and I like it. I manage a nervous smile. "Thank you for the rose, Sam."

He reaches for my hand. "You are welcome. A pretty flower for a pretty peach rose!" His smile is infectious. He kisses my hand and notices my bracelet. "I love that you are still wearing the graduation bracelet I gave you."

I hold my wrist up, allowing the heart with the delicate stones to shimmer in the light. "I loved it then, love it now, and will always love it, Sam."

He grins showing that tiny space between his teeth. "The heart for the girl with the big heart."

Michael is coming up the front stairs, right on time for Ruby. I can feel their nervousness. "You look pretty, Ruby!" He sheepishly tells her.

"Thank you." She timidly answers, like she is so shy. I know better.

Ruby just turned fourteen. I have swept her hair for her up to one side, and with a beaded barrette that matches her dress, to hold it in place. I did her makeup with a little extra rouge and lipstick. I used an extra thick mascara, so her eyelashes seem unusually long. On her eyelids I put a sparkling blue eyeshadow I bought at King's. It matches the blue in her dress perfectly. She looks darling.

Uncle Joe gave Ruby a camera for her fourteenth birthday. Mama uses it to take their picture and hands it to her so she'll have it for the evening. She gives Ruby a hug as she tells her she loves her. She whispers in her ear, "You be a good girl now, hear?" We all know Ruby needs to be reminded often to be good. Ruby chuckles and we are ready to go.

Sam will drive us all to the school and home again.

I am impressed that Sam looks so distinguished in his suit. He keeps telling me he is old at thirty-four. That's ridiculous. He is young and vibrant. He is also outrageously handsome. He has put on weight and looks muscular and healthy. I know what is happening between us, yet it is like something trapped under too many blankets, it can't get out. I know for sure he no longer looks at me as a little kid. When I turned twenty-four in October, he gave me a bottle of wine with a pair of earrings. He is very aware the little girl was gone long ago.

Upon entering the school, Ruby and Michael are met by a group of their friends. They hurriedly gather at a table together. Ruby is already busy taking pictures of her friends.

Sam and I have our own little round table in the corner, with some other chaperones in the same area. There is a lot of laughing and giggling among the kids. When the music starts, all the kids start to dance, especially Ruby and Michael. He seems to really like her. They dance to "Sh-Boom." When "Rock Around the Clock Tonight'" begins, Ruby kicks up her heels and jumps around the floor swirling and laughing. Sam and I giggle as we watch her. Then a slower song begins, "Mr. Sandman." Sam and I watch intently as Ruby and Michael dance close. We can see the spark between them. Sam looks at me. "Time to let Ruby grow up, I'm afraid." We both know it is true. We can't stop time. "Earth Angel" is beginning to play. Sam is staring at me. "Would you like to dance, Miss Patsy?"

"Oh, I don't know, Sam, I've got two left feet!"

"Then we'll make a good pair! My feet are both left too!"

He takes my hand and we enter the dance floor as he draws me close to him. I snuggle my nose into his neck and can feel him holding me tight. His grip is unusually tight, but it feels good. He smells wonderful of musk. The warmth of his body goes through mine. Sam is singing along with the music, softly. "Earth Angel, Earth Angel, will you be mine. My darling dear, love you all the time. I'm just a fool. A fool in love with you."

He is singing it to me? I melt with each word. From the corner of my eye, I see Ruby snapping our picture. She doesn't seem surprised that Sam and I are dancing together.

When the song ends, I don't want it to. He smiles at me and the cute lines at the corners of his eyes appear. "Thank you, Madam. I guess I haven't lost my touch."

"Indeed, you have not, Mr. Kaminsky!"

The night ends and we pile into Sam's car to head home.

"Did you kids have a good time?" I ask.

"Sure did!" Ruby chimes. "How about you and Sam?"

Sam chuckles. "Does a bear like the woods?"

Ruby is puzzled. "Bear like the woods? What kind of answer is that!"

Sam laughs. "You'll understand all these sayings someday. Michael, do you have someone coming to pick you up?"

"A friend will come for me. My daddy doesn't own a car."

Sam is curious. "No? Why is that?"

Michael paused a moment. "Because when my daddy was young and reached the age to drive, he was already a drunk. He told me he had to make a choice between drinking and driving, he chose drinking."

Sam was sorry he asked. "I'm so sorry, Michael. When you need a ride, you call me!"

We both like this Michael. He must have a rough life, yet he is mannerly and sweet. I think kids who grow up like that are stronger than most. Ruby was right about those Sagamore boys! Ruby has made a good choice for her first full-blown boyfriend.

Sam takes us to our house. Michael will wait for his friend to come for him. I am not ready to go home. "I'll go over to the house with you, Sam. Ruby, tell Mama I'll be right back."

Ruby opens the back-car door to get out. "Don't you kids do anything I wouldn't do now!"

I look at her sternly. "Just don't you worry about us Ruby. Now get in the house!"

Sam parks the car and we walk up the front steps. He is staring at me. "Let's have a beer on the back porch."

We walk through the living room and then the kitchen. Sam grabs us each a bottle of beer. We sit on the swing on the back porch. I am quiet. He is staring at me. "What are you thinking about, Patsy?"

"I was thinking it seems like yesterday I had my first beer here with you, and two years have passed already!"

His face is lit by the moonlight. "Time is going WAY too fast!"

Each of us take sips of our beer in silence. Conversation is hard. I am nervous. "Looks like Ruby and Michael are an item, Sam."

"Yep, looks like it." He is daydreaming, staring at his beer bottle. "Guess we have to let her grow up; you know?"

"Yep, seems so." I hate to admit.

I finish my beer through a few more one-line sentences. I put my beer down. The silence is deafening. Finally, I turn to him. "Sam, I have to ask you something. What is happening between us?"

Sam leans over to put his bottle of beer on the banister. He answers while his head is turned. "I'm sorry, Patsy. I know I am too old for you. I am ten years older than you. I don't mean to put you in this position. Yet, I can't help myself. You are everything to me."

My face breaks into a smile. "Don't be sorry, Sam, I'm not sorry." He looks at me. His expression is blank at first, then he breaks into a sweet smile. He glares into my eyes. His blue eyes are piercing. He puts his hands on my cheeks. His touch is soft and gentle. My heart is jumping out of my body. He draws my face to his. When our lips meet, I consume the warmth of his body and the velvet touch of his lips. He is gentle and slow. The kiss is long. I can hardly catch my breath. My body is enflamed.

Sam whispers as he withdraws from the kiss. "Should I apologize for that?"

It took me a second to talk, "No, you only need to apologize if I'm not going to get another one." With that, he draws me in even harder with his arms fully around me, kissing me with a sensation that tingles my spine. His lips are so warm and soft. I am melting like butter. I am electrified. He is strong, yet soft and intense. He is delicious! I want to consume him. I hope this goes on forever.

He finally withdraws but keeps his face close to mine as his hands stroke my face. "I didn't expect this, Patsy. But I fell in love with you a long time ago."

My cheek rubs against his. I talk into his ear, "I waited a long time for this. I fell in love with you, too."

He kisses me again with even more determination. My body folds into his. I feel the love pour out of him. I am feeling things I never felt before. It is a warm ocean breeze and a hot bubbly bath put together. This time as he withdraws, he looks into my eyes. "I love you, Patsy. I love you more than life!"

Those were the same words he had used when he described his love for Betsy. He "loved her more than life." He had said that about her. Now he has said it about me! He loves me the same. My body is on fire.

He reaches into his sport coat pocket and brings out a little black box. "I've been carrying this around, waiting for my moment to come. My moment is here, now. Patsy, I don't want to be without you, ever. Not for one more day. You make me so happy. Please tell me you will be my wife."

I am in shock and euphoria all at the same time. Getting out from all those heavy blankets came fast and feels wonderful! We both knew this, why did we wait so long? I look at his face with the moonlight hitting it. "I thought you'd never ask, Mr. Kaminsky! Yes, I will marry you!" I give a little squeal of delight, as I fold into his long passionate kiss.

I don't want this night to end, but I know I have to go home now; Mama will be worried. He takes my hand as I stand up. We embrace. We walk hand in hand to my house. At the front door he throws me passionately against the porch wall. The kiss is hard. A good kind of hard. It lasts forever. In this standing position I can embrace his body into mine. My body is screaming with delight. I feel like I've been plugged in and the electric is running through my veins. I put one leg over his thigh as he strokes it as he kisses me. We finally break apart, with his face close to mine he whispers, "I love you."

"I love you too, Sam. More than you can ever know."

He whispers in my ear. "I am a lucky man!"

He looks at me. "Can we have Ruby live with us too? We can be a family."

"That would make me so happy, Sam." As I throw my arms around his neck, he twirls me around on the porch and I laugh as we spin. Mama and my sisters hear the commotion and come down the stairs and out onto the porch in their pajamas, "What's wrong?" Mama asks.

I am squealing like a school girl. "WE'RE GETTING MARRIED!" Everyone starts cheering and hugging us both.

Mama is laughing as she hugs me. "You found him a long time ago, you just didn't know it."

"We've got wedding plans to make!" Dee says. "You'll be the prettiest bride ever, Patsy!"

I look at Ruby. She doesn't look puzzled as I would have expected. "What do you think, Ruby?"

She laughs. "I think it's about time!"

thirty-seven
I Never Thought She'd Leave Me

I can't wait for the sun to come up in the morning. I had so much trouble sleeping last night. Thinking about Sam is consuming me. The feel of his touch has brought my body to life. I know now how long I have loved him. And he has loved me that long too! Finally, I skip down the stairs, singing as I go.

Something isn't right. Mama isn't up yet. That's odd. She is always up at 6 a.m., every day. Is she delivering another baby? No note here. She always leaves us a note. I peek out at the garden, she isn't there. I walk to the front porch, no Mama. My heart is leaping out of my body as I race up the stairs to Mama's bedroom. She is in her bed. She is still asleep. I shake her. "Mama, wake up!" She doesn't wake up. I scream for Bella and Ruby. "GET DOC GRIFFITH!!"

It took several minutes for Doc to get here. He quickly puts a sugar tablet in Mama's mouth. After a minute or so she starts to moan. She is coming around. Doc asks us to step into the hallway. "Girls, your mama is very sick. She is in a diabetic coma."

My stomach does a flip. "But she is starting to wake up. You saw her!"

Doc's face is serious. "That doesn't mean much, Patsy. She could go in and out of consciousness. Her condition is serious."

I feel like I'm going to throw up. Doc rubs my shoulders as he talks to me. "We are going to take her to the hospital. Her sugar is out of control. We don't know what this outcome is going to be. You need to prepare yourself for the worst."

Listening to his voice is like hearing it through a tunnel, like it is coming from somewhere else. I cannot comprehend what he is saying to us.

Doc calls the ambulance. I will go in the ambulance with her. By now Ruby has run to Sam's and he is here to see us off. "I'll bring Ruby and Bella to the hospital, Patsy. I'll see you there."

I can't even answer. I just stare at him. "Okay."

At the hospital, Mama wakes up somewhat. She is weak and saying just a word here and there, in a very low voice. Bella, Ruby, and Sam arrive. Ruby won't stop crying. Sam keeps his arms around her and lets her sob into his chest. Medical people are everywhere. They check her vitals. They order tests. They start another IV. After an hour or so, Doc sits down with us in another room. All my brothers and sisters are here now. "We can't get her sugar under control. Her organs are failing. She cannot survive this. She may last a day, a week, maybe a little more, but not a lot more. Prepare yourselves. I am so sorry."

I collapse into Sam's arms and Bella holds onto Ruby. The devastation is just too much. Sam rubs my back, "I'm here for you, Patsy." It feels good, as I sob.

By ten o'clock I convince everyone to go home, I will stay the night. Sam insists he will bring Bella and Ruby back first thing in the morning. I will then go home to get some rest and come back. I sit at Mama's bedside all night, holding her hand. I must have dozed off. My head is down on the bed when I feel her squeeze my hand.

I look up and Mama is smiling at me weakly. "Patsy, we need to talk."

I sit up and wipe my hands across my eyes to get them open. "What is it, Mama?"

Mama hesitates. She is weak. "It's Ruby."

"Ruby? What about Ruby?"

Mama asks me for a sip of water. After that she seems to be able to say a few more words. "Mrs. Matteo. Go see her, Patsy. About Ruby."

"Yes, Mama. Mrs. Matteo gave you Ruby." I am thinking she is confused.

She made a motion with her hand left to right. "No, no. You must know the truth. Go to Mrs. Matteo. Go right away. Please, Patsy!"

"What?" Now, I am confused. "What truth? She gave you Ruby because she didn't want her. Remember? So why would I go, Mama. Why?"

Mama has tears rolling down her cheeks now. "It's not true. Go Patsy. Ruby needs the truth. She needs to know."

I can see now that she is of clear mind. She knows what she is saying. "I don't understand, Mama. It's not true? What's not true?"

"Not true." She says as she fades back into unconsciousness.

I shake her. "Mama, tell me, mama! What's not true?"

Her eyes opened slightly. "God forgive me."

Mama went back into a deep sleep and I was left alone to think. "Forgive you for what? Go see Mrs. Matteo?" I think out loud. "What is it? What? What?"

I am left alone with my thoughts. My mind races.

Sam shows up with Ruby and Bella at 8 a.m. Sam kisses my cheek. "You need to get home and get some rest now, Patsy. Bella is here to take you home."

"I guess." I stare at Ruby.

She notices. "Why you staring at me?"

"No reason. I'm just tired, Ruby." I am wondering who she is. I am scared. What will I find out?

I pick up my purse. "I'll be back by afternoon and spend the night again, Sam."

Sam pulls me to him for a strong loving embrace. "We will be here with her until you come back. Get some rest." He gives me a soft kiss on my cheek. I need his warmth; I need his arms around me. I fold into his body again. He keeps his arms wrapped around me. I need this. I will go home now and get some rest.

I can't wait to walk out into the fresh air. What is it Mrs. Matteo is going to tell me? Maybe I am just having a bad dream. What if I say nothing to nobody and just continue on like it has always been? After all, I am the only one that knows there is something else.

But I think some more. "What if it was me? Would I not want to know the truth? And what is the truth? WHAT??" It is all just too much to think about. I arrive home and fall into my bed. I kick my shoes off. My clothes are still on. I fall into a deep sleep.

I am awakened when a soft hand touches mine. Someone is sitting beside me. It is Sam. He is stroking my hair. My heart is pounding out of my chest. "What's wrong?"

Sam's face is drawn and sad. "It's your Mama, darling." He pauses, pulling me into him. "She's gone, Patsy."

I feel numb, blood rushing to my head. I feel his embrace. He is holding me together so I don't crumble apart.

"Ruby and I were with her. It was peaceful." He tells me softly in my ear.

I let out a wail and my tears start to flow. Sam holds me in his arms for the longest time as I sob. I struggle to regain some composure. "Did she suffer?"

Sam speaks softly. "She had no pain, Patsy. She was just sleeping. Just sleeping. She never woke up. Ruby told her how much you all loved her. It was beautiful. God took her easy. She just stayed asleep and eventually quit breathing. No pain, Patsy. None."

I sob into his shirt as I feel my tears wetting the soft cotton. "I never thought she'd leave me, Sam!"

"We never do. Patsy, you had a wonderful life with your Mama. You made her happy."

"I know. I know." I wipe my eyes. "Where's Ruby?"

"She is downstairs. She needs time to accept it. Your Mama was taken to the funeral home. There are arrangements to make. Now come wash your face and we'll join the others."

By now my brothers and sisters have arrived. The house is full. As each one enters, we hug and cry some more. Dee makes a pot of coffee and we all sit around the dining room table speechless. Ina starts the conversation of what to do next. Through our grief we begin to plan Mama's funeral. My head feels like there is a watermelon inside.

Three days later we are standing in a funeral home. The funeral service will soon begin. I stare at Mama. I wish she would wake up. I know she won't. I am trying to soak her in. Her face, her smile, her laugh. I don't want to forget any of these things. I am greeting the people who come to pay their respects, but we are all numb. I somehow mutter thank you. I feel like I am hearing my voice outside my body. Ruby mostly just cries. Her friends surround her. She leans her head on Michael to weep. The preacher talks about Mama and says so many nice things, but I think to myself, "You could never be able to tell it all. Mama was so wonderful in every way."

At the end of the service, as they take the casket out the door, we sing to Amazing Grace. It was her favorite hymn. I break down sobbing and Sam just holds me. He has me on one side and he has Ruby on the other side, sobbing. His arms around both of us is the little bit of comfort we can hold onto right now.

Many people come to the house after the funeral. Everyone has sent in food so there is plenty to eat. I just want the day to end, but it goes on into the night. Sam stays with me until everyone leaves. I tell everyone to go to bed. Sam helps me clean up. Only the two of us are doing dishes in the kitchen. I need this time alone with him.

I look up at him with the dishtowel in his hand drying a plate. He is smiling. "You had a great Mama, Patsy. You must hold onto the good memories. You are the one who taught me to do that. Remember? Your Mama will always be in your heart."

"I know." I whisper. "I just never imagined life without her."

"I know, it will be hard, at least for a while. You have had so many people you love in your life, and have loved you. You must know how lucky you are, Patsy."

"I agree. I am lucky." I think of Sam's loneliness all these years and how he waited for Betsy to come back. He has had so much more to face in life that I have. "Sam, can you do me a favor tomorrow?"

"Sure! Anything, Patsy."

"Can you go with me to Mrs. Matteo's house?"

Sam's face becomes drawn. "Why, Patsy? She is the part of my past I am trying to forget. I don't know if I can look at her face again! Why do you have to go there?"

I understand his feelings. "Mama told me when she was dying that I need to talk to Mrs. Matteo about Ruby. That was all she said before she went back into the coma. I'm scared. I don't want to go alone. I can't take any of my family until I figure this thing out. Won't you please go?"

His face softens into a sweet smile. "If you need me, then I'll be there for you. What time do you want to go?"

I feel bad that I've asked him to go, but I need him. I can't face this on my own. "Let's say 1:00, okay?"

He folds his dishtowel onto the counter. He seems troubled. "Okay."

We put the last dish away and go onto the front porch. I will kiss him goodnight and tomorrow will be another day. As soon as we walk out the wooden screen door, letting it bang twice, as always, he grabs me and draws me into him. His kiss is strong with that soft, long kiss that tickles my spine. I feel so safe in his arms.

The kiss ends and he is stroking my face. "I have felt alone for so long, Patsy. My soul was lost. You have brought me back to life. I love you so much."

I throw my arms around him. "I love you too, Sam!"

Falling asleep is hard. I think of Mama. I can see her face and hear her laugh. Then my mind goes to marriage and wedding plans. Mama won't be here to see me get married. I cry until I drift off to sleep.

In the early morning hours, Ruby awakens me. "Wake up, Patsy. Wake up! I was just thinking, Patsy, are we orphans now?"

I can't help but smile at Ruby. "No, Ruby. We aren't orphans. We have each other, don't we?"

Ruby begins to cry. "Just feel like I'm alone. No Daddy and no Mama now."

I am sad for her. "I'm here for you, Ruby. Me and Sam both. You know we will always take care of you. Always!"

Ruby fell onto the bed with me and sobbed. I hold her tight and stroke her back until she is done crying. "You know what, Ruby? When Sam proposed to me, he asked me if you could live with us, so we can be a family!"

She sat straight up in bed speechless for a moment. Then she throws her arms around me and cries. She is doing a cry laugh. Me too.

"Mama would want us to be strong, Ruby. We can do that, can't we?"

"I suppose so, Patsy."

"I have to go out today at 1:00, Ruby. Are you going be okay here by yourself?"

She pulls herself together and turns onto her back. "Sure, but Shelly wants to come down today. Will that be okay?"

"Of course, it's okay, Ruby. She can keep you company while I'm gone."

"Where you going, Patsy?"

"Just have to take care of some business. That's all." It isn't a lie. I am taking care of business. Just don't know what business!

Ruby falls back into a deep sleep. I sneak out of bed to prepare for what? I don't know.

Sam picks me up at 1:00 sharp. I jump in the car and he can see my troubled face. "You okay, Patsy?"

I tell him I am, but I'm not. "I don't know what I'm facing. Mama told me I had to go see Mrs. Matteo for the truth about Ruby. You remember how we got Ruby, right?"

"I remember." He turns the corner to go up the hill. "Mrs. Matteo had her. You don't suppose she wants her back, do you, Patsy?"

"Not at all. There is something else. Mama couldn't say."

"Okay." He answers in a serious tone, "Whatever it is, you sure you want to do this? You are in a fragile state right now you know. Should you wait awhile maybe?"

I love his concern for me. "I have to, Sam. It is just too important to let go. It was Mama's last request. She said to do it right away. I must do it."

We start up Mrs. Matteo's driveway. My stomach is in my throat.

thrity-eight
Truth Revealed

When we arrive at Mrs. Matteo's house, it looks a lot like it had when I was here years earlier, except everything has become even more overgrown. The same rusty bikes are in very high grass. The sidewalk now barely showing. The chickens are still running around. Knock, knock, knock. Mrs. Matteo comes to the door. She has aged. Her hair is white and her skin is badly wrinkled. There doesn't seem to be any of her kids around anymore. They would mostly all be grown and out of the house by now, I suppose.

Time shows on her face. When she sees me, her face drains of color. Her voice is weak. "Hello." She just stands there. She stares at us. She seems nervous. Very nervous.

"I need to talk to you, Mrs. Matteo." I say curtly.

She hesitates. She puts her head down and opens her door wide to let us walk through. "Come in, I'm glad this day has come".

I am puzzled by that. What does she mean?

Sam is nervous. I feel bad for him. I grab his hand as we enter.

"Please, sit." She points to her couch.

Sam and I sit together. Mrs. Matteo sits in the chair across from us.

She looks at me. "I'm so sorry about your mama, Patsy. She was a good woman."

"Indeed, she was, Mrs. Matteo. Do you know what her last words to me were? She told me to go see Mrs. Matteo for the truth about Ruby. What does that mean?"

She seems to be having trouble speaking. "Your mama said that?"

"Yes, she did. So, what did she mean? What is it about Ruby we don't know? I can tell you one thing; you aren't getting her back!"

With this she puts her head down. The silence is deafening. As she looks up our eyes meet. "She isn't mine, Patsy."

"Not yours? NOT YOURS??" How can that be? My Mama came here and delivered her!"

Sam's body stiffens. My heart is beating out of my chest. I am infuriated! He looks at me and readjusts himself on the couch. He knows to say nothing.

"No, she didn't, Patsy. I wasn't pregnant." She rings her hands in her apron and looks away.

"What is going on here? Mama would not have lied to me!"

Mrs. Matteo is silent, just staring down at her hands. "She lied to you because she had to. It was not something she wanted to do. When she came that night expecting to deliver a baby, Ruby was already here, in my arms. She was not my baby."

"NOT your baby? What do you mean? CAN YOU PLEASE LOOK AT ME?"

She raises her head. "Patsy, please stay calm. This day was a long time coming, so please just listen. It is not a simple explanation. My husband threatened your Mama."

"Threatened her? Really? Why?"

"I can tell you why in a minute. But please don't blame your mama. She was scared at that moment like I've been scared my whole life. She cared about that little baby. She would not have left here without her. She could see my husband was the devil!"

Mrs. Matteo stood up and stared out the window as she spoke, "When your mama came that day, she saw me with a black eye and a cut down the side of my face. I was standing right here at this window, holding little Ruby. My husband ordered your mama to take the baby home. He told her she was to say she was ours. He told your mama his niece had the baby. He told her that his niece was only thirteen and she was no good, and that she gave Ruby to him to give away. He threatened your mama that she had to say that I had the baby. He threatened your family. Your mama was afraid for me. She was afraid for herself and all of you. I got that black eye because I fought with Sal. He beat me up because I used my leverage."

"Leverage?" What are you talking about?"

Her voice quivers as she speaks. "Years ago, I found your Uncle Frederick's wallet and a bloody knife wrapped in a rag behind our shed."

I gasp as Sam throws his arms around me. "Oh Sam, poor Uncle Frederick! I always had hope he'd come home, and now......."

Her head is down. "I'm so sorry, Patsy. When I found that, I knew Sal had killed your uncle."

A basketball just dropped into my stomach. "Why didn't you turn him in, WHY?"

"So many reasons, Patsy. Had I turned him in, we would be in worse danger than ever, as another Blackhand would come after me and my kids. The Blackhands are bigger and more evil than you know. I wanted Sal dead my whole life. But between the danger of other Blackhands and me being able to feed eleven kids, what was I to do?"

I can't answer that. "So, what do you mean, leverage then?"

"I buried the wallet and knife deep in the woods. Then I wrote a letter to Father Berto, to be opened only in the event of my death. In the letter I told where to find the wallet and knife. Sal would go to prison. Through the years it was my leverage, but I was saving it for something I deemed so important I needed to use it. That so important thing was Ruby."

"Ruby?" What do you mean?"

"Sal was going to throw her in the dam, Patsy."

I gasp. I can't speak. I can't breathe.

"I used my leverage. I told him how I buried the wallet and knife and that the priest has my letter. If he killed me, he would be exposed. I told him he would have to kill me to take Ruby."

She sits back down in her chair and takes a deep breath. "He gave me a black eye and a broken rib. He didn't kill me, though. When he was done beating me up, I told him to go get Isla if he wanted to stay out of jail. He did."

I try to collect myself and stay calm. "I am so sad for my mama that she was pulled into your web, yet I suppose I need to thank you for saving Ruby. But I am sad for what these lies did to my mama."

Mrs. Matteo looks beaten. "I do know what that did to her. But please understand why your Mama had to lie for me."

I feel sorry for her in some way now. My heart wants to pity her, but anger has taken its place. "Who and where is this niece then?"

"There was no niece, Patsy."

I swallow hard. "OH MY GOD! WHY did you tell Mama a niece had her then?"

"To protect your Mama, Patsy. She did not know the real truth. Not the REAL truth. Your Mama was already dealing with the lie that I birthed Ruby. I thought it was better to let it go. To let that lie be the story, as I could not tell the real truth. Ruby was healthy. Her life was good with your family. The story we told was working." She took a deep breath and exhaled. "Your mama knew no good would come for that baby here. The minute she held Ruby, she loved her. She knew she had to take her. She saved both Ruby and me that day."

I glare at her. "Please give me the truth! I AM WAITING!"

She stands up and goes over to an old wooden chest and opens it. She comes out with a small book, looks like a journal. She holds it tight in her hands. "The story about the niece was just that, a story."

She grows silent as she looks at Sam with incredible sorrow. "I will explain. I'd like a minute to talk to Sam about Betsy right now."

I want to talk about Ruby. What is she trying to do? Yet, for Sam's sake, I have to let her talk. Even though, I don't understand how or why we are going from Ruby to Betsy.

Mrs. Matteo sits on the front edge of her chair. "Sam, Betsy didn't go with Bruno on her own. I know that is what I told you. But it wasn't true. Bruno took her. But I told you she went on her own, so you would quit looking. You would have been killed!"

His face is pale. "She was his prisoner? His PRISONER? How could you have kept that from me? I COULD HAVE SAVED HER!"

"No, you could not have, Sam. There were so many Blackhands in on it, they were all watching you. Bruno took her, thinking he could make her fall in love with him. I knew she was not being abused in any way. So, it was better to tell you she was not his prisoner, so you would quit looking, and therefore, live."

Sam's eyes are filling with tears. "My poor Betsy! A prisoner! Oh My God!"

"No Sam, she was okay. Please believe me. He was treating her fine. He was trying to win her affections. It is true he wouldn't let her leave the house, but she was okay. She was just biding her time until she could get home to you."

Sam is bent over, hands folded across his waist holding in the pain, his body shakes.

Mrs. Matteo straightens and wipes her eyes. "After she went missing, I tried what I could to find her to get her back without Sal finding out. I couldn't find her. Then one day the phone rang. It was her. Our conversation was brief. He allowed her to tell me she was okay and that was all. Then she quickly said, "Tell Sam I love him and I'm coming back!" That was all she said. The phone went dead. I still didn't know where she was."

Sam is having trouble talking. "Oh my God! Oh my God! I searched for so long! But everyone convinced me she went because she wanted to. They made me believe that!"

She looks at him with pity in her eyes. "I needed you to believe that too. You were smart to believe that and stop looking for her. Had you continued to look for her, you would not be sitting here right now. After the call Sam, I did everything I could to try to find her. I had to be careful. Our lives were in danger."

"Why didn't you go to the police. WHY?"

"Oh Sam, some of the police are Blackhands, honey. Why do you think they wouldn't help you very much back in the beginning when she disappeared? It was all so dangerous."

"I don't understand why she couldn't get away from him. Why?"

Mrs. Matteo's face drops. "Because she died before she could, Sam."

Sam is crying but his anger is greater than his tears. "Did he kill her? Is that what happened? DID HE KIILL HER? I will find him. I will find him and KILL HIM!"

"He didn't kill her, Sam. And you wouldn't find him anyways. He is dead. He was shot by police last May robbing a bank in Toledo.

Sam is angry and devastated. "The bastard deserved more than a quick death from a bullet! He deserved to suffer!"

"I know he did." Mrs. Matteo's voice is soft and loving. She puts her hand on his and rubs his hand. "But he is gone, Sam. He is gone."

"AND SO IS MY BETSY!" He shouts. "AND SO IS MY BETSY? HOW DID SHE DIE? TELL ME!"

Mrs. Matteo swallows hard. "She hemorrhaged, Sam."

"Hemorrhaged? HEMORRHAGED? From what?"

"From childbirth, Sam."

Sam stiffens. He looks like the blood has drained from his body. He is quivering. "Oh My God! She had a baby to him? To that filthy Bruno Matteo? My poor Betsy!"

Mrs. Matteo struggles to speak. "No, Sam. She did not. She had a baby to YOU! It was your baby!"

The blood rushes to my head as I grab Sam. His body is shaking. "My baby? My baby? "How do you know?"

"Because she told me, Sam."

He cries as he shouts. "She told you and not me? YOU and not ME?

"Please listen, Sam. I was at the company store that day he took her. Betsy had just come from Doc Griffith's office across the street. She had just found out. Betsy was always kind to me when no one else was. She told me that she was two months pregnant. She was so excited. She didn't mean to tell me first. She was just so excited. She was in a hurry to get home to you. She was so happy. She bought the bread your Mama had sent her for, and turned on her heel to run home to you. To tell you, Sam."

Sam seems to crumble into himself. "She didn't COME home that day!"

Sam looks up, his eyes are glassy. I put my arms through his arm and hold him tight. I feel him crumbling. He is sweating. His face is white. He can't talk.

I glare at her. "How do you know the baby was Sam's?"

"Bruno was in a terrible accident at age ten. It left him unable to father a child. It nearly drove him crazy. The baby could not have been his. The most hope he had was that she could love him and, therefore, he would be a father. That would never happen." She grabs Sam's arm. "Sam, look at me. It was yours. The baby was yours!"

'DON'T TOUCH ME!" He screams.

I embrace him. I lean my forehead on his forehead and look into his eyes. "Let's try to stay calm, Sam, it will be okay." My heart aches for him. "Continue, Mrs. Matteo. We need to know everything now. And the truth, please! You owe us that!"

She knows Sam needs to know everything now. "This will all be the truth. I have nothing to fear now. I only have myself to live with." She sits straight up to begin her explanation.

"Bruno had to have been outside the company store waiting for her that day. When I went out to go home, I saw the loaf of bread she had bought lying in the dirt. I've spent so much time thinking about it. If I had seen him doing that, I could have stopped it. I think I could have reasoned with him. Maybe, just maybe, I could have done something." She starts weeping, but I have no sympathy for her tears.

Mrs. Matteo sobs. "Then a month after Betsy called me, Bruno called me telling me I was going to have to deliver the baby when it came. He couldn't dare call a doctor. He would go to jail. I was happy because, finally, I will know where she was. I began to plan getting her out of there, just waiting for the call for me to go. A little over five months later, I got the call. Sal took me there. It was a cottage in the woods outside of Youngstown. Seemed as though a Blackhand friend of his let him use it. He had lost his wife and didn't want to go there anymore. I packed a knife and one of Sal's guns in my purse. I would do what I had to in order to get her out of there. I didn't know if I could kill them, Sam. I wanted to, but I feared so much for my children. I didn't have a plan, but I would have done what I had to. I got there as fast as I could. Her labor was long. I spent hours with her in the bedroom alone. I assured her you knew she was coming back. I even told her you told me to tell her how much you loved her. That you could not wait until she returned. While she was in labor, she talked to me, Sam. She told me she refused to love Bruno back. He thought if he kept her captive until the baby was born, she would fall in love with him, and this would be the child he could never have. But Betsy would have nothing to do with him. She hated him for keeping her locked in her room, but she assured me he had never physically abused her."

Sam can't stop crying. "I should have kept looking!"

"No, Sam! If you remember, you looked months for her. She only lived seven months from the day he took her. She was gone and had you kept looking, you'd be gone too."

Mrs. Matteo's face is drawn with guilt and shame. "After she called me that one time, she never knew I didn't tell you. I never got to talk to her again until she was in labor. She assumed I delivered her message to you. She stayed connected with you through that thought. But I couldn't deliver her message, Sam. My evil husband would have killed me AND my kids!"

She rubs her hand over the front cover of the book she is holding. "Betsy had this diary under her mattress. She told me to give it to you, if something happened to her." She lays the diary on his lap softly. "Sam, can you ever forgive me?"

Sam won't answer. He glares at her like he is looking into the darkness of hell.

"She wrote you notes every day in this diary, Sam." He wrapped his hand around it and brought it to his chest, now sobbing uncontrollably.

I have both my arms around him as his body jerks with sobs.

She keeps talking, though I know Sam needs her to stop. "I couldn't tell you as long as Sal was alive. I feared for my life. Do you understand?"

I can't bring myself to calm down. My anger is bubbling over. "Sal died months ago! Why not then? Why would you continue to keep that secret?"

She seems embarrassed now. "Because I lived so long in fear, I didn't know how to live without it."

She continues to defend herself. "I did tell you that Betsy had died, Sam. At least that much! You needed to know in order to give up on the hope she would walk through your door."

He glares at her. "Don't flatter yourself, you evil woman! Had I known I would have gone to the ends of the earth to find her. You took that from me! What a fool I have made of myself! Talking about the red ribbon coming. Hoping and praying. All the time she was gone, GONE!"

"Hope is never a bad thing, Sam." I embrace him as he cries into my shoulder.

Sam rocks back and forth clutching the diary.

Mrs. Matteo tries to take his hand. "I SAID, DON'T TOUCH ME!" He yells again.

She withdraws quickly. "Sam, Betsy had the baby. She saw her baby, held her, and loved her. Bruno was too ignorant to even come into the room."

Mrs. Matteo cries as she speaks. Every detail of the truth is pouring out. "She delivered a beautiful little girl. Betsy held her. She talked to the baby. I heard her say to her, "We are going home to Daddy, I promise you." After the birth, I took the baby from her when Betsy fell asleep. Next thing I knew, Betsy was bleeding, bad. I screamed for Bruno to get a doctor. He did, but it took too long for him to get there. He couldn't save her. She didn't suffer."

Sam let out a muffled wail. I hold onto him. I am afraid he shatters into pieces. Suddenly he stops. He withdraws from me. He looks at her. "How do I know she didn't suffer?"

"She did not suffer, Sam. She was sleeping when the bleeding started. She never woke up. She passed in her sleep. It was peaceful. Once she was gone, Bruno ordered me to get rid of the baby, so you need to know Betsy never heard those words. With Betsy gone, I didn't have to murder them. And I wanted to bring the baby home. I knew someday that I could tell you about the baby. That day has come."

Sam is exhausted from all the emotions he is feeling. He stops crying. He is staring. Then, he looks at her with piercing eyes, "WHERE'S MY BABY? WHERE IS SHE?"

Mrs. Matteo pauses, wipes her eyes, and gets on her knees in front of Sam. She puts her hands on his hand clutching the diary and this time he lets her. "Don't you see, Sam? She's at Patsy's house. Sam, it's Ruby. Ruby is your daughter!"

Sam drew back. He isn't breathing. "Ruby? RUBY? Oh My God!"

The room is silent. It feels like we are suspended in time. No air to breath. My head is going to explode. My heart is beating out of my chest.

Mrs. Matteo puts her hand on the diary still on Sam's chest. "I think this diary will explain a lot. Her love for you and the baby. That has to mean something, Sam. And through all these years, I knew of the love between you and Ruby. Even though I couldn't yet tell you, I found comfort in knowing she was part of your life."

She put her head down, as she continues to talk. "Bruno and Sal wanted no one to know she had your baby. So, when I brought the diary home, I had to hide it. I was scared, just scared to death." She pauses. "Bruno threatened me to never tell the truth about Ruby. I agreed. My only goal was to get her to a safe place."

I feel like there is an elephant sitting on my chest. "So, this brother-in-law of yours cared about nothing! Not even a wee little baby! How cruel were these men! And you are cruel too, to have kept this from Sam. Do you have any idea what you have done?" ANY IDEA??"

"Yes." Her body hangs in shame. "I have asked God every day since to forgive me. Can you forgive me, Sam?"

He is just staring into the still air. He doesn't answer her question. He bends over with his elbows on his knees glaring at her. "Where's my Betsy? Where is she?"

Mrs. Matteo reached into a tiny drawer beside her and brought out a card. It said '*St. Andrew's Cemetery, Youngstown, 516 Meridian Road.*' "I made sure she was buried properly, Sam. Thirty years ago, I had hidden some money my mother had left me. I took it with me. I didn't know what Betsy and I would need to escape. Since Sal had gone home before the baby came, I didn't have him to deal with. Bruno had just enough heart to allow me to bury her properly. I used the money for Betsy. Bruno stood and cried at her grave. He really thought she would learn to love him. He was delusional. He drove me and Ruby home the next day and we never saw him again. He disappeared. You can go to her grave, Sam. She is buried near the big oak tree at the back. I had the headstone engraved with: BETSY KAMINSKY, LOVING WIFE AND MOTHER.

We sit in silence. I rub his back as I look into his eyes. I see pain, guilt, grief, and questions all at one time. I wipe his eyes. I take his face into my hands. "Sam, we'll go there. We'll go there and get her, and bring her home to St. Mary's Cemetery, so she is close to us."

He nods his head up and down slightly. "Okay, Patsy."

I have one more question. "Why my mama? Other women delivered babies around here. Why her?"

She smiled. "Because I wanted Ruby to grow up near Sam."

I give him time. Several minutes pass by. The silence is deafening. Finally, he looks at me. "Patsy, Ruby?"

"Yes, Sam. Ruby is yours! You are a dad, Sam!" He cannot answer, his face is white, and blank. Finally, he blinks his eyes. With his hands he sweeps across his eyes and shakes his head like trying to wake up.

He opens the first page of the diary. There is the red ribbon, coiled on the page. He looks at her.

"Yes, Sam. The ribbon was in her hair. I took it off after she died and put it in the diary."

Sam broke down in immense grief. He grabs the red ribbon and clutches it tightly in his hand. I just hold onto him and let him cry. Mrs. Matteo is crying too, but I don't care.

Finally, he stops crying. "Ruby, Ruby." It is all he can say.

I put my hands on his cheeks, so he will look at me. "Sam, Ruby is yours! She's YOURS!"

He is staring at me. His eyes are blank. Suddenly, he shakes his head again like he is loosening cobwebs. "How will we tell her, Patsy?"

I embrace him as he embraces me. "We'll figure it out, Sam."

I help him stand up. "We are done here, Mrs. Matteo,"

She sinks into her rocker. "I'm so very sorry."

I cannot forgive her. "You have to live with what you have done."

We go out the door and to Sam's car as if we are walking in deep water. Our bodies are numb, our thoughts scattered.

We go back to Sam's house and sit on his porch swing. He is still clutching the journal. "I can leave now Sam, so you can read it."

"No. Please stay, Patsy."

He stares at the journal in his lap. The leather cover is a softly worn burgundy with a delicate border of embossed rose vines. His fingers tenderly caress the length of the vines. I know he is tracing the roses, just as Betsy must have done over the many times she wrote to him in this diary. Finally, he stops and brings the journal to his cheek. His eyes are closed as his tears fall. I lean my head into his shoulder. "It will be okay, Sam."

He brings the journal back to his lap, lying his palm on the soft leather. He takes in a deep breath. "She kept a diary for me, Patsy."

I know, Sam. She loved you so much!"

He opens it. His hands are shaking. He takes the red ribbon into his left hand and pauses, holding it tight. He begins to read.

Day one: **I don't know where I am, Sam. He pushed me into his car at the company store and put a blindfold on my eyes. I'm so scared. I was in the car I think over an hour, so I'm not too far from Yatesboro. I am in a bedroom that someone has been in before. There is jewelry here, yarn, and women's clothing in the closet and in the drawers. There are shelves of books. I found this blank journal among the books. I will make it my diary where I will write daily, and that will keep us connected. Sam, my love, we are going to have a baby!**

Day two: **I hate being here. There is one window but he closed it in with wood on the outside and inside. There are three locks on my door. I don't hear cars or dogs or anything, so I think I'm in the middle of the woods. I'm so scared. I love you. Keep praying.**

Day three: **He brings me my meals and leaves me alone otherwise. I hate him for taking me. He told me today I will learn to love him. NEVER! During the night last night, I heard what I think was a coyote, so for sure I am in the woods. I hope God is listening to me. I love you.**

Day four: **I tried to get out today, Sam. I miss you so badly. The wood on the window is impossible to budge. I tried picking the locks on the door with no luck. There are no tools in here I can use for anything. If there were, I would kill him with it. He even took the bathroom mirror out. I could** have broken it to make a weapon. He knows that. I will think of something. Love you, Sam.

Day five: **He brought me a little television today. I get only three channels and one is an Ohio news channel. So, I know that I am in Ohio. Not very far into Ohio though, since I was only in the car an hour or so. I'll keep trying to figure it out. I'm okay, Sam. I love you.**

Day 19: **I suppose I should be glad I have what I need here. A bathroom, a shower, a television, books, yarn, clean clothes and food. But I don't have you. I love you, Sam.**

Day after day, for weeks and months she wrote. Sam kept reading and I kept quiet, letting him read, page after page, reading each slowly, then turning to the next.

Day 29: **He asked me today why I don't take the red ribbon out of my hair. I won't answer him, but you know why. It is my love for you. It will stay in my hair until I get home to you! I started to use the yarn I found here. It is an odd color, purple. I am making booties for our baby. I love you, Sam!**

He stops reading and chuckles. "She made purple booties for Ruby." He went back to reading. My mind goes back to the day Ruby came to us. She was wearing purple booties! I know Mama would have saved them. She saved everything. I have some searching to do.

Day 38: **Bruno called Mrs. Matteo today. Then he let me talk to her to tell her I am okay. I told her to tell you that I'm coming home. He grabbed the phone out of my hand but I know she heard it. Now you will know. Our baby should be born with you at my side, not him. I hate him so bad. I love you Sam!**

Day 56: I heard Bruno on the phone today telling Mrs. Matteo she has to come when the baby is born, to deliver it. He doesn't dare call a doctor. He'd go to jail. I'd give anything to see him in jail. I'll be okay, Sam. I love you

Day 87: I am sad I have not escaped yet. I've tried everything I know how. I realize now it is impossible. I'm scared, Sam. I don't think he would hurt me, but I'm scared that you are alone. Please wait for me, Sam. I love you.

Day 94: I thought about Mrs. Matteo today. She will help me escape when the baby comes. I know she will. She is my friend. I have a little hope now. I'm reading the books that are here. I'm okay, Sam, and I'm coming home. It might not be until the baby is born, but I'm coming. I promise. I love you.

At this entry he closes the diary and pauses to cry. After a few minutes, he reopens the diary and continues to read. There was an entry for every single day. Betsy had tried so hard to escape but never succeeded.

Day 180: Our baby is kicking a lot today. I'm really big. I yearn for you to be near me. We are going to love this baby to death! It will soon be here and then I will be home. Gotta go, hear Bruno coming home. Love you!

On the last page she wrote, "I'm having pains today, I think the baby is coming. I heard him call Mrs. Matteo to come. I will soon be home now darling. She is going to get me out of here. I know it for sure. If our baby is a boy, I will name him Samuel after you. If our baby is a girl, I will name her Ruby. I am so excited to be back home with you, Sam. I love you so much!

He has had the ribbon in his hand this whole time. He closes the diary. He stares at the porch floor. He pulls the diary to his chest. I let him sit in silence, so he can grieve Betsy. He continues to clutch it. His head is down. He weeps. I lay my head on his shoulder. His hand comes across my lap. I feel his warmth and love. I feel his grief. With the red ribbon clutched in his hand, he brings it to his face and smells it. With his right hand, he lays the diary beside him on the swing. He looks at the red ribbon again. He kisses it. He lays it on top of the diary. "Goodbye, my love."

I mourn for his loss. I remain silent, weeping quietly with him. My head lying on his shoulder, I am overwhelmed by the love that this man holds. His hand grabs mine. Our fingers entwine together. I feel so lucky to have him in my life. This man, who loves so deeply.

Finally, he straightens up. As if awakening out of a deep sleep, he repeats. "I have a daughter. I have a daughter. I have a daughter." Then he stops. "Patsy, what are we going to do? How are we gonna tell Ruby, Patsy?" The color came back into his cheeks. "Ruby, who I love already and she loves me! At least I think she does!" He cry-laughs.

I am cry-laughing too, "You KNOW she does, Sam!"

He starts to prance back and forth on the porch. "How we gonna tell her, Patsy? How?"

"I don't know, Sam. Especially, since Ruby doesn't even know she wasn't Mama's child. This is all very complicated. I am not sure what a fourteen-year-old mind can handle. It will not be easy." I see the fear in his eyes. "Don't worry, Sam. We will find a way."

Sam and I need to take time to understand all that has taken place and get our heads around it. But Sam doesn't give me much time. He wants to tell her tonight. "We need to tell her now, maybe after dinner. There is no sense in waiting. The secret has gone on too long already."

I am troubled, "Just not sure I'm ready, Sam. I don't know yet what to say."

He throws his arms around me and holds me. "I need this, Patsy. I can't wait. She is mine and I need her to know. Let's make this happen!"

thirty-nine
You Are Mine

I run home to get dinner and cannot think straight. I somehow manage to put food on the table. I feel like there are cobwebs in my head. Ruby helps me do the dishes. I find myself staring at her again. "Ruby, we'll go visit Sam for an hour when we're done here, okay?"

She chuckles. "Not tonight, Patsy. Michael is coming to see me tonight!"

I have to get serious with her. "Ruby, you will need to tell Michael not to come. There is something very important going on with Sam. You need to go over there with me."

Now she is paying attention. "What's wrong?"

"We'll talk about it there." We finish the dishes and I grab my sweater. "Come on, Ruby, let's go."

We walk in silence to Sam's. I am going over in my head what I need to say. I have changed the conversation a hundred times. I am not confident I can say the right thing.

Ruby stares at me. "Why are you so quiet, Patsy?"

"Just thinking, Ruby." I force a smile. "You will understand soon."

"Mysteries!" She laughs. I hope she is laughing an hour from now.

THE CREEK DON'T RISE

As we enter, Sam meets us at the door. He smiles at her with love as he always does, "There's my girl!"

"Hey, Sam. This better be good! I had to tell Michael he couldn't come down tonight!"

Sam puts his bottom lip out in a fake pout. "Ruby, you mean I'm not more important than Michael?"

She just laughs and gives him a shove.

"Sit down, Ruby." I direct her. Ruby sits on the couch and Sam and I pull two chairs forward and together so we are sitting across from her.

"Gee willikers. Must be serious!" She laughs.

I don't know where to start. I take both her hands in my own. "I need you to be serious, Ruby. I have something to tell you and this won't be easy for you, but it is time you know the truth. Now keep in mind as we talk that we love you so much. Both Sam and me. Try to process what we have to tell you and take time to think, okay Ruby?"

Ruby is looking sideways at us. "OOO-kay?"

First, please promise me you will not be mad at Mama. She made the best decisions she could, under hard circumstances."

Ruby looks puzzled. Her tone changes to worry. "Mama? What's going on, Patsy?"

I take in a deep breath. I stare into her eyes and I can feel my eyes filling with tears. My voice is shaking. "Ruby, Mama is not your biological mother."

Ruby pulls her hands quickly out of my hands. "WHAT? What do you mean?"

She seems like a wounded animal. I want to explain it quickly so she will calm down. "Mama brought you home from Mrs. Matteo's house in 1941. She went there to deliver Mrs. Matteo's baby. When Mama returned home, she had you with her."

She stops me from talking. "Stop. Just stop!" She is upset and confused. "My Mama really isn't my Mama? What are you saying? All this time I didn't belong here?"

"You belong, Ruby. You are ours. Ours! That is all that matters. Mama didn't want you to know. She never wanted you to feel you didn't belong. Mama did the right thing. She loved you to the moon and back, like all of us do. You are loved! Period!"

Ruby draws her knees to her chest and starts to rock back and forth as she sobs. "I belong to Mrs. Matteo? To a Blackhand family? Oh my God, Patsy!"

I have to continue. "Ruby, listen. Please! Mrs. Matteo was not having a baby that day. Mama didn't know that when she went. When she got there, you were there. A tiny beautiful little girl baby. Sal Matteo told Mama that his niece had you and couldn't care for you. He asked Mama to take you. She did. She loved you from the minute she saw you."

"A niece? Does the creature have a name? TELL ME!"

I try to stop her from rocking, but she withdraws again by pushing me away. I take a deep breath. "First of all, don't you forget that Mama loved you with all her heart. We all do. When she got there and saw you, she wanted you. You were chosen by Mama, you were! You were chosen!"
Ruby pitifully sobs. "Chosen or stolen, which is it Patsy? Who is

my Mama, who? WHO PATSY? What was her name? The name of the creature who threw me away!"

"No one threw you away, Ruby. Your mother wanted you!"

"Stop it, Patsy. She didn't want me! I hate you for keeping the secret! I hate you!" I try to put my arms around her. She throws me off. "I came from a Blackhand family. Ain't that great!"

"No, you did NOT come from a Blackhand family. There is more to this. I need you to calm down. I will tell you the rest when you calm down. Can you do that, Ruby?"

She stares at me with horror. She stops rocking, but holds her troubled stare on me.

"Okay now, Ruby. One fact at a time. Mrs. Matteo was holding you when Mama got there. Sal Matteo threatened Mama to keep the secret of your birth. She was to pretend that Mrs. Matteo had you. Mama said she'd take you, she loved you the minute she saw you."

"So, a person can just give a baby away, just like that?" She goes back to crying and rocking. "What did I do that she didn't want me? Was I so horrible?"

"You weren't just 'given' away by your mother!" I assure her. "There were circumstances Mama did not know. She was afraid for your welfare. She brought you home to us. She kept you safe. We made you ours. We have loved you ever since."

"Doesn't matter!" Ruby sobs. "I wasn't yours! Who am I? What kind of a mother would give her baby away? Tell me that, Patsy! What kind of mother would do that! What's her name? ANSWER ME!"

We are all three sobbing now. I look at her with love, "You were not born to a niece. That story was made up too. He didn't even have a niece."

Ruby jumps to her feet. She walks to the kitchen. She walks back to us. Back and forth, back and forth. "Oh my God! That's just great! What's the next story going to be? Is my mother a troll that lives under the Kittanning bridge? WHO IS SHE? WHO is my mother? She must have been horrible!"

Sam looks like he is beaten. He just sits silently weeping. He is staring at Ruby. I make her sit down again. "Sit, Ruby! I will tell you when you calm down!"

Ruby sobs harder and louder. Now as I put my arms around her, she lets me. Her body trembles with each sob. My heart breaks for her. I hold her tight and talk into her ear. "You were born to a wonderful mother. She wanted you with all her heart. She wanted to be your mother. She saw you and loved you. She gave you your name. She would have been the best mother. You would have been her life."

Sam is crying harder now. Ruby looks at him. "What are you crying about? It was me no one wanted! Not you!"

She picks up her head. She looks at me with contempt. "And you all knew it too! All my sisters and brothers with their little 'secret' about Ruby. Isn't that sweet? You all hoped I'd never find out. Well, I have! Why did I have to wait so long to find out? Why, Patsy, why?"

This is becoming even harder than I thought it would be. "None of us knew, especially me. We just found this out this morning."

Her sobs grow louder. "I've been living a lie! I DON'T EVEN KNOW WHO I AM!"

She is demanding an answer. "If you know who my mother is, then tell me, JUST TELL ME WHO MY HORRIBLE MOTHER IS!"

Sam is up and out of his chair. He grabs her and pulls her into his chest. Ruby sobs into his chest as he strokes her hair as he talks to her. "I know who you are, sweetheart! Your mother was NOT horrible. She was wonderful. You had a beautiful mother. She loved you. She would never have given you up, Ruby, NEVER!"

"How do you know so much?"

Sam tries to stop crying. He takes his hands and puts them on her shoulders to push her back so she has to look at him. "Ruby, because your mother is Betsy. My Betsy."

Ruby's backs away. She stares at Sam, then at me. Her face is blank. "YOUR BETSY?" She is still. "How can that be?" She stops. She is thinking. "Oh my God, I'm the daughter of Bruno Matteo! I AM the daughter of a Blackhand!" She doubles over with uncontrollable tears.

Sam grabs her. He is suddenly calm. He enfolds her in his arms. "Ruby, listen to me, Ruby! You are NOT the daughter of a Blackhand. Ruby, you are MY daughter, you are MINE!"

Ruby jerks back. She looks into his eyes. His words were hanging in the air. They stare at each other for what seems like an hour but was only seconds. Ruby runs out the door. The screen door bounces twice and bangs shut. Sam grabs me and holds on tight. We cry holding onto each other.

The moment was just too much for everyone. Sam and I fall onto the couch. We sit wrapped in each other's arms for what seems like forever. The sun is going down and darkness is falling through the house. We don't move. We just stay on the couch, embraced. The front door opens quietly. It closes softly. Ruby is standing in the doorway with the light from the street light illuminating her silhouette. Her face is wet from tears, with black streaks running down her cheeks from the mascara she is wearing. She just stands there staring at us. Sam and I part, and stand up. No words are spoken. Ruby just stands there in the doorway, staring at Sam. He is staring at her. Finally, she breaks into a short run and throws herself into his arms. No words are spoken. They stay embraced as I join them and we all cry-laugh at the same time.

When Sam stops cry-laughing, he looks at Ruby, and with love he says, "I always knew those blue eyes of yours looked familiar. You have my eyes. And your hair. You have your mother's hair!" He takes his fingers and pulls on one of the ringlets falling next to her eye. "Betsy had the same curls, the same thick and beautiful auburn hair! There was always a feeling from the moment I saw you that you were special. And now I know why. It is because you are mine!"

Ruby remains in his embrace. Sam's smile is warm. "I am a lucky man. I have a daughter that I have enjoyed her whole life. I truly wasn't robbed."

Ruby and I stay with Sam until midnight talking. She asks him so many questions about Betsy. Sam loves telling her. "I want you to read her diary. You can let me know when you are ready."

When I see Ruby's eyes getting heavy, I insist we go home. She bends over and kisses Sam. "So, what do I call you now?" She asks softly. "Can I call you Dad?" I can see his heart melt.

"Can you keep a bear out of the woods?" He answers with his voice cracking with joy.

Sam walks us home holding her hand on one side and mine on the other.

I talk to her as we walk. "Ruby, this could not have ended any better. Sam is your dad! Do you see how lucky you are to have such a good dad? And he has been there for both of us for years. I feel such contentment. Don't you, Ruby?"

"Don't know if contentment is a strong enough word." She laughs.

He smiles and looks down at her. "We are going to be a family, Ruby. All three of us in the same house. Do you like that idea?"

"Does a bear like the woods?" She laughs. "As long as you let me have my boyfriend!" She is beaming. She leans her head into Sam's body and his arm pulls her in. She is smart beyond her years. I am so proud of her.

As we are passing the alley just before our house, we see a figure of a woman. She walks out of the shadows towards us. It is Mrs. Matteo. We stop. We are silent. We stand like statues. Frozen. She stares at all of us. We stare at her. Ruby releases Sam's hand and walks towards her. She puts her arms around her. "Thank you for giving me my dad." I hear her say. The smile that formed on Mrs. Matteo's face was one of love. The tears flow down her face. Ruby releases from her embrace and returns to me.

Sam walks up to Mrs. Matteo. He stares at her. She stares back at him. Sam reaches down for her hand. "You saved my daughter. For that I am grateful. I forgive you."

forty

Forever After

The days that follow are happy. Sam, Ruby and I talk a lot. She wants to know everything about Betsy, her mother. Sam is very happy to talk about her. "You would have loved your mother, Ruby."

"I know I would have. I am ready to read her diary. May I?"

Sam is happy to give it to her. "Take your time, honey. It was seven months, so it is a lot of reading. I know you will know her better after you read it."

I begin making plans for my wedding and Ruby is about town telling everyone she is Sam's daughter. She takes pictures of the three of us with her little camera. She reads the diary with great intent over several days. I catch her crying in her room as she reads it on her bed. To know that Betsy wanted her and loved her is everything to Ruby.

I take Ruby along with me to pick my wedding dress. We go to the Kittanning Arcade. I choose a simple but elegant dress. The soft satin falls to the floor softly. The top is satin up to and across my breasts, then chiffon covers my arms down to my wrists and up to the top of my neck. At my neckline are tiny white roses. Simple but beautiful. I choose a veil that is edged in tiny white roses also, with a beaded headband on top. My hair has gotten long and somehow it has gotten a little darker as I've aged. The headband and veil are perfect.

"Ruby, I want you to be my maid of honor." I announce as we are eating lunch at the Five and Dime Store.

Ruby almost chokes on her burger. "You mean it?"

"Of course, I mean it, silly. What is your answer?"

"Yes! Yes, yes and yes some more!""

I love her energy. "Now let's pick your dress. I'd like you to be in blue. Sam always liked you in blue."

We walk back up the street to The Arcade to fit Ruby with a dress. We picked blue satin to her knees. The skirt flares out after the tiny beaded belt. She will be adorable.

"I can't wait, Patsy, we are going to be a family!" She beams.

"Indeed, we are!" I kiss her forehead. "In two weeks, we will be a family!"

Two weeks slide by and it is the night before our wedding as I sit with Sam on his front porch swing where our story began. Tomorrow I will be his wife. I cuddle into him. "I have something for you, Sam."

"You do, do you? Is it bigger than a breadbox?" He laughs

I hand him the box I wrapped so lovingly. He stares at me, puzzled. He pulls the ribbon to release it, and slowly opens the paper. He lifts the lid. He stares at what is inside. He is silent. He is thinking. He looks at me.

"Yes, Sam. Betsy made them. Ruby was wearing them the day she came to us."

He smiles softly and takes the booties out of the box. He brings them to his nose and smells them. He is smelling Betsy. He embraces me and whispers in my ear. "Thank you, Patsy. I will cherish them."

Finally, the wedding day is here. We will be married at my church. The Yatesboro Presbyterian Church. Rev. Murphy will marry us. My sisters and brothers adorn the aisles with flowers and ribbons. The church is beautiful.

I have a moment with Ruby alone before we get in the car to go to the church. "Ruby, I have loved you since the day you were born. So has Sam. Don't you see? He fell in love with you not because you are his daughter, he simply loved you from the minute he met you, because you are you. We are so very lucky to share the love we three share. Now we can live as a family. Do you see how lucky we are, Ruby?"

"I do, Patsy." she beams. "I am as happy as you are, and I have forgiven Mama for keeping the secret."

I throw my arms around her. "That means everything to me, for Mama to be forgiven. She loved you so much!"

Ruby starts to cry. "I know she did, and I was so lucky that she took me that day. I wish she were here."

We hold each other and cry-laugh. "Now stop crying, we'll ruin our mascara!"

It is time to go. Ina takes us to the church. There are children sitting in the yard, like I used to do for weddings. There are many young girls and several boys. Two of the boys are holding their baseball bats and gloves. They love baseball, like I did. I smile remembering those times I loved so much. I am nervous. I get out of the car. Mrs. Blose is on her porch applauding, like she did when Doug returned from the war. I look down the street to the company store. Bumble Bee, Mr. Conti, and Lena are outside waving to me. Mrs. Shevencko is on the sidewalk with Mrs. Carenini. Mrs. Shevencko is smiling! It is good to see her smile again. I hear the Catholic Church bell chime. I turn right and see Avi's Tavern and Shy's Barbershop across from it. Shy is walking towards the church with Norb. Norb is waving a silly top hat. I laugh and wave. The outhouse at Mrs. Snyder's house next door to the church is still standing, used only to store tools now. The half-moon still carved on the door. I remember the fun I had chasing the honeydippers. I smell the boney dump burning. My eyes fill with tears. I love my town and the people in it. I love Yatesboro. Yatesboro made me who I am. We are a melting pot, and we make a mighty fine soup!

I enter the church.

My brother Sid is waiting for me. He will walk me down the aisle. Ruby is at my side. I can see my old friends are all here; Slick, Ike, Utz, Husker, Spike, Norma Jean, Margaret and Tubby. I see Pee Pee in the back pew, she has grown into a woman! On the end of one row, I see Ethel sitting with Gibs. She looks at me, smiles, and does a sweet little wave as she beams. I have missed her.

I grab Ruby's hand. "You go ahead honey. I love you, Ruby."

She is quick to reply, "I love you too."

The music begins. She begins to slowly walk up the aisle. She is beautiful today, with the wreath of flowers on her head with the faint wisps or curls around her face. Her thick hair trails down her back to between her shoulder blades. She walks slowly between the rows of pews adorned with ribbons and flowers. The sun is shining through the stained-glass windows. As she starts up the stairs to the alter, Sam extends his hand to hers and leads her up. He kisses her on her cheek as she takes her place.

Sid looks at me and smiles. "You ready?" I nod yes.

I begin the slow march up the aisle. Mrs. Davison plays the wedding march loud on the organ. Sam is waiting. He looks so handsome in his black suit. I can see his eyes welling up. He tries to compose himself. I feel so happy and lucky. Sam keeps staring at me the entire time I walk. I stare at him, and I am trying to realize that soon I will be Mrs. Kaminsky. I finally reach him. He takes my hand. "You are beautiful." He whispers.

Sid kisses me and sits down. I hand my bouquet of red roses to Ruby. Rev. Murphy begins and I try to soak in every word. "We are gathered here today to witness this union between......" and my mind wonders. I am not hearing the words; I am dreaming of Sam and I being together forever. When it is time for my vows, Rev. Murphy speaks my name. I come back to reality. Sam and I are facing each other, hands joined, and I begin, looking directly into his eyes. **"Sam, I love you. You are my best friend. I found you a long time ago, sitting on a lonely porch. From the child that I was, I grew into an adult, and my love for you grew with me. I give myself to you in marriage. I promise to encourage and inspire you. To laugh with you. To comfort you, in times of sorrow and struggle. When life seems easy and when it seems hard. I promise to cherish you and to always hold you in my heart. These things I give to you today, with unending love.** I take his hand, and slip the gold band onto his finger. My hands are shaking. **"I, Patsy McDonald, take you, Sam Kaminsky, to be my husband. To have and to hold from this day forward, for better, for worse, for richer, for poorer, in sickness and in health, to love and to cherish, until death do us part; as God is my witness, I give you my promise."**

Sam is next, as he holds both my hands. **"The day you walked onto my porch was the best day of my life. You give** me a reason to live. You make me happy and fulfilled, at the start and finish of every single day. I choose you to always be by my side. Knowing you and loving you have been the greatest gifts in my life. I can't believe that I get to keep knowing you better, and loving you more, every day for the rest of our lives. I choose you, Patsy. I choose you to be my wife and I will love you forever."

He then slips a beautiful narrow gold wedding band onto my finger, squeezing my hand and smiling. "I, Sam Kaminsky, take you, Patsy McDonald, to be my wife, to have and to hold from this day forward, for better, for worse, for richer, for poorer, in sickness and in health, to love and to cherish, until death do us part; as God is my witness, I give you my promise."

He lifts my veil from my face and folds it over my head. He kisses me softly.

He then turns to Ruby. He takes her hands in his, "I dedicate these vows to you, my daughter. I am so lucky to have been with you as you grew up, into the beautiful young woman you are today. I love you, Ruby, with all my heart. I have been made whole having you in my life, my daughter. Today I want the world to know that you are mine." Sam takes a thin gold band with a tiny ruby on top, out of his pocket. "Ruby, this ring signifies our bond as father and daughter and the love that we share." He slips it onto her right hand, and they embrace.

Ruby whispers to the preacher. "Can I speak?" He nods: yes. She takes one of Sam's hands and one of mine. "The love you both have shown me is beyond anything I could have ever dreamed of. From this day forward, I look ahead to the life we will share. We must keep all those we have loved in our hearts forever." She then reaches under her long hair at her neckline where she had hidden Betsy's red ribbon. She takes

Sam's hand and turns his hand face up. She holds the ribbon up by its end and lets it coil onto his hand. She then takes my hand and lays it on Sam's hand palm down, covering the ribbon. She then puts her hand on top of mine and continues, **"I promise to love you both forever and that we hold my mother Betsy always close to our hearts. I thank her for giving me life and giving me an amazing father. Today I pledge to her that I will make her proud."**

Sam throws his arms around us both as we embrace. We are crying. Our guests are crying, Even the preacher is crying as he speaks. **"I now pronounce you man and wife. I pronounce you a family! May I present to you Mr. and Mrs. Sam Kaminsky and daughter!"**

The people in the church stand up and applaud, as Sam kisses me softly. My life is complete. Sam takes our hands to descend the altar. He is beaming. I am crying. This is the best day of my life.

Our reception is in the church basement. It is wonderful. People are so happy for us. Sam, Ruby and I stay together to greet people and mingle. Ruby breaks away now and then to take pictures. We are a family now.

When it is over, Ruby asks us to go to the Roundtop. She wants to take our picture from the Roundtop. We gladly trek up the winding narrow road in Sam's car to the Roundtop. Sam and I stand at the crest of the Roundtop, looking down over the Valley. The Valley we love. His hand around my waist is warm and loving. "I love you, Mrs. Kaminsky." He kisses my cheek.

"I love you back, Mr. Kaminsky!"

I am lost in the moment when I hear Ruby's camera click from behind us. She is laughing. I look back at her. "What's funny? Is there a squirrel crawling up my dress?"

She is cry-laughing. "It just hit me, that's all!"

"What just hit you, honey?"

She grins. "Don't you see? The good Lord was willin' and the creek didn't rise!"

*The bride and groom on the Roundtop
overlooking the Valley on their wedding day.*

Author's Notes

I was born in 1950 in my grandmother's house in Yatesboro PA. We moved up the street to Rural Valley where I spent my childhood. My mother's family, the Enterlines, resided in Yatesboro for over 100 years. We visited Grandma almost every night of my young life. Over the years, I relished the true stories told by my mother and her sisters about growing up in Yatesboro in the years before and during WWII.

I have always loved to write, but life took many different paths while raising two boys and working as a small business owner, a hair stylist, and then a high school secretary.

The times that I ventured from my roots, the more homesick I became. My longing for home beckoned me back and gave me the inspiration to finally write. In my retirement, and with no formal training, I began to write the stories I could recall and those shared more recently by my 90-year-old Aunt Peggy, who delighted in the process of sharing her memories. I was fortunate to have people in my life that were able to help me with the process of writing.

I love to write about the past. With the future feeling so uncertain, I find a comfort in the history of the past. Patsy's story invites us into her childhood escapades to experience small town life in an era long passed. My hope is to write a sequel to this novel with more history of our area, in a fictional story, which is learning history a fun way.

My husband, Mike and I, happily reside in my family homestead in Rural Valley. A coming home story of its own.

About the Author

Mary Kathryn Koma was born in YatesBoro PA, the setting of this fictional small-town story. At age 68, she began to write inspired by her sense of place and by shared tales of an earlier time. With the completion of this novel at age 70, she has fulfilled her wish to write perhaps the first of many stories.

Mary lives in her family home in Rural Valley with her husband, Mike.

They most enjoy spending time with their two sons, two daughter-in-laws, and seven grandchildren.

WA

Made in the USA
Monee, IL
20 April 2021